Liz A. Stratton is the kind of woman who regularly gets letters asking her to run for president: she's the host of a *Spare Me!* a wildly popular national talk show. Plus, she's edgy, beautiful, and doesn't take crap from anyone. However, she never expected her friend Cal, the head of a women's rights organization, to ask her to run. Even though she said "yes," Liz and her team don't think they actually have a chance at winning the election. Then she is invited to a national debate. Things go well at first, but then an opponent makes the mistake of patronizing Liz about her plans to end the war in Mesopotamianstan. She sees red, and an idea flashes into her mind. She asks every woman in the United States to stop having sex until the war is over. Period. The men in the audience and watching on television all realize with a sense of dread that Liz isn't joking. And that's when the fun begins…

KUDOS for *Closing the Store*

In *Closing the Store* by Maren Anderson, Liz Stratton is a popular TV talk show host, who is convinced to run for president by a friend who is the head of a national women's organization. Running on a platform of ending the war in the Middle East, Liz asks every woman in America to go on a sex strike until the men in charge in Washington DC decide to get off their butts and end the war. The men laugh at her, at first, but as more and more women develop headaches or other excuses, and "close the store," the men begin to panic, thinking that Liz might actually win. The story is cute, funny, and clever, the characters delightful. Add in a couple of sweet romances and some dirty political tricks, and you have a fun, exciting, and completely entertaining read. ~ *Taylor Jones, Reviewer*

REGAN MURPHY SAYS: *Closing the Store* by Maren Anderson is the story of political corruption and one woman's quest to end a senseless war in the Middle East that is being prolonged so that big business and corrupt governments can continue making money off of it. Popular daytime TV talk show host, Liz A. Stratton, is approached by a long-time friend Cal Talmadge, president of a national women's organization, and asked to be their candidate for president. The story takes us through the campaign up to the election and beyond, as Liz rallies the women of the world to "close the store" and deny sex to their men until the war is over. Women respond in mass, and men are left high and dry. Even the hookers "come down with the flu," so men have nowhere to go. *Closing the Store* is a delightful, intriguing, and entertaining romp through the world of politicians and election campaigns—one that will have you in stitches from beginning to end. *~ Regan Murphy, Reviewer*

ACKNOWLEDGEMENTS

I want to thank my husband for giving me a model to aspire to, my daughters for teaching me how to manage time, and Aristophanes for being a wise, old sage.

Closing

the

Store

Maren Anderson

A Black Opal Books Publication

GENRE: WOMEN'S FICTION/CHICK LIT/ROMANTIC COMEDY

CLOSING THE STORE
Copyright © 2016 by Maren Anderson
Cover Design by Rebecca MeCannell
All cover art copyright © 2016
All Rights Reserved
Print ISBN: 978-1-626945-52-4

First Publication: OCTOBER 2016

Published by Black Opal Books **http://www.blackopalbooks.com**

DEDICATION

For my daughters.
They will (eventually) know
they have more power than they think.

Preface

L iz A. Stratton, presidential candidate, peeked from behind the curtain. In front of her stood a crowd of thousands of horny women who had given up sex to show support for her effort to end the war in Mesopotamianstan. They expected her to say something that would inspire them and keep them from going to bed with their husbands or lovers—or both—until the war was over.

But Liz kept thinking about that…that…*man*—a secret service agent, no less—who was currently in her room on the bus waiting for her—as she'd left him, she supposed—naked and half-crazy with desire. Honestly, she didn't know whether she was going back to him once she was done with the crowd. What could she possibly say to those women to keep them on track if she wasn't even able to contain herself?

She slumped in a folding chair and flipped through her talking points, not reading them. She was thinking of Dion's floppy hair, his sexy sunglasses, his lopsided grin, what his cock must look like. She sighed and swore.

Maybe this sex strike thing was more trouble than it was worth.

Chapter 1

Earlier that year:

Liz Stratton made it a policy not to have bad days, but at 9:15 a.m., this one was already testing her optimism. An overnight blackout had jinxed every electrical device in her house, including her alarm, which unhelpfully blinked *12:00* at her when she eventually opened her eyes. She stumbled to her car to find that despicable yellow light glaring at her, daring her to attempt the highway with an empty tank. Once she was at the studio, her new hairdresser had to rush—because Liz was so late—and tugged on her tender scalp in new and excruciating ways.

And now, a timid little assistant was informing her that Ethan Falconwright, that day's show guest, had cancelled. The star's son had broken his arm and was at the hospital. Liz had to admit that this was a better excuse than she usually got for a last-minute cancellation. But now she had to find a new guest for her show, *Spare Me!*, who would be interesting and would show up on time—a tall order in Hollywood.

She glanced her reflection as the girl tugged—yanked—at the back of her head. Liz scrutinized her long, coffee-colored hair for stray grays, but didn't see any.

Her tall frame was a tad too long for the chair, but at nearly six feet tall, Liz was used to not quite fitting in the world. She sighed, peered over her glasses at her makeup, and decided that she was presentable to a television audience.

Her cell phone rang. It was her producer, so she answered it with, "Zeke, please tell me something good."

"You're as beautiful as ever," he answered, and she had to grin. "Are you smiling? Good. We've lined Cal up for your interview today. How's that for last-minute tricks?"

"Zeke, you're a peach," she replied. "Have her come by my dressing room as soon as she's here."

"She wants to, anyway," Zeke said. "She says she's got some great ideas for 'The Future.'" He said this last part in a spooky voice that made Liz laugh.

"That's Cal," she said and hung up.

"Good news?" asked the hairdresser. She shoved a pin deep into Liz's sensitive scalp.

"Yes. My friend Calliope Talmadge is going to be on the show today."

The girl dropped her comb. "You know Calliope Talmadge?"

Liz took a closer look at her. "What's your name?"

"Amber Hastings," the girl said. Her hair was chopped in a short bob, and she wore trendy clothing in all-organic cotton. "Calliope Talmadge is a hero of mine. I've been a member of WAP since I turned eighteen."

Liz assumed that was last year, but didn't say anything. "I'll make sure you're introduced, Amber," she said, and then winced at the girl's squeals of excitement. "Now, don't pull my hair so hard. I'm not a lawnmower, you know."

♥

Spare Me! was the highest-rated afternoon talk show on the West Coast and second only after *Ellen* east of the Rockies. It was named after Liz's catch-phrase. During a radio interview with a state senator in Arizona, she said, "Spare me!" so much that everyone at the station called her "Spare Me Stratton" from then on. She re-named her radio show *The Spare Me Hour with Liz Stratton*, and shortened it simply *Spare Me!* when television finally called.

Ten years ago, Zeke Rowan heard her as he drove through the Southwest on an assignment for a news show he was assistant producing, and "fell in love." That's what he said when he called up her station and demanded a lunch with her that day.

The short, handsome, soon-to-be producer insisted

that he could get her a daytime talk show in LA if only she'd give him her phone number and a handful of headshots. She had done so, though, knowing what she knew now about LA, she'd never be so trusting again. She had been lucky that Zeke had been the real deal.

At first, Liz had no aspirations for television because she didn't consider herself beautiful enough for the small screen. Who would want to watch an Amazon interview anyone? Liz had played basketball in high school and had gone to prom with a boy of equal athletic prowess and low social standing. They were the knees-and-elbows couple. She couldn't imagine being graceful in front of a television camera.

Zeke was persistent, though, and convinced her to fly out to LA for a screen test—a fake interview with an actor. After an hour in the hands of a talented makeup and hair stylist, even Liz had to admit she looked good. The camera loved her expressive face and caught the loveliness of her blue eyes against her dark hair. Once she relaxed into her typical interview mode, her forceful and lively personality even made the cameraman smile. She was a natural.

Of course, television was different than radio. A million decisions had to be made about the set, the format, and Liz's wardrobe. She didn't know how she would have survived if Zeke hadn't been there every step of the way, helpful and attentive.

One of her first shows aired right after Congress reinstated the draft. She invited the local Congressman and any representative of the U. S. Army who would come. When she walked onto stage that afternoon, the two men sat confidently on her sofas. She began by questioning them carefully about the justification for the draft.

"Well, you see, it's like this," said Congressman Miller. "If we have any hope of winning this war, we need to attack both fronts with as much force as we can muster."

"Right," said Lieutenant Archer. "So the army asked the government to reinstitute the Draft so that we could send the reserve and national guard troops home and have fresh recruits for the field."

"So, you're telling me that in order to send the US Army Reserve and National Guard home, you began the Draft, so that you could just conscript them again for as long as you like?" Liz asked. She tried to keep a mocking tone out of her voice, but she wasn't sure it worked.

Lieutenant Archer looked a little stricken, so Congressman Miller jumped in. "Now, Liz—"

"Ms. Stratton," she said shortly.

"Uh, right, Ms. Stratton, this is a necessary step in our quest to win this war."

"And why do we need to do that?" Liz asked, as innocently as she could.

"What do you mean?" the congressman said.

"I mean what I said. Why do we need to 'win' this war? What has being in this war gotten us so far? What does it promise to give us if we 'stay the course'? I've always wondered this, and now it seems really important to know."

"Well," said the lieutenant. "I mean, think of the consequences of not winning."

"You mean 'losing'?" Liz spat at him. "What are the consequences of losing, Lieutenant? Giving up ground on a rock I'll never see? Paying more for gas? I'm already doing that. Being threatened by terrorists? I'm still being threatened by them. Losing Mesopotamianstan democracy? So what? We're not missionaries, or at least, we shouldn't be. I don't feel any safer than I did ten years ago when this thing started, do any of you?" she asked the audience.

A great "no!" was the reply.

"Gentlemen? Response?" Liz asked.

The lieutenant stared at her like the proverbial deer in high beams while the congressman glared at her meanly. Finally, he said, "I didn't come here to be ambushed by you, Ms. Stratton."

"Then you shouldn't have voted to reinstate the draft or agreed to come on to my show." Liz stood and stepped toward the audience. "And now, gentlemen, I have some people I'd like you to meet." She gestured to the wings and groups of women began walking across the stage.

"This is Soledad, whose husband returned from a two-year rotation in the Middle East six months ago. He's been drafted and is leaving in a week to go back."

Soledad stepped up and shook both men's hands as she held a squirming infant on her hip.

"Soledad works part-time to help support their five kids, but daycare is killing her budget. Her husband is an engineer, but the army only pays him a tiny percentage of what he could get at home."

Another young woman stepped forward.

"This is Mindy, gentlemen. Her eighteen-year-old fiancé Bill was killed in Mesopotamianstan a month ago. She's pregnant with his child."

An older woman stepped forward.

"This is Ann. She had four sons, but now she's down to a single boy who's seventeen. The rest were killed in action. She's terrified that her lone son will be next."

"That's enough," snapped the congressman. "We had hearings that lasted two months. We've heard all these stories and others that were worse. We still decided that the draft is needed. Nothing you can show me will change my mind."

"Oh, I'm not here to change your mind," said Liz. "But perhaps you're right. These ladies may have the saddest stories, but maybe not the most convincing ones. You may go sit, darlings." Liz waved them to the front row seats. Then she turned to the opposite wing off stage.

Four men in suits walked on stage and sat in chairs opposite the couch the congressman sat on.

"Who are they?" the lieutenant whispered to Congressman Miller who shook his head.

"Gentlemen, meet Adams, Tappan, DeFord, and Malvadkar of the Winchester Research Institute. They study money in Washington."

Miller shifted a little in his seat.

"Would you tell us what you've found, sirs?" she asked.

"Well," said Malvadkar. "It's quite fascinating, really. The amount of money the oil companies are making off of developing the reserves in Mesopotamianstan are quite astounding. There is more oil and natural gas in that part of the world than any other. The American presence in the area has kept OPEC countries from controlling the resource. It's very lucrative."

"That's nice for the oil companies," said Liz. "How does that affect Washington?"

"Oh, there are all kinds of donations to both major parties by oil companies."

"Thank you," she said, turning to another man. "DeFord?"

"My department researches contractors working on the 'rebuilding' of the infrastructure of the area. Again, very lucrative and big contributions to leaders in both parties who decide where the contracts go."

"Wow. Anything else?"

"Well, many Washington leaders are major stockholders in such companies."

"Now, wait a minute!" Congressman Miller stood. "Are you accusing me of something? If you are, out with it!"

Liz's eyes flashed so brightly that the sparkle could be seen on a thirteen-inch black-and-white set with rabbit ears in Alabama. "Spare me, Congressman Miller," she hissed.

The crowd cheered and Miller sat back down in surprise.

"I could accuse you of taking bribes from the oil companies to vote in favor of this war and of supporting it for the last ten years," she continued. "I could accuse you of voting in a way beneficial the companies you own stock in, companies that make huge amounts of money *not* building schools and roads in the Middle East. I could accuse you of taking 'campaign money' from Russian sources whose interests in the northern oases of Mesopotamianstan are suspect, as Dr. Adams here has studied. I could use information Dr. Tappan has collected and accuse you and all of Congress of lining your pockets with taxpayer money earmarked for armor and ammo for the troops already in that God-forsaken land, the troops who are the lovers and husbands and sons and fathers of ladies like those who face you in the front row here, and who face you in the rest of the studio audience, and who are peering at you from behind their television screens all across the country. I could accuse you, Congressman Miller, of all these things, but I don't have to. These things are all true, and documentation proving them are on my website for my viewers to see. The address is on their screens right now. So spare me your self-righteousness, and get off of my stage. Now."

Congressman Miller sputtered angrily but then faced the audience, which was jeering loudly. He sat down and scowled at Liz until the hissing stopped.

"Listen here, Ms. Stratton," he began. "I will not be ordered around by the likes of you. You and your media-dog cohorts have no idea how Washington works. You haven't been there. True, it is difficult to extract oneself from the rat's nest of loyalties. Besides that, many of the people in your audience are probably just as 'heavily invested' in those companies as I am because they are commonly part of mutual funds in 401Ks. Most of the things you accuse me of are true, but you forget that not everyone in Washington is the greasy, corrupt slime ball you make us out to be. Some of us actually try to make the broken system work to the benefit of our constituents. That includes protecting them with a strong military. Now, if you'll excuse me—" Congressman Miller stood, stripping the microphone off of his tie and dropping it to the floor as he left the stage.

The audience taunted him again as he left. This was fortunate for Liz, who was speechless for the first time in ages. Zeke kept the camera on the audience and not on Liz's stunned face. The lieutenant sat frozen to his seat, looking so frightened that Zeke signaled a commercial break so he could get both of them off stage.

It was looked like young Stratton's finest moment on television, but the congressman's words stuck with her.

♥

The day was definitely looking up. Liz sat in her green room, re-reading the last press release from WAP, or the Womyn's Achievement Party, of which Calliope Talmadge was president. When Liz and Cal were friends at Mt. Holyoke College, you wouldn't have guessed that Cal was going to take up a cause. For the first two years of school, she claimed that she was majoring in Amherst men. Liz was the one who worked at the school paper and wrote angry letters to the Boston Globe about the treatment of women under the Taliban.

It took one required Women's Studies course to change Cal, although her reaction was very different than Liz's.

After reading a speech by Susan B. Anthony, Cal stopped "chasing boys." After reading a book by Gloria Steinem, Cal cut her waist-length strawberry blonde curtain to a bob. Liz wasn't as drastic. She stopped fretting about what her boyfriend thought about her wardrobe. After all, he was a Philosophy student, always dressed in black, and didn't know a thing about cut and drape.

That summer, Cal interned at WAP's political office in DC while Liz worked at a newspaper copy-editing the ed-op pieces. The roomies reunited the next fall with very clear ideas of where their lives were going. Liz was going to win a Pulitzer by the time she was twenty-five, and Cal was going to be the first woman president.

Today, Cal tapped at Liz's dressing room door and peeked in, all grins. "He—ey!" she squealed. "Lizzy!" Cal was the only person in the world who could get away with this nickname.

"Cally!" Liz squealed in return and the two hugged in the doorway. "Come in, come in! How the hell are you?"

Cal, still sporting a short blonde bob, but dressed in a trim beige suit and shoes that showed off her sexy calves, perched on a make-up chair. "Oh, Liz. Big doings! Big doings this year! This is the year, I tell you."

"What's up?"

"WAP is going to have a candidate for president this year!"

"No way! You're kidding! Cal, I'm so pleased for you!" Liz leaped up and hugged her friend. "You will be fabulous!"

Cal laughed. "No, no, you misunderstand! I'm not running. We have a much better candidate in mind."

"Really?" Liz asked. "Who?"

Cal got a sly look in her eye.

"Okay, Cal. Spill it. Who's your candidate?"

Cal drum-rolled on the make-up table, then leaned in to whisper into Liz's ear: "You."

"You're kidding."

"No. Hear me out, Liz." Cal tucked her legs underneath her and leaned in. She had practiced this speech endlessly over the last two days. "The idea struck me when I was in the shower," she said. "What if *the* Liz Stratton ran for president? She has the name recognition, the platform, the well-defined political bent. It would be perfect!"

"Cal."

"No, listen before you say 'no'." Cal wrinkled her brow. "We could finally end this war."

Cal knew just which buttons to push to convince Liz. The "It's your civic duty" line wouldn't have worked, but Cal knew that Liz was angrier about the futile war than anyone.

Liz's eyes sparked. "What? How?"

"Well, that's our main platform. Our talking point. We bang that drum, get the word out as far and wide as we can. We *make* an issue out of it so all the candidates have to take a position on it," Cal said through a toothy grin.

Liz nodded then smiled. "So, what's next?"

"You and I and the WAP team will discuss policy, and you'll have to study the issues like you're taking the bar exam. Can you do that?"

Liz grinned. "Are you actually asking if I can pull all-nighters with my best friend in the whole world? As long as there are Oreos, I can learn anything!"

Cal laughed. "This is the *real* reason I picked you, Liz," she said. "We don't hang out enough."

"Jesus, Cal," Liz said. "Just invite me out to a movie next time!"

They laughed and, after the last giggle, Liz looked her friend in the eye. "So, are we going to win?"

"Oh, probably not," Cal said casually. "But we'll make as much noise as we can as we go down."

"But, Cal," Liz said a little urgently. "What if we *do* win?"

Cal' eyes lit up. "Then we'll change the world, my girl. We'll change everything!"

There was a tap at the door, and Liz's hairdresser came into her dressing room shyly. "Ms. Stratton? You need to be on stage in two minutes."

"Yes, yes. I'll be there," Liz said, but the girl continued to stand at the door awkwardly. Then Liz remembered. "Oh, right. Cal, this is…" Damn it. What was that girl's name? "This is my new hairdresser…Amber! Right?" She nodded. "Right. She heard your name and just went to jelly in admiration, didn't you?"

Amber blushed, but stepped forward and shook Cal's hand. "I am so honored to meet you, ma'am."

Cal smiled kindly. "I like your hair."

Amber's blush receded and she smiled in pride. "I modeled it after yours," she admitted. "I'm the president of my WAP chapter in Anaheim. I would love to talk to you about a couple ideas we've had about the upcoming presidential election."

"That would be wonderful," Cal said graciously. She pulled a card out of her purse. "Give me a call this week and we'll talk."

Amber could hardly contain her glee. "Thank you, thank you, thank you!" she said as she backed out of the room, clutching the business card to her chest as if it might try to escape.

Cal grinned at Liz. "You get this more than me," she said. "Is fame always like that?"

"Amber is a sweetheart, but if she does your hair, bring a branch to bite on," Liz said as she glanced at her watch. "We need to get on stage."

♥

The theme music of the show filled the studio and the audience began to clap and cheer. Liz made eye contact with Zeke who gave her five…four…three… two…

"And now, here's the host of *Spare Me!*, Liz Stratton!" cried the taped announcer.

Liz took the stage, waving to random people as they stood and cheered for her.

"Hello! Hello, everyone! Welcome to *Spare Me!*, the show where…" Liz waited a beat for the audience to hear their cue.

"…we don't take any baloney!" they cried happily.

"We've got a great show for you today. My dear friend Calliope Talmadge, the President of the Womyn's Achievement Party, is here with a big announcement!"

There was genuine applause, not as exuberant as they might have been for Ethan Falconwright, who was presumably waiting for his clumsy boy to get a cast on his arm, but that didn't bother Liz.

Liz looked for Calliope in the wings. Cal winked at her and smiled, signaling that she was ready for the show.

Liz spread out her arms. "Here she is, my dear friend Calliope Talmadge!"

Cal strode onto stage, waving and smiling as if she were running for president. The ladies in the audience cheered and the men smiled, because, despite her position in life as the short, unmarried leader of a women's organization, Cal was as poised and beautiful as a movie star.

Cal and Liz sat on the comfortable upholstered chairs in the center of the soundstage, a contrast in femininity. Compact and bubbly, Cal was not the picture of a feminist leader, and rangy, athletic Liz did not fit the image of a woman who made her living talking.

"So, Calliope Talmadge, President of WAP, what are you here to announce today?" Liz asked her friend.

"Liz, I am here to announce that WAP will have a candidate in this year's race for the President of the United States!" The crowd clapped and cheered as Cal smiled. "It gets better," she said when the audience quieted. "I'm here to announce our candidate today on this show!"

The crowd whooped in excitement.

"That's marvelous!" Liz said.

"It is marvelous, Liz. And the best part, everyone, is that our candidate will be our own Elizabeth Ann Stratton!"

The audience erupted out of their seats, cheering and applauding. Some of the younger women were actually screaming and jumping up and down, demonstrating how poorly their bras fit. Liz stood and waved to the crowd, smiling.

Then Liz caught Zeke's eye. She and Cal hadn't told him what they were planning, so he stood next to the camera with his headset wrapped around his neck and his jaw hanging open like a mailbox lid. She gave him a little wave and he blinked slowly at her.

He mouthed the word "Really?" and she nodded. He cued a commercial and sat down heavily on the floor.

Chapter 2

Maureen Bach squealed and jumped and down like a cheerleader, which, in fact, she had been in high school. Liz had to grin at her friend's enthusiasm. Maureen may have started out as a lowly intern at Liz's show, but her "spunk" gave her a rocket-ride to Liz's inner circle. There was no one who else who could entertain quite like Maureen and her tales of growing up young, ginger-haired, and pert in the Valley. Plus, she was always ready with a dirty limerick to liven the day. One of her classics was:

> *There once was a girl from the Valley*
> *Who went to a political rally.*
> *She blew the committee*
> *That ran the whole city,*
> *And now she's called Mayor O'Malley.*

Right now she was saying "omigodomigodomigod" while bouncing bra-less in her tiny tee shirt. Zeke could barely contain himself, though Liz did admire his efforts.

When Maureen was done expressing her excitement, Liz said, "So, I take it you're willing to take the position?"

"Oh, *yes*, of course! Oh, you'll be so proud of me, Liz. *Spare Me!* will be in very capable hands." Maureen was nodding seriously as she returned to her seat. Liz loved that Maureen could turn herself on and off like that. It made her very hard to pin down sometimes, but Liz was jealous of the ability to switch roles so effortlessly.

Liz continued with the briefing. "You've handled the show very well when I've been on vacation, so I know you'll do fine," she said. "But that was with Zeke at the helm. I'm a little worried about leaving you with a new producer, though."

"Oh, where's Zeke going?" Maureen asked.

"I'm going with Liz as her, what do you call it?" Zeke said.

"You're my handler," Liz answered.

"M-row!" said Maureen with a saucy grin on her face. "I bet it didn't take long for you to convince him to 'handle' you!"

Liz laughed and missed the micro-second that Zeke looked undone by Maureen's remark. "No, he was eager for the job, all right. But I love Zeke. I couldn't do any of this without him," She smiled at him like he was a trusted retriever, and that's exactly how he felt.

Maureen didn't miss any of this. But she changed the

subject. "So, how can I help with the campaign?"

"We'll have you come out for some of the rallies and things, but mostly, you need to keep the show focused on our issues so we can keep this audience engaged," Zeke said. "And keep us informed about the issues your, um, peers are interested in."

"Peers?"

"He means people under 30. He's just being polite in my presence," Liz said. She stage whispered, "He doesn't think I know that by running for president, I'm admitting I'm over 35."

"Well, as your handler, he has to protect you from the big scary world, doesn't he?" Maureen said. "He's doing a good job."

"Are you finished?" Zeke said.

"Not even close," Maureen said. "But I'll just save some of this awesomeness for later. You two get along and don't worry at all."

Zeke stood and pointed a finger at her. "You'd better get the show to bed before bedtime on school nights. It gets cranky otherwise."

Liz laughed. "And no pop after 9 PM."

Maureen arched an eyebrow. "You guys are seriously weird."

♥

A couple of days later, Liz sat backstage and re-read the same sentence of her acceptance speech over and over. Why was she nervous? Hadn't she been in front of a live studio audience taping a national show every day for ten years? Why did a room full of supporters and some press give her butterflies all of a sudden?

She couldn't talk herself down because she knew that her talk show was just a forum for the conceited and was watched by people who didn't work during the day and had no better use for their time. This was real. She might be a "name," as Cal put it, but she wasn't a politician. Liz began to pant and her contact lenses felt like they were burning. She yelped as she pulled them out, so Cal ran in.

"What the hell, Liz?" she cried when she saw Liz leaning over the make-up table with tears streaming down her face. "Oh, honey! What's the matter?"

"My contacts went toxic in my eyes," Liz sniffled, hoping to cover her panic. "I need to find my glasses. I can't wear my contacts anymore today." She pulled out her glasses and slipped them on. She sighed in relief when she realized that they masked her fear just a little, too.

Cal looked at Liz in the mirror for a moment. "Actually, Liz, that's good," she said. "They give you that 'sexy librarian' look. That'll go over well with the men and the lesbians in the press room." She gave Liz a sly wink. "We will need to work the whole 'she's single, everyone' angle, don't you think?"

Liz couldn't help but grin. "A woman for all the people, huh? I'm not sure that's going to fly in Omaha, Cal."

"Oh, fuck Omaha," Cal said. "Like we'd win

Omaha, anyway. Now bring your sexy self along. We have a room to rile up."

Liz took one last look at herself in the mirror. She did look like a sexy librarian, so she pouted and put her fingers in front of her lips in a silent "Shush! Madame President needs quiet," and minced out of the dressing room.

♥

"...and that is why I, Elizabeth Ann Stratton, am running for the office of the President of the United States of America!" Liz finished her speech with as much enthusiasm as she could muster, and the crowd began its applause. At the last moment she added, "Because I mean, really, *Spare Me!*"

The crowd leapt to its feet and let loose a high, throaty, decidedly female howl as Liz stepped back and waved, a moment before Cal came on stage and hugged her. Cal took the podium and shouted over the melee, "How about a hand for the future Madame President?"

The room erupted again and chanted, "*Spare Me! Spare Me!*" as Liz and Cal waved and left the stage.

Cal grinned. "I think that went well," she said. "I mean, I was a little worried when they began chanting your name, but I think you really got them when they began chanting your name, you know?" She nudged Liz in the ribs.

Liz was high on endorphins, so she giggled like a seven-year-old, but her inner critic was already in high gear. "You don't think the speech was a little stilted or…trite?" she asked quietly.

Cal looked at her as if making a decision. "Well," she began. "We can work on your delivery. You're best when you're improvising, you know. Like throwing in '*Spare Me!*' Brilliant. We're going to have to work that in every time you talk."

"Won't that get repetitive or boring?"

"That's politics, honey," Zeke said stepping up from behind them. "Let's get to the green room for some champagne," he suggested. He took a deep breath, put his fingertips on the small of Liz's back, and exhaled when she didn't pull away.

Liz noticed Zeke could open a bottle of bubbly better than anyone. Barely a burp so the bubbles stayed in the wine. He poured three glasses and then raised his in a toast. "To our girl!" They clinked and drank, and then Zeke said what he always said: "In celebration of a successful show, please come to dinner with me tonight!"

To which Liz responded the same way she always did: she laughed lightly and said, "Some other time, I promise!" and sipped some more champagne.

This had been their ritual for the past ten years.

Zeke watched as the two women chattered in agonizing ignorance of their effect on him. He held the wine under his nose and peeked at them over his dark-rimmed glasses. After ten years, he was used to the way he felt about Liz and the way she felt about him. He hadn't meant to be categorized as brotherly: just the opposite, in fact. When he heard her radio show all those years ago and then saw her headshot, he had recognized her potential, but mostly he had wanted to get into her pants.

The "assistant producer" line had worked for him before. Zeke was handsome, but he was not tall or remarkable-looking, and recently he'd begun shaving his head to hide unfortunate early balding. In LA, you had to be remarkable-looking and have great contacts to make girls pay attention to you. Or you had to be somebody who could help a career.

At least Zeke had been an actual assistant producer when he met Liz. He'd found that he liked the work, and the line was useful for picking up girls in bars. But it hadn't worked on Liz. Maybe it was because she wasn't in or from LA, but she hadn't reacted in the way the bimbos on the strip did.

She didn't scoot her chair closer to his or start making eyes at him over her drink. She just began talking about her ideas for a television show. Her excellent ideas for a show. Zeke was smitten with her, but the casting couch remained unused.

He snapped out of his head when he heard his name.

"Zeke. When is the first debate?" Cal was asking.

"Debate? Well, we won't be actually debating the other candidates until after their conventions in August," he said. "Until then, we'll be just setting up press conferences, buying ads, and campaigning. You know, spreading the message."

"Fine," said Liz, stretching her long, long, ever so long, legs out so they almost touched Zeke's polished shoes. "What's our 'message'?" she asked.

Cal pulled a legal pad out of her case. "Besides our usual 'break the glass ceiling,' and 'keep your legislation out of our uteri' platforms, WAP is calling for the end of the war in Mesopotamianstan. 'War is a stupid man's game,'" she read from the pad. "Present company excepted."

Zeke waved a hand.

Cal smiled. "We need to brainstorm some ideas on how to end that fucking mess."

Liz sighed angrily. "I've been talking about that stupid war on the show for six years now," she said. "And I get angrier every time I do. The amount of money spent! The continuous tours of duty for the soldiers! Do you know, I interviewed a girl last year who had only seen her husband for a month before he was shipped back to Mesopotamianstan for another two-year stint?" Her blue eyes flashed.

Zeke thought "angry Liz" was the sexiest beast there was.

Cal was nodding. "WAP has statistics on how many families have lost primary breadwinners to the war, how many have lost sons or husbands."

"Do you have numbers on how much these missing men are straining the economy?"

Cal flipped through a stack of printouts on her lap as she took a sip of champagne. Smiling she said, "Yup," and held up a sheet with a downward-sloping graph. "Right here."

Liz leaned farther back in the soft chair and sipped

her bubbly, too. "Does it seem to you, Cal, that the war has robbed us of all the men?"

Cal glanced at Zeke. "Sometimes. Zeke, how did you escape the army?"

Liz looked up to see if Zeke had taken offense that she had forgotten that he was in the room, again. He hadn't. "I have flat feet," he said. "You should see my footprint. It's like an outline of a shoe."

Liz smiled at him, and that was enough for him, for now.

♥

Liz was not a rock star, but now that she was on a bus tour, she felt a little more empathy for them. Granted, her tour only needed two busses, and required no semi-trucks full of guitars and such, but after only two hours on a luxury coach, Liz felt a bit stir-crazy.

Her bus was even a deluxe special model with a private bedroom for her in the back. The driver made sure to show her the door that closed for "privacy." He was immensely proud of his coach. Liz could hardly turn around in the "bedroom," and the bunk was a cramped fit for her six-foot frame, but she made a big deal out of it for him. She knew better than to upset a bus driver.

Once she was settled, the support staff mounted the steps and occupied most of the seats of the bus, including the two "booths" with little tables.

The driver had also shown these off to Liz on her tour. Soon, all the staff were busy tapping away on their laptops, tablets, and smart phones, completely absorbed in their electronics.

Liz wasn't expecting the staff to be so…technologically savvy.

"Gosh, they're quiet," she whispered to Zeke.

He looked up from his yellow notepad. "Hmph," he snorted. "If I ever get a Twitter account, make sure I'm shot the next morning."

"Is that what they're doing?" Liz asked. "I mean, I have email, and the show has a Facebook page that I sometimes post on, but, I mean…" She trailed off sadly. "Am I actually so old that I can't understand the new generation's mode of communication?"

"Oh, my poor girl." Zeke smiled at her. "You are worse than that. You are so old that once you get a Twitter account—and that's part of our plan—you will make it passé."

"You really know how to hurt a girl," she said.

♥

Liz's contact lenses were officially out of commission. Even if the smog died down and she were able to wear them again, her "handlers" had decided that glasses would become her presidential "signature." Now she had three dozen pairs and one person in charge of picking which she was to wear when.

"Where does WAP get the money to do this, again?" Liz asked Cal as the "eyewear technician" considered the options for today's open-air rally.

"We've got an endowment that the Ivies envy," Cal whispered. "One of the Rockefeller widows left everything to us instead of her simpering children."

Liz nodded and peeked at her notes again. She felt like she was getting the typical rally and press conference routine down. She hadn't really focused on how much repeating politicians running for office did, but she had said mostly the same thing every day. It was Saturday, the beginning of a new week in a way, and she was studying her new script.

"Where are we today, Zeke?" she asked, glancing out the bus window. The parking lots all looked the same.

Zeke knew, but he glanced at the calendar, anyway. "We're just North of San Diego." He saw Liz frowning, instead of being pleased with the news. "Frowning Liz" was another sexy beast he loved.

"But where, Zeke?"

He glanced at the calendar again and saw what was irking her. "Oh, we're near Camp Pendleton."

"Shit," Liz hissed between her teeth.

"What is it?" asked Cal.

"Military wives."

"Liz, focus on the script. We've outlined a few things—" Cal began.

"This is bullshit, Cal, and we know it. I don't want to go out there and look at those faces without a *plan*." Liz paced up the aisle of the bus. "Can we postpone this rally?"

"No. You'll just have to do the best you can, Liz. Remember, we're the only ones who are indignant and angry about the war. It's enough for now just to say it has to stop."

"Maybe for you," Liz said, flopping back in her seat. "I want to be able to tell them that we know how to end it."

"Well," Zeke said. "When you have an idea, let us know."

♥

Liz walked onto the stage inside an old gym, complete with basketball hoops suspended from the ceiling. The crowd that had gathered to see her hardly filled one corner of the room, but they seemed enthusiastic.

The local media had set up across from the stage so three cameras and bored reporters faced her. The cameras didn't bother her nearly as much as the faces of the young, mostly female faces that stared up at her. Alarmingly, there were several "Support Our Troops!" tee shirts polka-dotting the audience.

"We entered this war for the wrong reasons," Liz declared and waited for the high-pitched whoops to die down before saying, "We continue for the wrong reasons."

The crowd cheered again and seemed perfectly happy to respond to her cheerily, regardless of the hot, stagnant air in the gym and sticky, stale mat smell. Liz felt like a parrot, mouthing words that had no meaning and blinking blankly at the faces before her. She felt sick.

Her speech done, Liz shook hands and kissed babies. This was the last stop today, so she could afford to linger a little. As she hugged a particularly chubby infant for a picture, someone tugged on her sleeve. She turned to face the oldest woman in the room. "Yes?" Liz asked. "What can I do for you?"

"You can tell me how you propose to stop this stupid war," the crone rasped at her. Her faded sweater had a yellow ribbon pinned to the lapel. "I've been voting for a half century, and I'm ready to stop because not one politician has done what he's said he was going to do. Most've just stopped saying what they're going to do, so I've taken to asking. What are you going to do to get us out of this war?"

Liz stared at the old woman for a moment, stunned and angry that she didn't have a ready answer. Finally, she sighed and put her arm around the elderly lady. "Honestly, I'm still working on a plan," she said, suddenly feeling very tired. "I *will* tell you that I would give up anything to get us out of this war."

"So would I," said the old lady.

"Me, too," said another woman.

A number of other women also agreed.

"That's great," said Liz. "Now, we need to figure out what we could sacrifice to make the war end."

The ladies surrounding her laughed.

"If any of you come up with a plan, please send it to us," Liz said. "We're ready to listen to ideas."

Zeke nudged her and handed her a pen and paper with a wink.

"Actually," she said, "how about we just start with brainstorming session now?"

"Beer!" came the first suggestion, followed by snickers.

Liz wrote it down carefully. "Beee-eer. Next?"

"Oil changes!"

"Taxes!"

"I think we're missing the spirit of the exercise, here," Liz said, but wrote the items down, anyway.

"Chocolate!"

Liz laughed. "*Now* we're getting somewhere!"

"Pantyhose!"

"New shoes!"

"Ice cream!"

"Let's not get crazy," Liz joked.

On the sidelines, Cal congratulated Zeke. "Great idea, man. Those ladies are eating up the brainstorming thing! Where'd that come from?"

Zeke shrugged. "It's the way we write the show, Cal. Someone writes down every crazy idea that pops into our heads because one of them's gotta be a winner."

"You always get winners?"

"Not every time, but it only takes a couple of winners to make the difference."

"I'm glad you came along, Zeke," Cal said, bumping him affectionately.

"Me, too."

They smiled as they watched Liz work the crowd.

♥

Maureen Bach wasn't Liz Stratton, but she was entertaining in a different way. Cute and bouncy and normally bra-less, Maureen filled up the small screen like an off-duty stripper in a smoky bar. Liz watched Maureen's first segment in awe and disbelief. It was titled, "I Don't Get Any Since The Army Took My Lover Away." Maureen had eight women come on stage and tell her in great, graphic detail how they hadn't seen an actual penis in months and were resorting to a number of "Plan B's."

"Zeke," Liz called. "Zeke, what is this?"

Zeke peered over Liz's shoulder at the little flat-screen mounted on the wall of the bus. "That's Maureen doing your show," he said.

"But, Zeke. She's said, 'cock' and 'dildo' at least three times already!"

"Really?" Zeke sat down. "I'm surprised Kevin let her to do that. He's a bit of a prude."

They watched as Maureen interviewed another woman who was describing in thinly veiled detail how to make a "pleasure device" from frozen vegetation.

"I don't believe this," Liz cried. "This is on during the daytime, Zeke!"

"Calm down, Liz," Zeke said soothingly. "I think this might be very helpful." He started scribbling on a nearby yellow pad. "I mean, if you mention an interview with a woman who was resorting to her vegetable bin for lack of a lover, I think you might get some attention—"

"But what would I lose?" Liz wailed. She watched as Maureen turned to the camera and said, "We'll be right back," somehow bouncing her pert breasts at the camera without moving a muscle.

Zeke put a hand on Liz's shoulder and caught a peek down her blouse. "Honey, I think this will be good for us. That's why I approved the segment. You know we're using the show as a platform, right? We need it to stir up the issues we want to talk about."

"I know," said Liz. "I just see my journalistic ideals flying out the window."

"This isn't journalism. It's politics," Cal said from her seat. "We're not aiming for the highest common denominator. You know that."

The memory of Maureen's nipples made Liz turn off the television. "Just make her wear a bra, okay? I'm depressed enough about not being twenty-five anymore. I don't need her rubbing it in."

Chapter 3

Liz tried to keep from shaking from nerves. She stood on the stage with the other candidates waiting for the "show" to start. The debate was about to begin.

She had spent the last week stumping all across the country during the day and cramming for the debate at night. She didn't expect to win the election, but she would be damned if she'd look like an idiot on national television.

There was so much to learn! She had had plenty of guests on *Spare Me!* who talked about the economy and the military and so on, and she had done her prep work for them. She'd read the books, the briefings, and the research from her team. But she'd been the one asking the questions! It was much different being on the other side.

She allowed herself a stack of ten index cards to help her remember the talking points and facts that she, Zeke, Cal, and the various advisors had constructed as the platform for the WAP party. The rest of it was in her head, she hoped. She cleaned her glasses again to hide her restless hands.

Her opponents were chatting with each other amiably. As senators and governors of middle-of-the-road states, they had all met before at one time or another. Liz had never interviewed any of them, nor had she met them at any other events. One detached himself from the group, ambled over to her, and thrust out his hand.

"Ms. Stratton? I'm Oscar Beckinger, senator from Indiana. I'm the Democratic Party candidate." He was tall and handsome and 40-ish. His impish charm reminded Liz of every successful politician she'd met.

"I know who you are," Liz said, shaking his hand and smiling.

"This is quite a set-up, don't you think?" Senator Beckinger said conversationally. "There's a few more people on stage than I expected."

Liz nodded. "I certainly didn't expect to be here," she said. "The WAP and Green Party candidates don't usually get invited to national debates."

The senator rocked back on his heels, hands in his pockets, and smiled. "It's a sign of the changing times," he said.

"Could be," Liz said, smiling back. She tried to remember if the good senator was married and blushed when she realized she was doing it. She pretended she didn't notice her rising color, and the senator had the good taste to pretend he didn't notice, either. But he did.

The lights on the cameras blinked and the audience began applauding. Patriotic music swelled and a disembodied voice announced the opening of the show. Senator Beckinger smiled in farewell and ambled back to his podium. Liz realized she had been holding her breath and tried to regain her composure before she was introdu—

"Ms. Elizabeth Stratton, talk show host from Los Angeles, California!" the announcer shouted.

Liz smiled cheerily and waved to the polite applause.

"Senator Oscar Beckinger!"

Liz let out the rest of her breath and dabbed her forehead. She looked up just as Oscar winked at her. She willed herself not to blush again as the other candidates were introduced. Then Liz focused all her energy on answering the questions.

The moderator, Robert McNally, was an old friend whom she had met early in her career at a journalists' party when she first got to LA. He was a venerable warhorse, and he wouldn't pull his punches for her, but she could tell from his smile that he was pleased she was there.

"Welcome to the first nationally televised debate of the election season featuring not only the Democratic and Republican parties, but also candidates from the WAP and Green Parties," Robert announced to applause.

Liz felt a little chill run between her shoulder blades.

The first questions were warm-ups. First, Robert asked them to give a brief statement on how they would improve the economy.

"We need to eliminate the glass ceilings of this country either by legislation, or regulation, or cultural revolution. Frankly, I think the last option would be ideal, but I'm not opposed to the first two. If women and minorities can compete with everyone else on equal footing, productivity will increase, as will consumer spending," Liz said when it was her turn.

The audience applauded politely, and the next candidate ignored her comment completely.

Next was the obligatory question about alternative energy solutions. Jack McNerny, the Green Party Candidate went on a while about all of his party's ideas on alternative energy. When it was finally Liz's turn, she said, "The less petroleum this country uses, the better, given that we cannot seem to produce enough to fulfill our needs, and most of us are unwilling to continue this war to fuel our SUVs. I think women especially are willing to try alternatives that will ultimately save their households money like solar power and wind turbines, as well as fuel-cell and electric cars. Funding this kind of research is vital."

Liz was feeling pretty good about herself at the midway break. She sipped some water and smiled at the moderator. So far the debate had been friendly enough, although all the candidates' answers were predictably similar.

The music swelled again, and Liz put her water bottle away.

Robert looked up into his camera and said, "And now we'll turn our attention to the war in Mesopotamianstan. Candidates, the question we put to you is how will you end the war?"

Liz was ready for this one, but she wasn't prepared for Robert to look at her and say, "Ms. Stratton, you may go first."

First?

She smiled at him and reminded herself to rib him about this later. "Of course, Mr. McNally." Liz looked into her camera. *I am ready.* "This war must end. Now. The drain on our national resources has been obscene. The drain on our populace has been devastating. A whole generation of young men and women has been sent on this fool's errand so a very few people can become immensely wealthy. Reinstating the draft has ripped apart families already under the strain of the bad economy and mortgage crunch. This needs to stop. Ending the war will take aggressive negotiations with the warring parties in Mesopotamianstan, and as president, I'll personally spearhead those talks so that we can get our people home and focus on repairing our own country, not someone else's. Thank you." She heard her supporters' heartfelt applause in the back of the auditorium over the more polite clapping.

Robert grinned at her and turned to the next candidate. "Senator Beckinger?"

Oscar Beckinger rocked back on his heels and smiled

warmly at the moderator. "Robert," he said. "I know that the WAP party candidate has her heart in the right place—"

Liz's face froze and a chilly knot seized up in her gut. *Oh, no*, she thought. *Please don't let the handsome man patronize me.*

"—but," he continued. "I don't think hosting a talk show has prepared her for holding talks between the Iranians and the Mesopotamian separatists." To Liz's horror, there was a general chuckle from the audience. "I mean," the senator continued, smiling. "Can segments on celebrities and novelists be any sort of preparation for negotiating with terrorists?"

Another chuckle of approval.

Liz felt the color draining from her face as Beckinger went on to babble about not negotiating with terrorists and measured response. Suddenly, she wasn't in a packed auditorium full of members of the press and privileged audience members, she was in her seventh grade science class with her old nemesis, Mr. Tory, standing in front of her with a mean grin slashed across his face.

"Say that word again," he said.

"I can't," Liz had said, blushing.

"Do it."

"Anem-mem-mem-y."

"An-nem-o-ne," he said, a look of triumph on his thin face.

He had finally found one thing Liz couldn't do. She might ace every test he gave her, but she couldn't pronounce the name of a soft-bodied sea creature.

That was not the first time Liz had seen red, but it was the first time it had landed her in the principal's office. Throwing the book at Mr. Tory had felt good, though.

Robert McNalley turned to the Republican candidate. "Governor Ostrem?"

Bill Ostrem shook his jowls in mirth as he chuckled to himself. "Mr. McNally," shouted the Governor of Georgia. "I am also not one to negotiate with terrorists, nor interview novelists."

The audience was now warmed up and laughed outright at this pathetic joke.

"In fact," the governor went on. "I'd venture to say that I'm in a unique position to help Ms. Stratton learn how to negotiate a lot of things—"

"That's it," Liz shouted. Her head pounded and the world had a distinctive scarlet cast. She was so angry that she didn't know what to say, so she just started talking. Or shouting. Whatever.

"Ostrem, you sack of shit. You are in a unique position to kiss my ass and the asses of taxpayers. You own fucking Nortramal. That company beat out Haliburton for the school building contract in the Middle East. There aren't any schools there yet, and it's been five years. We all know that you're neck deep in this war because you're making so much money that you can't afford for it to end. How would you keep your mistress in new furs if it did?"

"Ms. Stratton, will you wait your turn?" Robert McNally was trying to regain order, but Liz ignored him.

"And Beckinger? You voted to reinstate the draft. Why did you do that? You have two sons. Could it be because you have ties with the industrial military companies that make their livings making body armor, tanks, and gas masks?"

"Liz, please," Robert McNally was standing, pleading with his eyebrows.

"Robert, I'm sorry, but these two patronizing assholes have no business running for president. They are up to their armpits in dirty money, direct profiteering from this sticky, smelly mess of a war. They have no intention of ending it because they are making too much money, and they have no moral fiber at all."

The Green Party candidate started clapping, but Liz shot him a withering look that made him stop.

"Well, what do you propose?" Ostrem sneered. "Negotiating with the terrorists? That'll work."

Liz glared at him, but he did not cow like McNerny. "Fine," she said. "You want a stronger tactic? You want a tactic that will work? You want a strategy that will guarantee an end to the war, no matter which of us takes office in January?"

"I'd love to hear it," said Ostrem.

"I spoke to a barracks full of women near an army base who said that they'd sacrifice anything to end the war. Absolutely anything. At the time, I couldn't think of anything they could give up that would change things, nothing that would convince the powers that be that the population was serious about ending the war. But I now know what needs to be sacrificed to end the war."

"What's that?" asked Beckinger smugly. "Television? Eating out? Driving to work?"

"Sex," Liz said.

The room was suddenly quiet. Then someone tittered. Then the whole room roared in laughter. Liz waited until they quieted down, working out in her head how this spur of the moment plan would work.

Finally, Robert McNally, wiping a mirthful tear from his eye, said, "Ms. Stratton, would you mind explaining how giving up sex will end the war in Mesopotamianstan?"

"I'd be delighted, Robert," Liz said sweetly. "Firstly, let's review something. What do men love? Fighting and sex and maybe a sport or two—perhaps not in that order. If you take one of those things away, the man becomes unbalanced. I think that given a choice between sex and fighting, men will choose sex. It's that simple."

Robert McNally blinked at her. "You're serious," he said. "You're seriously suggesting that women start a sex strike to blackmail men into ending this war."

"Blackmail is such an ugly word, Robert," Liz said.

Senator Beckinger was chuckling. "Well, it wouldn't work, you know," he said. "I mean, my wife likes our, um, recreation. Certainly too much to give it up for the war."

"Oh? You're willing to bet on that?" Liz asked. "She's never 'closed the store,' so to speak, to get something she wants?"

The senator looked uncomfortable. "That's a little personal, don't you think?"

"Ha-ha. That's your answer," Governor Ostrem said. "You pussy-whipped bastard!"

"Oh, Governor. It's not like you've ever passed legislation to help out one of your mistresses, especially the one who dabbles in speculative real estate?" Liz had to remember to send her research department to Hawaii as a thank-you present. "Robert," she said, turning back to the moderator. "I am saying that if each woman in this country got a headache every night, if she were on the rag for weeks on end, if she suddenly needed to see her sick mother for a month, if she closed the store to her husband, those men would very much want to know how to open it again. And if the same thing happened in Mesopotamianstan, this war would be over in the matter of weeks—if not in *a* week."

The cheering that rose from the crowd had a perceptively higher pitch than earlier in the evening, as only the women were applauding. The men in the room and in the television audience had a sickening feeling of dread as they considered what it would be like if, indeed, every woman in America decided to ignore them. Then they tried to laugh it off, but they checked their stashes of porn, just in case.

♥

When Liz stepped off stage, Zeke was waiting and fell into step beside her. His brow was so furrowed his eyebrows hit his glasses and pushed them down his nose.

"Liz," he said, shoving up the black frames. "A sex strike, Liz? Really?"

"It just sort of slipped out," she said.

Before Zeke could respond, Cal burst in from the green room where she'd been watching. "Liz!" she cried when she saw them and ran over. Liz braced herself. Cal flung her arms around Liz and laughed. "A sex strike, Liz? Brilliant! This is gold!"

Liz and Zeke looked at her in disbelief.

"You can't be serious," Zeke said, closing the dressing room door behind them. "There's no way this idea can help a serious campaign."

"Oh, Zeke," said Cal. "What if we aren't out to win? What if we're just out there to stir things up and maybe get one issue out in front?"

"But isn't this too...I don't know...vulgar for politics?" Liz asked.

Zeke had to laugh this time. "I'm no political historian," he said. "But I do remember a certain cigar and all the trouble it caused. Sex and politics go hand-in-hand, Liz. I have to agree with that."

"You did so good!" Cal said, hugging Liz again. "You should always say what's on your mind. From now on, we'll give you notes about the party's position, but you are to tell it as you see it, darling!"

Liz was still flustered. "But haven't I just ruined our chances of winning?"

Cal sat them both down on the moth-eaten couch in the dressing room. "Honey, we had a snowball's chance before. So now we're a melted snowball. Who cares about the office? Now we have their attention!" Her eyes sparkled. "I can't wait for tomorrow's paper! Oh!" She jumped up and switched the television on. "Let's see what CNN has to say about you."

♥

They watched the debate coverage for an hour in the dressing room and turned it back on once they got to the hotel. They gathered in Liz's room and marveled about what was happening in front of them.

While they were still in the dressing room, the twenty-four-hour networks had stuttered and babbled incoherently in utter confusion. Had Elizabeth Stratton really just asked American women to stop having sex? Did she mean it euphemistically or literally?

By the time they were all sitting on the edge of Liz's bed, the talk had turned to speculation about whether or not the sex strike was a planned strategy by WAP. A few pundits were adamant that Liz had simply gone off-script and said the preposterous idea as it flew through her head—as, indeed, she had.

After room service had been ordered and eaten, they watched the talking heads wonder if people would vote for someone who flew off the handle like that and suggested such crazy ideas.

Around midnight, a pert blonde suggested that a sex strike might actually work.

Then things started to get silly. One ugly male pundit speculated that WAP had an agenda, like the gays, and planned to eventually have an Amazon-run government and castrate all the men in the country, except for "breeders." That was when Cal turned off Liz's TV and shooed people back to their own rooms.

She turned to Liz as she left. "Honey, that was amazing," she said softly.

"What?" Liz asked in a daze.

Cal beamed. "The national news networks have just spent the last four hours talking about you and WAP."

"Cal, they think we're nuts. They think I'm a crazed Amazon who wants to chop off their balls."

"There is no such thing as bad advertising," Cal said. "We couldn't buy exposure like this. The phone is going to ring off the hook tomorrow. Get ready for the big leagues!" With that, Cal shut the door and left Liz alone.

Liz took off her stockings and brushed her teeth on automatic pilot. Before she knew it, she was beating her pillow and snuggling down in the cold sheets. Slowly, the day sank in. Cal was right. No matter how famous Liz had been before, nothing she had said or done had brought her the attention her performance tonight would.

She swore and whacked the pillow in frustration. Cal might be delighted by the attention, but Liz had worked really hard on not coming off like some harridan, or shrill harpy, or, worst of all, an idiot. The ugly pundit who was worried about his balls invaded her thoughts.

"How can I fight an image like that?" she wondered.

She surprised herself by crying. Tears of frustration wet her cheeks as she sobbed into her pillow and mourned the loss of her credibility. She hadn't realized that she had wanted this so much. This was the end of the campaign, and the thought of packing up and going home in disgrace made it clear that this whole time, Liz had wanted to win. Cal might be satisfied with promoting a message, but Liz wanted to walk into that big, white house and belong there, dammit.

She sat up in the big bed and turned on the light. She wasn't going to sleep anytime soon, and she dreaded turning on the television again for fear some jowly monster would hurl her back into tears. She couldn't concentrate enough even to read the trashy romance novel or study the policy notes she'd brought along. Finally, her eyes fell on a yellow pad cast aside among the papers on the desk.

Liz fumbled for her glasses and grabbed the pad and a pen. She went back to bed and turned to a clean page. She hadn't written in bed since college when working under the covers was a compromise between sleeping and studying.

At the top of the page, Liz wrote her name and circled it. Then she wrote the names of key cities in the country: LA, Chicago, New York, Miami. She circled those and below them wrote the names of influential people–and their wives—she knew there. When Cal found her the next morning, half-sitting, glasses askew, snoring, Liz had filled eight pages with notes. It was the beginning of her plan.

Chapter 4

Cal shook Liz awake at seven a.m. "Dearie, I've let you sleep as long as I dare. You've got to see this." She held a newspaper by the masthead in front of Liz's unfocused eyes.

Even without her glasses, Liz could read the headline. *LIZ STRATTON CLOSES THE STORE!* it exclaimed in gigantic capital letters.

"Oh, God," Liz moaned and tried to roll facedown in her pillows.

"That won't do," Cal said, pulling her back. "Here, have a mocha. Chocolate will do you good." She thrust the hot paper cup into Liz's unwilling hands.

Liz sighed and took a swig of the chocolaty goodness. "I still don't feel up to this," she said. She put her glasses on, anyway. "Gimme," she said and read the article on the front page.

It read, in part:

Ms. Elizabeth A. Stratton, presidential candidate for the Womyn's Achievement Party, called for women in America and Mesopotamianstan to give up sex until the war is over during the first presidential debate last night.

The call to "close the store" seemed to be in response to condescending and patronizing remarks made by the Democratic and Republican candidates, Oscar Beckinger and Bill Ostrem respectively, during a question about ending the war.

Liz skipped the painful recap of what she said, and scanned ahead in the article.

There have been unofficial anecdotal reports of women actually denying their husbands access coming from many parts of the country. A quick survey of staff at this newspaper implies that the idea of a sex strike may have more staying power than most pundits may think.

Liz put the paper down and looked at the grinning Cal. "I don't believe it," she said. "Am I reading this right?"

"Yes!" Cal was giddy. "It's a positive review. Plus, it looks like women might actually do it."

"Or not do it, as the case may be," Zeke said as he stepped into the room. He noticed with disappointment that Liz slept in full-length pajamas, but he could still see her cute little toes. "You know, this hasn't won you any friends in the male camp," he said, sitting in a chair.

"Oh, pooh," Cal said. "What man would vote for a WAP candidate, anyway? And like I said last night, winning isn't everything. In fact, we probably shouldn't be trying to win at all."

"Why's that?" asked Liz.

"If we try to win, we need to make as many people happy as possible. If we just attack this one issue like a tenacious pit-bull, we could end the war without having to appease the majority."

Liz sat silently for a moment and then reached for the yellow pad that still lay on her bed. She flipped through her increasingly incoherent notes until she found the page she was looking for. "I think we might be able to do both," she said.

Zeke blinked. "Both?"

"Yes. Both. I've got a list here of, well, basically everyone I know with connections. And their wives."

Even Zeke had to smile at the idea. "That's kind of a cruel thing to do to your friends, isn't it?"

"The girls will understand, and the boys will understand when their sons come home from the war," Liz said. She lifted her cell phone from the bedside table and scrolled through the numbers.

"Who are you calling first?" asked Cal.

Liz grinned and held the phone up so they could read the name. Zeke's jaw dropped and Cal began to giggle. "Hello, Liz," said the voice on the phone in a slow drawl. "I was expecting you to call, just not quite so soon."

♥

The sex-strike phone tree quickly spread support for

the idea among many of the wives of the most influential people in the country. Ginny Ostrem, the dear governor's wife, was instrumental in launching the operation. Liz had met her at a fundraiser for a women's shelter, and they had bonded lightly over stories of various cats they'd each had. They had traded cards and worked together peripherally on shelters for both humans and animals. They had not crossed paths since then, but Liz had read the accounts of the governor's affairs for years and guessed that Ginny might be a willing participant.

In fact, Ginny was more than willing, and she said she was pretty sure she could "convince" Bill's current mistress to jump on the bandwagon as well. If Ginny had concerns that Liz might threaten her chance at being first lady, she overlooked them and sent Liz an email bursting with the contact information for the wives of members of congress south of the Mason Dixon. Cal made a note to send Ginny the deluxe WAP gift pack.

Liz's other sources were just as fruitful, and soon they had the unofficial support of women attached to other governors, senators and even more local officials. By early afternoon, the WAP headquarters was awash with phone calls offering support from women from all walks of life.

By evening, it was certain that the newspaper reporter had been right: this idea had legs that could carry it. The question was, how far?

Liz had to admit it was fun watching the news that night.

The male anchors seemed distinctly uncomfortable

on the topic of the sex strike, but the anchorwomen could barely contain themselves. Even Katie Curic couldn't keep a smirk from curling her cute little mouth as she described unofficial reports of groups of congressmen's wives suddenly going on week-long spa vacations together.

Liz and her staff toasted themselves with champagne in the hotel lounge that evening. As the wine flowed, the songs got louder and the jokes cruder.

Zeke was the only man in the group, and he was returning the light flirting of an intern when a group of men drunkenly approached them with mean swaggers.

"You're that bitch from the debate last night," said the leader. He was a tall, good-looking man in a rumpled dark suit, tie askance. Liz smiled sweetly at him and stuck out her hand.

"Liz Stratton, candidate for president," she said.

The man swatted her hand away. "You bitch," he repeated, leaning a little to the right. "You know my wife called me tonight to say that she's going to visit her mother?"

"How would I know that?" Liz asked, her head muddled with bubbly wine.

"My wife won't be there when I get home!" he said threateningly. "I can't fuck her if she's not at home, bitch." He leaned in too far and had to catch himself on a chair. Somehow this didn't diminish his menace.

It dawned on Liz that she might not be very safe, but she felt her staff close ranks around her. Still, no point in provoking anyone. "I'm sorry your wife needs to see her mother—" Liz began, but another man in the group interrupted her.

"My wife is going to see her sister," he growled.

"My girlfriend said she wanted some 'space,'" said a third.

"Well, I'm sorry about that," Liz began again. She saw the bartender on the phone and prayed he was calling security.

"We were thinking," the first man said, a leaning tower of hate. "We were thinking that you're a girl. And you've got lots of girl friends here. And since you all caused this mess, maybe you should finish it."

Zeke suddenly pushed his way between Liz and the drunk. "Mister, I don't think I like what you're implying to my lady friend here," he said, thrusting his chest out like a bantam rooster. "I think you should be on your way before things get out of hand."

Zeke, though a full foot shorter than his adversary, exuded "Do you feel lucky, punk?" juice through every pore. Liz was impressed. She didn't know he had it in him.

The evil drunk swayed left, then right, and looked at Zeke with surprise. Then he vomited on his own shoes. His friends dragged him away. At the door of the lounge, the drunk managed to turn back and shout, "Bitch! You owe me a fucking—fuck!"

Once the men were out of sight, Liz sat down hard and started shaking. The room spun and she panted as the situation sunk in. Zeke put a protective arm around her.

Three security guards appeared at the bar and spoke

to the bartender. Two quickly left to find the drunks while the third stayed to get a report from them all. Cal gave him the full details.

"If we catch these guys, do you want to press charges, ma'am?" he asked finally.

Liz looked up. "Press charges? Maybe. We'll have to think about it."

"Think about it?" Cal was shrill with indignation. "Those men are dangerous! How could we let them get away with this?"

"If we don't press charges, the media doesn't have to know," Liz said. "I'd like to keep control of the issue, Cal. Besides, no one was hurt. Maybe they are just harmless assholes."

"I'll write down 'maybe,'" said the guard. "We'll at least tell the police that the hotel wants to press charges for disorderly or drunken conduct."

"That's fine," Zeke said. "Just keep the campaign out of it for now, please."

Liz rested her head on Zeke's shoulder, grateful for his presence in a way she hadn't been before.

The next morning, the secret service finally gave Liz the same security detail that they afforded to the "major party" candidates.

♥

Liz stood backstage of the first rally since the debate, and she was nervous. The drunk men at the hotel lounge had really shaken her. They hadn't been denied anything they had been expecting, not even for a day. But they were so angry. Liz tried not to think about the kinds of things that might have happened had Zeke not acted or if the aggressors hadn't been so very wasted.

The crowd gathered in front of the stage was predominantly women, as was normal for a WAP event, but they seemed a bit more varied than before. A few more "regular" girls were in attendance in addition to the normal crowd of crew-cut women's libbers and 1970s era bra-burners. There was an anticipatory buzz that might have made Liz excited. Today it made her jumpy.

"Stop being so nervous," Cal said, walking up behind her. "This is *your* crowd. They *like* you. They're going to hang on your every word. You know that choir people preach to? Well, that crowd is about to sing out 'Halleluiah!'"

"You're right. I know you're right," said Liz. "Friday night still has me rattled."

"I know," Cal said. "But look over there." She gestured to the far corners of the crowd.

Liz could just make out men in dark glasses. Cal pointed out the others in the secret service security detail behind the stage.

"They kind of stick out in this crowd, don't you think?" Liz asked.

"They're supposed to be obvious, but not alarming," said Zeke. "You're safe, though. That's the point."

"Okay," Liz said with a deep breath. "Showtime."

When she stepped onto the stage and began waving, the crowd cheered. By the time she arrived at the podium, the cheering had dissolved into a chant. "Close the store! No more war! Close the store!"

As she waited for them to calm down, her eyes scanned the crowd, looking for faces to talk to during the speech. She found the sunglass-ed face of one of her secret service agents standing close to the stage. She had shaken all of their hands when they arrived Saturday morning, but she had not slept that night and had a hangover to boot, so even though she recognized him, she didn't remember his name. She didn't remember him as being so handsome, either.

He gave her the slightest of smiles and a wink.

Liz didn't have time to try to interpret this as the crowd quieted and waited for her to speak.

"Kind supporters," she began. "This is, indeed, a new day. For millennia, women have taken a back seat in shaping world politics. But that 'backseat,' shall we say, has been a place of influence for women everywhere." The audience tittered appreciatively. "Acknowledging the fact that pillow-talk has shaped policy since the beginning of time, we are willing to undertake a coordinated effort for one purpose: the end of this stupid war and the resulting draft that has torn our families apart." Liz waited for the clapping to subside. "In order to end this fruitless war, we need women everywhere to give up the one thing we hold more dear than anything except our children. Intimacy. Women are creatures of intimacy. We create strong, intimate bonds with other women, we have those bonds with our children, and, yes, with our lovers. To give up the intimacy with our loved ones is very painful for us, so to give up sex is also very painful for us. We live for that intimacy.

"However, the greatest sacrifices for the greatest causes are painful, but worth it. By giving up the intimacy with a lover, we might bring back the son or father and re-kindle those bonds anew.

"But why sex? Why must we give up this particular joy? Well, it's because of the male. He lives to fight and fuck. No, no, really, that's what men are programmed to do, and we forgive them just like they forgive us for being programmed to wear shoes that match our purses and to turn off the television during dinner.

"The American male is highly competitive and wants to win. They have the mistaken idea that if we decide not to fight in Mesopotamianstan, that we will lose, and that is anathema to the American male, especially the ones in politics.

"The answer is in their dicks. No, really, it is. The one thing men like better than winning is fucking. They would rather fuck than anything. Try this: make a man a steak dinner and as you serve it, offer to fuck him on the kitchen floor that instant. The dog might steal the steak, but the man will be happy.

"So, ladies and other audience members, remember this: leverage. No sex until there is peace. We might love being intimate, but we have the resolve to win this standoff. Use the time to pick up a new hobby…knitting perhaps? Sharp needles in bed to make your point? Or go on vacation with your girlfriends. Or, better yet, your mother. I'm sure she misses you."

When the cheering died down, it was time for questions. Liz watched as a thin girl approached the microphone. She held herself carefully and spoke softly. "Ms. Stratton, what if, what if he's—stronger than you?"

Liz felt her blood boil. "I don't want anyone to get hurt because of this," she said firmly. "But, my friend, I think you have been hurt before, haven't you? No, don't answer, there are cameras. Anna! Get over there and help her." The crowd closed in around the woman protectively as she began to cry. A few WAP staffers made it to her and lead her away to talk to one of the campaigners who specialized in abuse.

"Let me repeat, ladies. I don't want anyone to get hurt here. I don't want a litany of martyrs in my wake. But you can always call the WAP campaign and be put in touch with people who can help you. This kind of abuse is the kind of thing that I will fight against if I am elected!"

The cheering subsided when another woman approached the microphone set up in the crowd. "Ms. Stratton, I have to be frank," she said. "I like sex. I mean, I really, really like sex. I'm not sure I can give it up."

Liz smiled. "I know what you mean." Her eyes flitted to the secret service agent standing in the front row. He grinned at her, and she tore her gaze back up to the questioner. "We had a show on *Spare Me!* about that very topic. You know, some people might say things about me, like how I've been single for so long that I don't remember what it's like to have sex. Well, it hasn't been *that* long." She laughed. "But it isn't by choice, and

I certainly wouldn't ask any of you to do something that I couldn't do myself. In case you were wondering, every person on my staff has sworn off sex until the war is over!"

The next speaker was a man—a flamboyant gay man. He leaned in close to the mike and said, "But Liz, honey, are you 'master of your domain'?"

The crowd laughed at the old television reference.

Liz grinned. "Well, I never said *that*." Wild cheers and applause. "I mean, it's a sex strike, not a pleasure strike, lovey."

Chapter 5

"All we have to do is idly sit indoors
With smooth roses powdered on our cheeks,
Our bodies burning naked through the folds
Of shining Amorgors' silk, and meet the men
With our dear Venus plats plucked trim and neat."
From *Lysistrata* by Astrophanes

Governor Bill Ostrem eased his flabby body down into an easy chair and groaned as his feet throbbed in relief after bearing his weight all day. He'd been pressing the flesh all night at a $2,000 a plate fundraising dinner. He hated those things because the food was always terrible and a tiny part of him was ashamed that he was too cheap to hire a caterer who would do a decent job.

He watched as his mistress, Honey, padded around the room in her short skirt and plunging neckline. He liked her better than most of the mistresses he'd had over the past twenty years. She was a treat to watch as she bounced atop him since her breasts, though large, were actually real. He'd popped in tonight unannounced, so she was "straightening up" the apartment.

"That's enough," he said gruffly as she passed by. "Come here." He pulled her down and kissed her.

She smiled as she pulled away. "Oh, this place is still a mess, Billy," she cooed. "Let me just pick up a little more." She squirmed away and dropped to all fours to pick up some magazines on the floor, pert ass waving in the air. Bill cursed his fat when he realized that his dick would never reach her in that position.

Instead, he reached over and fondled her ass. "Come on, pet. That can wait. Papa can't."

Honey sat up on her knees and smiled at him. "Oh, but I'm so ashamed of the mess," she said. She rolled up onto her feet and fetched a duster. She began dusting the bottom shelves of her bookcase by bending at the waist, not the knees.

"You little minx," Governor Ostrem moaned. "You're killing me. Come here!"

Honey moved toward him, but dropped the duster. She bent to pick it up, flashing him a grand view of her cleavage. She pivoted and sat primly on his knee, but repelled his hands gently.

"Bill," she said sweetly. "I know you think I'm a bit dim—"

"Nonsense," Ostrem muttered absently. He was inches away from her best parts.

"Could you please explain to me why we're at war in the Middle East?"

Ostrem had one hand up her shirt. "Later."

"Now," she said, pulling his hand away. "Please?"

He looked up in Honey's face and was mildly surprised that she had brown eyes. He'd thought they were green. "Uh," he began. "It's complicated. Can't we do this later?"

"We could," she said. "But this question will bother me so until it's answered, I just don't know if I can get into the mood."

"Harumph. The Iranians made a land grab and we repelled them. Now we have to stabilize the region. Satisfied?" He lunged for her shirt again.

"No, not really," Honey parried. "I thought I heard the TV say that the Iranians hadn't invaded anyone, but we thought they might, so we invaded."

"Mebbe," Ostrem said. He tried kissing her neck, but Honey moved away.

"You mean we invaded a country without provocation again?"

"Mebbe," he muttered. "Please, Honey, can we just forget this for now?"

"Sure, Billie," Honey cooed and cuddled up to him. "Just 'cause I know you'll fix it once you're president."

"I'll fix it," he murmured into her hair.

"How?" Honey looked up at him with those—brown, yes, brown—eyes.

"Oh, I suppose we'll stabilize the region and pull out eventually."

"Eventually? Why not right away?"

"It's complicated, Honey," Bill snapped. "Lots of people, powerful people, rich people, don't want the war to end right away."

Honey hopped out of his lap. "Billie! You're not making money off the war, are you?"

"Not as much as some," he huffed. "Now come back here."

Honey stood in front of him for a moment and then said loftily, "Bill, I think you should leave now."

"You're kidding," he said. His eyes grew wide. "You're not kidding. Honey, you can't do this to me!"

"Can't I?" she said. "Just watch me!"

♥

A few days later found Ostrem in Washington, DC, where he had a known penchant for strippers and masseurs.

But when he'd gone looking for some entertainment the other night, he'd found that all the girls at his favorite place were sick with the flu. The next night he'd tried a different place, but those girls were sick, too. Tonight, in desperation, he'd called his state's congressman for ideas.

"I'm having the same trouble you are, Bill," Congressman Less Nausbaum said. "I've got three numbers and everyone is sick, or on vacation, or found religion. I've talked to Keller and Whiskerman and they're out in the cold, too."

"Do you mean that DC is fresh out of whores?" Ostrem said, astounded.

"It looks that way," Nausbaum said. "You don't suppose your lively little tart of an opponent is behind this, do you?"

"I don't know," Ostrem growled. "If she is, she's going to pay."

♥

All Jack Riddel wanted was his customary blowjob before he started his twelve-hour shift at the factory. His wife, Amy, had been good for one every morning of their married life. Even though she wasn't the prettiest girl he'd ever dated, her warm heart and willing tongue had won him over all those years ago.

But today, Amy was taking a long time in the bathroom. Jack sat on the bed with his pants folded beside him, waiting impatiently. He was going to be late for the bus. Finally, he called out to her.

"Amy? I'm going to be late!"

"One moment, dear!" The door of the bathroom opened and Amy stepped out, dressed in some sort of polyester uniform. She was putting in an earring and walked past him, even though he was naked from the waist down.

"Ahem," Jack said. When Amy turned, he tilted his head and asked, "Aren't you forgetting something?"

"I'm sorry, honey. I don't have time today. I'm late, too."

"Late? For what?"

"I'm late for my first day of work. Isn't it too, too exciting? I'm the new day manager at the Burger Hut!"

"You don't need to work. I make plenty of money. Now, please—"

"Of course you do, my darling," Amy cooed and kissed the thin spot on his head. "I just have nothing to do now that Mark and Kyle are at college, and I wanted to save a little money for a cruise next summer. Won't that be fun!"

"Still," Jack said. "Don't you have time for...uh, me?" Jack resorted to pointing at his stiff member.

"Not today, dear!" Amy called as she sailed out of the bedroom. A moment later, Jack heard the door slam behind her.

He was two minutes late for the bus and got an earful from his equally frustrated boss when he finally got to work.

♥

Liz was washing her hair in the sink when someone knocked on the door of her room. "Come in!" she shouted. She watched in the mirror as Zeke stepped in. "In here!" she called. "I'm almost done!"

Zeke closed the door and sat on the bed to wait. As he did, he allowed himself a little fantasy that he was sharing this room with Liz and that she was getting ready for a night out on the town with him. He knew exactly which dress she'd wear: the little strappy blue number she wore to the Daytime Emmys once. They'd dance, share some champagne, and then end up back at the room for a game of twister, sans mat.

"I'm nearly ready," Liz said as she came into the room wrapping her hair in a towel. She was in the hotel bathrobe, and it killed Zeke to think that she was naked under there.

"You don't look ready at all," he said, crossing his legs nonchalantly.

"Pooh," she said. "I just washed my hair. It'll take five seconds to put in a ponytail. I just need to find my hair bands." She bent at the waist and rummaged through her suitcase.

"Damn," Zeke said to Liz's heart-shaped ass.

Liz looked over her shoulder at him. "What?"

"Oh, television," Zeke lied. "Uh, that CNN story was just, so...damn!"

Liz frowned at him and found her hair bands. "I don't know why I keep that channel on. Everything that's on it makes me angry." She turned it off as she passed.

Zeke repositioned himself when she disappeared into the bathroom but denied himself the urge to peek in her suitcase just to see if any underwear was on top. Oh, she was killing him softly.

Liz appeared in a ponytail and trim pantsuit, looking as professional and polished as ever. "Let's go have breakfast with rich people," she cried and stepped out into the hallway.

Zeke trotted at her heels like an ever-adoring shi tzu.

Shame could do really awful things to people. The

first three times Zeke had asked Liz out, he was serious. He had fucked up the timing or the tone or the situation so badly, though, that Liz hadn't taken him seriously, and now she never would. He kept asking her out because now it was just expected. They would laugh about it and then go on with their days. He could tell himself and his therapist that he had tried again—though the therapist saw through this—so he was off the hook. Liz always got an ego-boost when Zeke asked her out, though she'd never admit it. The days she didn't see him and no one else asked her for a date, she felt a lot less confident.

Not that either of them would admit that they needed each other. Ever. To anyone.

♥

Senator Oscar Beckinger was home in Indiana briefly from the campaign trail, and he was frustrated. He'd come home in a good mood because the campaign was going well. The Democratic Party was behind him, and Ostrem, the Republican candidate, was a parody of himself, easy to ridicule. The campaign platform of helping the country by caring for the least fortunate was working like a charm. Compassionate Democrats were lining up to work on the campaign.

He found a little hole in the campaign schedule so he could go home and "recharge," as he put it. He wanted to spend time with his wife and kids, he said. The boys would be glad enough to see him, but they were both off with their friends most of the time. His wife, Megan, was always loving and told him how much she missed him. She was still delicious, and he was all set to ravage her affectionately as soon as his suitcase hit the entryway.

Then, of course, he'd ring up his mistress and ravage her, too.

But Megan wasn't at home when he got there. His dog Salvadore, a black pedigreed standard poodle, was ecstatic he was home, but it wasn't the same. Salvador bounced around him happily, which lightened his spirits and gave him an idea. He'd call his mistress, Rebecca. She was always happy to see him, too.

He picked up his cell phone, pushing away Salvador's amorous advances, and dialed Rebecca's number. The phone rang and rang and rang, but then clicked over to voicemail. "Hi!" it said. "This is Rebecca! Please leave me a message."

"Rebecca, this is Ox. I'm at home. Please call my cell."

Oscar hung up and flung the phone onto the bed in frustration. Now what was he going to do? He didn't want to jerk off, in case Megan came back or Rebecca called soon. But he was antsy and grumpy.

Salvador jumped up on the bed, and Beckinger shouted at him. *Damn dog probably hasn't been outside all day*, he thought. *He's going crazy all cooped up in here. We need to get out.*

He changed into his running clothes, loaded Salvador into the hybrid SUV he'd bought to "green up" his image, and drove to the dog park for the people who lived in his gated community. When he was home from sessions of congress, he ran here with the dog all the time. It was safe enough that the secret servicemen could follow at a leisurely distance, as they did now.

Salvador was nearly mad with anticipation when they pulled into the parking lot. He spun tight little circles in the cargo area of the car and whimpered piteously. When Beckinger opened the door, the dog launched himself toward the gate of the park. "Don't go running off, Sal," Beckinger called after him, knowing it wouldn't do any good.

As he approached the gate, a ragged man appeared before him. Beckinger realized he wasn't going to be able to avoid talking to him since the hobo had Salvador by the collar.

"This yer dog?" the man asked. "He's mighty fancy."

"Yes, he's mine," Beckinger said. He took Sal by the collar, shoved him into the dog park gate, and tried to follow.

The homeless man stepped in front of him. "No 'Thank you'?" he asked.

"Thank you," Beckinger said and tried to push past him again.

The hobo stood his ground. "Can you spare a dollar, mister, since I caught yer dog?"

"I don't have my wallet with me. I'm going for a jog," Beckinger snarled. "Let me by or I'll call the police."

The homeless man backed away from Beckinger, muttering an apology. Beckinger let himself into the dog park and whistled to Sal, who ignored him gleefully. Beckinger had to chase Salvador down and clip on his leash before they could begin jogging around the well-groomed park.

The homeless man went back to his own mixed-breed dog, which had been waiting patiently for him by his pack. He patted the mutt affectionately, picked up his belongings, and began to walk. The dog fell in beside his master without a leash, and the two marched on in search of their next meal.

Beckinger didn't feel less frustrated after the jog, though he was more tired. Once Salvador was on the leash, he behaved well enough, as long as he was in front, and they went where he wanted to go. Catching him was very challenging.

The only reason Beckinger had been able to get him at all today was because there weren't any other dogs at the park.

Salvador didn't seem tired at all. He spun circles once they were in the driveway and was out of the car like a bullet, racing to the front door. The house was still empty, and no one had called. Beckinger turned on the television and then turned it off again. He lay down on the couch and closed his eyes. He hadn't had a nap during the day in ages.

He woke to find Megan sitting at his feet on the end of the couch, watching a talk show. He sat up, rubbing his eyes. "Hi, honey," he said, kissing her cheek. "Where were you?"

"I've been at a meeting," she said vaguely. "I didn't

know you were coming home."

"It's just for the day. I'm off again tomorrow. I just wanted to see you," he said, shifting so he could lay his head in her lap. "Where are the boys?"

"Practice until four, then they usually hang out with their buddies until six."

"What time is it now?"

"Two-thirty."

"So, we have time." Beckinger grinned, slid his hands around his wife's waist, and buried his face in her belly.

"Oh, now, I couldn't," Megan said, pushing him away.

"Why not?" Beckinger whined. "I came home just to see you!"

"It's that time of the month," Megan lied.

"No, it's not," Beckinger said. "It was that time last time I came home."

"I have a headache."

"I won't touch your head. Please, honey?"

"Oscar, stop it. I don't want to. Isn't that enough?"

"Not really," he said, sitting up and pouting. "I'd like a reason, please."

"Well, there's a war on—"

"The war's been going on for years. So what?"

"Well, I'd sure like it to end."

Beckinger blinked. "Oh, hell, Megan. You're not doing that silly sex-strike thing, are you? Are you? Christ Almighty!" He stood and began pacing the room. "I don't know what you silly women think you're proving by doing this, but I've been horny for days—days!—and now my own wife is denying me, even though all I've done is pine for you. My lovely! My wife!"

Megan looked at her hands for a moment and then stood up. "Please don't shout at me," she said, eyes on the floor.

Beckinger stopped and looked at her. "What?"

"Don't shout at me. Every time you're unhappy with something, you pace and shout at me, and I'm tired of it."

He squinted at her as if it would help him understand. "What?"

"You shout at me, you never call the boys when you're in Washington, and you only come home when you're horny. I'm sick of it, Oscar. So, I'm cutting you off." She took a breath and met his eyes.

"You're what? I can't believe my ears. You're what?"

"Cutting you off!" Megan's adrenaline was ringing in her ears. The words spilled from her as if she had rehearsed them. "I do care about the world and the damage this war is causing, even if you fucking don't. I don't want our boys drafted into this stupid endeavor. You do realize that they'll be eligible soon, don't you? Don't you? They're your boys, your sons, for Chrissakes!"

"So, you're actually following my opponent's sex strike? Really, Megan? You're betraying me this way?"

"Betrayal? Don't talk to me about betrayal. You're the one who voted to reinstate the draft, you fuckwit," Megan screamed. "You aren't sending my babies to a war and then having your way with me! No. Either this war ends or your dick shrivels up and falls off from disuse! And don't think you'll just go to that tart Rebecca, either. She and I are in complete agreement on this."

"How—Rebecca?   Rebecca,   too?"   Beckinger stammered. He staggered backward and collapsed into one of the stuffed armchairs. "How do you know Rebecca?"

"You're not so smart," Megan said, sitting down and glancing away. "It's not like she's a secret."

A moment passed when all Beckinger could do was blink, and all Megan could do was count the seconds until he exploded in his usual tirade. She prayed nothing she cared about got broken this time, but the seconds kept ticking and nothing happened. Finally, she ventured a peek up at him.

He was staring at her with a new look of, was that respect? It made her blush. "What?" she said.

"Jesus, you're sexy when you're mad."

"Thanks, but that won't work, either."

"Damn. I do mean it."

"Thanks," Megan said. Then she stood up. "I'll set up the guest room for you tonight. I'll explain this to the boys if you'd rather not."

"No, I'd better," he said. "Don't want them to get the wrong idea." He watched her leave the room, admiring her motherly ass and wondering what had happened to bring back the spitfire he'd married. It wouldn't be the first time he'd slept with the dog in the guestroom, but it was the first time he'd done so with an increased desire for his wife.

♥

When Cal first saw Jerry Albright fifteen years ago, he was a rangy, bearded hippie in a power suit on the UMASS campus during an Activist Fair. He was running the Amazon Rainforest booth and was surrounded by long-haired, not-recently-showered hippie kids who were doing their sophomoric duty by spouting rhetoric from their Bible, a book called *So Few Trees, So Little Time*. Jerry had written it while he was doing research in the jungle.

He stood self-consciously behind the pile of books as his late-teen disciples bombarded passersby with unanswerable questions:

"When are you going to stop supporting the rainforest's destruction by eating meat?"

"How many trees have to die before you stop buying wood furniture?"

"Stop wasting paper!" a hippie chick hollered at Cal, as she shoved a leaflet into Cal's hands.

Hundreds of leaflets were strewn on the ground in front of the booth. Cal found this extremely funny and stood for a moment, giggling.

"Yeah," Jerry said from behind the wall of books. "That one gets me, too."

Cal looked up into his clear brown eyes and giggled again, shaking her head. "Talk about no self-awareness!"

She felt both very mature and a little self-conscious saying this since she was only a little older than the chickie.

To cover up her awkwardness, she thrust out her hand. "Calliope Talmadge. I'm running the WAP booth." She pointed to the far corner where the WAP banner was visible next to a PETA display. "I needed to take a walk to get away from the tortured bunny pictures."

"Jerry Albright," he said, shaking her hand. "I totally understand. I don't have the stomach for that, either."

Cal fingered one of the books and glanced at the small table display. She said "Oh," when she saw his picture on the poster. "You're *that* Jerry Albright!"

He smiled. "That makes me sound like a celebrity or something."

"In some places, you are. I read this book last year. It was required reading for WAP interns."

"Really? Why?"

"You outline techniques for getting attention—media attention. They work for most issues, I think."

"So, you're not at all concerned about rainforests?" Jerry sounded disappointed.

"Oh, no. I mean, yes. It's on my top ten list after reproductive rights and shattering the glass ceiling."

"I like people who fight for causes," he said. "People who care passionately. I think those are the best kind of people, Calliope."

Cal looked up at him and found that the note of interest she heard in his voice was reflected in his eyes, as well.

"Me, too!" she said once she realized she had been staring. "I like passionate people, too, Jerry."

After a first date at a Vegan restaurant that ended with them skinny-dipping in a lake in a city park, Cal knew she was in love. Jerry was about five years older than she was. Cal was still in graduate school when they met. He lobbied hard for her to quit—"What does one do with a PhD in Women's Studies anyway?" he'd ask—and follow him to Brazil on his long research trips. Even though it had been difficult to maintain the relationship over those years, Cal was later very, very glad that she had stuck to her guns and finished school.

He proposed to her on the one trip to Brazil she made before they were married, bending on one knee under an enormous tree in an endangered forest. She panicked when a little snake bit Jerry's calf as he slipped the ring on her finger, but after their guide had wrung its neck, he said that the snake wasn't poisonous.

A month after Cal graduated, they were married barefoot on a beach in Maine—a spot they found when Jerry was home from the jungle and Cal was between projects for WAP. The ceremony had a shaman instead of a minister and the invitations were printed on hemp paper.

Liz thought that the whole thing was out of character for Cal, but Cal was in L-O-V-E, so Liz kept her mouth shut.

Later, Cal was embarrassed to admit that they only actually lived together as man and wife for eleven months, tops. For rest of their three years of legal commitment, Jerry was in some part of Amazonia, and Cal was fighting the right-to-lifers or corporate America somewhere in the States.

They parted ways when Jerry found a nubile Brazilian who also liked passionate people. Cal didn't really blame him for wanting a partner who was not only passionate about him, but was passionate about his chosen cause. However, she was angry with him for telling her of the affair via email and his filing for divorce from Brazil. She hadn't figured him for a coward, but there was the proof.

Liz and Cal took a week's vacation together when the divorce was final. They put boxes of Jerry's things in a van and drove from LA to Yellowstone and back. They left piles of books and records and clothes at any charity shop they passed. On the way back, they left piles of things in front of the bathrooms at the rest stops. Cal returned to her half-empty apartment, feeling cleansed.

She was dismayed, but not surprised, to see Jerry's name on the list of people working for the Democratic campaign stop scheduled just after the WAP rally. She'd expected more Green Party work from him, but she wondered if he were actually radical enough for them.

Every time she walked into a building where the Democrats were holding a rally, especially an environmental rally, Cal held her breath and prayed that Jerry wasn't there.

Now who's the coward? she berated herself.

She was ashamed that she hadn't spoken to her ex for eight years. She didn't want to confront his crushing rejection in person. Plus, his new wife might be with him, and Cal was terrified that she'd be pretty, and twenty-five, and possibly admirable in other ways. Cal was torn between hoping she was an ugly hag and hoping that she was "better" than Cal in some ways so she could understand why Jerry left.

Cal hated herself for still having these feelings all these years later. She practically spat on the ground whenever Jerry's name came up in conversation, and she hated being the bitter ex who couldn't move on.

Still, when she saw him standing in the crowd at the Ohio State Fair, waiting to listen to Liz speak, Cal nearly swallowed her tongue. The woman standing with him was not his new, young wife—she was in her fifties and was consulting a clipboard. Plus, Jerry was openly enjoying watching the women in the crowd. He was never so crass as to do that in his wife's presence.

He looked good, although age had thickened his middle and thinned his top. His eyes still twinkled, but she could picture him in ten years with a paunch and long hair, balding on top, with streaks of gray in his beard. That look might be ridiculous on some, but Cal suspected that Jerry would be able to pull it off as somehow dignified and rebellious at the same time, just like when he wore that suit with his hippie beard to seem more like an "author" and less like a radical who couldn't sell books.

Her blood froze when his eyes found hers. He smiled and walked directly toward her. Cal's first instinct was to flee, but realistically, what would that get her? She gulped and willed herself to smile at him as he approached.

"Calliope! Fancy meeting you here," Jerry said, pulling her into a bear hug.

"Mph," Cal said, somewhat grateful that she could have this moment to pull herself together. She was disappointed when his familiar scent caused her knees to jellify.

Jerry held her out at arm's length. "You look good enough to eat!" he declared. "How have you been?"

"I'm really good," Cal managed to say.

"I'll say! I'd love to know how you convinced Liz, of all people, to run for president. If I remember correctly, in college you couldn't get that girl to run for dorm president."

Cal smiled at the memory. "Well, honestly, I ambushed her."

"I heard," Jerry said. He looked at her again appraisingly. "I meant it when I said that you look great."

Cal was mad at herself for dropping her gaze. "Thank you," she managed to say. "It's nice to see you, too. Where's your wife?"

Jerry rolled his eyes. "Brazil," he said. "That's where she always is. She's come to the States to visit my family once. I can't get her out of that country. It's like we're only married when I'm down there. I've got a life up here, too."

Cal managed to turn her ironic grin into something that resembled a sympathetic moue. "That's too bad," she said. "Long-distance relationships are difficult."

"Too true," he agreed. He looked her in the eye. "So, would you be up for drinks later?"

Cal's eyebrows shot up in surprise. "Really? Why?" She didn't mean to sound so incredulous.

Jerry scuffed the dirt with his shoe. "I don't know. Re-live old times? Be adults and keep each other company for a while?" He glanced up at her hopefully, a method she recognized from when they were married.

"I'll have to get back to you on that," she said. "The campaign has absorbed every second of my time, and promises to for the next several months. You understand," she finished.

"Oh, yeah, I understand," he said. He fished out a business card and jotted a number on it before handing it to her. "My cell," he explained. "Just give me a call when you want to get together," he said. He stepped up to her and gave her a kiss on the cheek. "I've missed you," he whispered, warm whiskers tickling her ear. Then he turned and walked back into the crowd.

Liz came up behind Cal once Jerry dissolved into the audience. "Was that as weird as it looked?" she asked.

"Yes," Cal said.

Liz took the business card from Cal, tore it in half, and handed one part back to Cal. "I'll keep this," she said. "If you really, really want it back, ask me for it, and I'll spend the next hour reminding you of all the crap he put you through. Then maybe I'll give you the other half."

"Sure," Cal said, too stunned to protest or thank Liz. "I'm going to go sit in the bus, okay?"

"Good idea. We have everything under control here," Liz said.

The bus was dark and quiet, exactly what Cal wanted. She turned the half-card over and over in her hands. One side had words like "environmental consultant" and "Jerry" on it. The other side had an area code and a "4" written in black ink in Jerry's surprisingly precise hand. She knew that Liz's trick of tearing the card in half was only a symbolic gesture: five minutes on the Internet and Cal could find Jerry's contact information. That wasn't the point, though. The point was that she shouldn't.

Cal dropped the scrap of cardstock onto the table and sat back to stare at the ceiling of the bus. She peered into the dark corners of herself and asked, "How do you feel, Calliope Talmadge? How do you feel about Jerry Albright?"

Ugh. It was dank and cobwebby in the corner of her heart where she stored the pain Jerry caused. She opened up that box and stared into it hard. She found hard little bits of anger and bitterness, dried up like currants. There were the little pips of the desperation she felt when she wanted him to love her again so badly. There were even the dried-up peels of her love for him. But nothing juicy or fragrant or viable still lived there. She had moved on, after all.

But she still wouldn't have a drink with him. She shredded her half of a card, sprinkled the pieces in the bus's commode, and flushed it with ceremony. That was the end of that.

Chapter 6

W hat's new?" Liz asked as she slipped into her seat for the breakfast meeting. They were well into the race, and she felt like she was getting the hang of this campaigning thing. "Where are we going, what are we doing, how are we doing it?"

"Let's see," Zeke said, consulting his notes. "We're going to visit a college this afternoon so you can shake hands with some young voters."

"They're letting me mingle with young people?" Liz said. "I thought I was a bad influence."

"You're telling them *not* to have sex," Cal said. "How can that be a bad influence?"

Liz grinned. "What else?"

"We got the sponsorship," Cal said.

"Which was that?"

Cal's grin got bigger. "The one from Good Vibrations."

"You mean the health-food chain, right?" Liz asked slowly. "Not the other place?"

"Silly. Of course I mean the sex shop! It's woman-owned and a long-time contributor to WAP causes."

Liz licked her lips nervously. "I don't see how this is going to help us."

"Oh, don't turn into an prissy biddy on us now," Cal said. "Look at the swag they sent us to pass out at our next rally." She hauled out a sample box full of gels and creams and tiny battery-operated devices. "This will help bolster the troops!"

Liz imagined her granny spinning in her grave. Actually, her granny used to say all you needed for a swimsuit was two postage stamps and a cork, so maybe not. Anyway, Liz thought that someone in her family ought to be ashamed of what she was doing in the national spotlight.

Her mother was probably upset. Mom always had a taste for the privately risqué, despite her prissy exterior. Finding her mother's racy novels on the nightstand mortified young Liz. Now Liz's show embarrassed her mom, who found it difficult to reconcile her pride for Liz's success with the public shame over the show's topics. Liz had been avoiding calling her mother since the announcement of the sex strike. She dreaded that conversation.

Liz's father was confused by the strike. He was more technical than her mother. Mom viewed the telephone as the end-all of communication tools. Dad had sent a one-line email the day after the strike:

Really, Liz? A sex strike? Really?

Liz had been amused by the similarity of this reaction to Zeke's. "Vibrators for peace from Good Vibrations, huh?" she joked on the bus.

"Oh, we can come up with a better slogan than that!" cried Cal. "I wish the '60's hadn't already taken 'make love, not war.'"

"How about 'Make love to me, not war?'" Zeke offered hopefully.

Cal grinned. "I love it. Let's think of others."

Eventually, they came up with a list that included gems like, "Vibrating for peace," "War kills my libido," and "Fuck me, not them."

"Oh, hey, I forgot about these." Cal held out a lavender rubber bracelet.

Liz took it and read the inscription. "What does 'WWLD?' stand for?"

"'What Would Liz Do?'" Cal laughed. "Do you love it?"

"Yes, yes I do," Liz said and put it on her wrist.

"They're going in the swag bags, too."

"Anything else?"

"We do have one last thing to talk about," Zeke said as he put on his bracelet. "Running mate candidates."

"Running mate? Oh, of course," Liz said.

"The Dems and Reps have their running mates already. We're a little behind actually," Zeke said. "Do you have any ideas about this?"

"Oprah leaps to mind," Liz said, "but I'm sure she wants to be the headliner when her time comes."

"No Oprah," Zeke wrote down.

"Um, I don't really know of anyone else who fits the profile, you know?"

"Well, I have some ideas," said Cal. She pulled a manila folder out of her bag and flipped it open. Inside was a stack of photos and biosheets of women from all over of all ages and persuasions. Cal pulled them out one by one.

"First is Isabella Terres. She's a Hispanic leader in New Mexico who began by opening shelters for abused women and now is a state representative." Isabella's picture showed a small, intense woman with long black hair in a dark suit seated in front of the New Mexico state seal.

"Next is Clementine Redfeather. She's a Native American advocate for the state of Texas. She's now the district attorney for the Dallas area." Clementine was not a great beauty. In fact, Liz caught herself thinking that she wouldn't want to find herself in a dark alley with her. But Clementine had a shrewd eye and somehow Liz knew she could trust her. Maybe it was the flag she was sitting in front of.

"Then, my personal favorite, Elektra Sampson." Cal flicked the picture to Liz who picked it up. Elektra was a distinguished black lady of a certain age who smiled kindly out of a headshot with an inexplicably pink background.

"She looks like someone's grandmother," Liz said, smiling.

"She is," said Cal. "But she is also a retired eleventh grade teacher from a boy's reform school in Harlem. In her spare time, she was the chairwoman of the NAACP chapter in Harlem and the foreign affairs editor at a small academic journal."

"Really?" Liz asked, eyes wide. "This sweet little old lady?"

"She's as sweet as they come," said Cal. "Just don't cross her."

"When do I meet them?" asked Liz.

"They're coming for meetings after dinner." Cal said. "Be prepared!"

♥

When Elektra walked into the lounge, Liz knew she was there, even though she wasn't watching the door. The mood of the room had shifted ever so slightly, and Liz could feel the weight of the eyes that had turned to watch the dignified lady walk across the floor.

"Ah, Elektra!" Cal said when she saw her. She stood, waved her over, and shook her hand when Elektra arrived at the table. "Elektra Sampson, this is Elizabeth Stratton," she said.

Liz stood and shook Elektra's hand. "It's nice to meet you, Elektra."

"How do you do?" asked Elektra as she closed her dry hand around Liz's smooth manicured fingers. "It is a pleasure to meet you, my dear."

Liz watched as Elektra sat, primly crossing her

ankles and folding her hands in her lap. Liz could see
how this little woman could control a room full of
degenerate teens as she was already desperate for this
woman's approval, and they'd only just met.

"So, we have the same initials," Liz said. "We'll be
forever mixing up our monogrammed luggage!"

Elektra smiled indulgently. "Yes, I suppose we
would." Her tone indicated that she would rather they
dispose with small talk and get on with things.

Liz glanced down at her notes and then pushed them
away. "Elektra, I get the feeling that you are a
very…proper…lady, am I correct?"

"Most days," Elektra said with a smile.

"And, you've been following our campaign, have
you?"

"Yes."

"Well, if you don't mind my asking, why would you
want to join me…uh…this campaign, given
our…uh…tactics?"

Elektra smiled again, and Liz realized that her smile
was the perfect mask. Liz couldn't read Elektra at all
behind that smile. It was a Mona Lisa smile, in that it
could be read so many ways that it actually had no
meaning. Liz was instantly jealous.

"I do not object to your…tactics," said Elektra,
"because I agree with the objective so strongly.
However," she said coyly. "I think you are not targeting a
large group that perhaps I could help with."

"Who's that?" asked Cal.

"Women my age," she said. Cal furrowed her brow

and Elektra scoffed. "Now, don't tell me you didn't think older ladies could help out? Not only are old men the ones you most want to influence, my dears, but old ladies have the most practice not doing what you want them not to do. Believe me," she said. "Nothing can torture an old man like an old woman."

"Please, please be my running mate," said Liz.

"Of course, my dear," said Elektra, clasping Liz's hand across the table. "As long as you promise that we're going to fight this one all the way to the end, tooth and nail. We're not going to give up and just rattle our sabers so that our cause is heard."

Liz smiled. "I want a change of address, too," she said to her running mate.

♥

Still here at last the water's drawn
And with it eagerly I run
To help those of my friends who stand
In danger of being burned alive.
For I am told a dribbling band
Of graybeards hobble to the field,
Great fagots in each palsied hand,
As if a hot bath to prepare.
From *Lysistrata* by Astrophanes

Elektra Sampson was a trim woman of sixty. She had a husband, Horatio; three adult children; and five grandchildren, number six on the way. Her gray hair was cropped close to her head and she wore gold hoop earrings and red lipstick. She came across as both grandmotherly and as a woman who had seen every trick in the book and was nobody's fool.

The campaign had taken Elektra's advice and searched for places to hold rallies that might focus on senior citizens. The best they could do for her first appearance, however, was an Indian casino in the Connecticut "wilderness." Elektra wasn't exactly pleased, but she knew that the attraction of the casino would certainly increase the numbers of people at the rally, given the short notice.

When she inspected the scene before the rally began, she asked someone with a walkie-talkie where the chairs were.

"I didn't get an order for any chairs. Usually at rallies and such, people stand."

"Not this time," Elektra said. "This is a rally for old people, and they're going to want to sit. You get on that talky thingy and get some chairs in here pronto!"

"Yes, ma'am." The man scampered off and chairs were set up right away. Twenty minutes later, the doors opened and a large group of white-haired ladies filed in, chattering to themselves. They all found seats, and soon, the chairs were all filled. With a word from Elektra, more chairs were found for those standing in the back.

As Elektra expected, the sea of faces waiting for her were predominantly white, with a few shades of black and brown peppered in. And she was pleased to see a full house. She hadn't expected that.

She stepped on to the stage to enthusiastic applause. She hadn't expected that, either. She smiled and waved as the crowd clapped itself out, which wasn't long given its age.

"Thank you for that wonderful welcome," she said. "I am so flattered and grateful to be here. I want to thank our lovely hosts here at the Lucky Seven Feathers Casino, especially for the seating they've provided. Isn't it nice to sit down at a rally?"

The crowd cheered again and a few canes were pounded on the ground for added affect.

"Now, why are we here today besides the bonus bingo and loose slots? We're here to show our support for Elizabeth A. Stratton, a woman who wants to be your next president!" She waited for the cheers to die down. "I plan on being your next vice president, myself. The first thing on our docket once we get there is to end this damnable war that's taken our sons, our daughters, and our friends. This is a war that was sold to us as a great war, but it isn't. It's a legacy from the old regime. It's a revenge-play from the ugly past, and it's got to stop!

"Now, those younger ladies are having a strike to make their point clear. They're giving up something vital and precious to them: sex. Then they looked to me and said, 'Elektra, how do the old ladies want to help?' I said to them, 'My dears, you imply that my good friends in this room don't know how to have a good time in bed. Or wouldn't miss it if they gave it up.'"

A good-humored chuckle moved through the crowd.

"I put them straight, of course. With Viagra now

given out with our blood pressure pills, old men are more randy than ever. What's more, I reminded those little girls that our old boys are the ones who run the show. I told them that a sex strike wouldn't work at all if it didn't include us.

"But, let's face it, girls. We can do more than that. Most of us are retired, or at the very least don't have a brood underfoot anymore. What more can we do? In the spirit of the generation that burned its bras forty years ago, I think we can recruit more to the cause, march in more parades, write more letters, and make more phone calls. We can stop having sex to end the war, but we can get off our keisters to break the glass ceiling, put down the bridge game to keep control of our uteri—or those of younger women—and tape our soap operas for later as we rally for women's shelters!"

As the crowd of blue-hairs cheered, staffers passed out bags of swag. As the old ladies opened their bags, a hush spread across them. Then a titter started and flooded the hall. A wrinkled hand shot up and out of teaching habit, Elektra said, "Yes?"

"I thought we were supposed to stop having sex? What's with the... goodies?" asked a crone of about eighty.

"Liz Stratton said it best when she said that it is a sex strike, not a pleasure strike. Enjoy the goodies, everyone."

♥

Liz was horny. No, she couldn't deny it, that was her problem. Her last date had been months ago, long before the campaign, and it hadn't ended well. The last time she'd had sex? Was it Easter? She'd been so busy that she didn't remember. But man, oh, man, did she ever miss it today.

She'd often wondered how she'd ended up thirty-five and single. Her five-year relationship with Evan Peterson didn't help, certainly. They'd always talked about getting married, but he kept finding little nineteen-year-old distractions. Evan was a daytime soap actor and had his pick of delectable young actresses, and he couldn't help helping himself, he'd said. Eventually, Liz got fed up and left. That caused a bit of a Hollywood to-do, but it had been three years ago. There hadn't been any naked pictures of them on the Internet, so the paparazzi got bored and moved on.

She rolled over in her hotel king-sized bed and stretched a hand to the other side, feeling how cold the sheets were over there. She wondered if she'd be allowed to date as president. Then she wondered whom she could date as president? How would she meet people? Were there available men in DC? How would a date as Madam President go? Would the secret service have to do a background check on any suitors? How fun would that be?

Secret service.

Her mind wandered to the handsome guard that had been standing at the edge of every stage she'd been on for the last two weeks. She'd had a couple words with him and found him extremely engaging. His name was Dion Young, and he had green eyes. Liz liked green eyes.

She imagined him there beside her in bed, and she liked the image a lot. She resolved to get his phone number before the end of the campaign. It didn't matter which way the election went. One way or another, she hoped to see him again.

♥

Pearl wasn't sure about video games. She had been old when the first ones came out thirty years ago, so she hadn't paid any attention to them. Now she was sitting in her wheelchair in her best wig and a white thingamajig in her hand, and she was bowling. Well, sort of bowling. She hadn't been able to lift an eight pound ball in a long time, but this game was very similar to bowling, minus the stinking shoes, heavy equipment, and, unfortunately, beer.

She swung her arm, let go of the button under her thumb, and watched the ball roll along the virtual lane on the screen in front of her. Her teammates, all women in their eighties and residents at her rest home, cheered as most of the virtual pins fell over with a satisfying crash. Pearl grinned and wheeled her chair back to her team.

"That ties us up!" cackled Angela, whose red hair was almost too much. "I'd like to see those old hacks win now!"

They all sneered at the group of old men sitting next to them. They lived in the next wing over and were frequent visitors. This computerized bowling tournament was just an excuse used by the activities directors to get the widows and widowers together. The activities directors didn't seem to realize that, especially since Viagra was invented, widows and widowers found each other quite easily, without the assistance of well-meaning young people. In fact, Pearl was making eyes at Teddy, who had most of his teeth and was very good in bed, according to Sheila who was taking her turn at bowling now.

"Knock 'em down, Sheila!" Pearl cried to her teammate. Sheila threw a gutter ball and then got four pins.

She sat next to Pearl and picked up an earlier conversation as if they hadn't left off. "I'm just ready to move on from Teddy, you know? He's sweet, but I'm looking for someone who's a little more dangerous, you know?"

"You haven't been dating during the sex strike, have you?" gasped Beth, the prude of their team.

"Well, dating, yes," Sheila said. "But I haven't slept with anyone since."

"I can attest to that," Teddy grumbled.

"Damn, it, Teddy, this is a private conversation," Angela snapped. "Turn your hearing aid down to normal levels. It's not nice to eavesdrop!"

Teddy grinned wickedly and wiggled his finger near his ear. He didn't fool anyone, so the girls changed the subject while the men took their turns.

"Did you see that Elektra woman speak at the

casino?" Angela asked.

"I saw it on the TV," Sheila said. "I like her. She's a firecracker."

"I like how she said that her family is having a sex strike, too," Pearl said. "A little solidarity from old marrieds."

Beth nodded sagely. "This movement might just end the war, you know?"

She was interrupted by snickering beside them. They turned to see all four men giggling at them.

"What's funny?" demanded Angela.

"You four old biddies." Biff laughed. "You think that you're helping by being all prim and abstaining. You old hussies. Who're you keeping yourselves from?"

"The likes of you, Biff Wickerman," Angela snapped.

"And just how does that help?" asked Tom. "You deny a helpless old man a few moments of joy for what? So he can stop the war how?"

"It's a matter of solidarity, you old sack," Pearl said. "What did it matter that I burned my bra forty years ago? The one act didn't make a difference, but all us doing it did."

"Don't go off on your old professor shit, Pearl," growled Ben, Pearl's former beau. She'd stopped sleeping with him when the sex strike started, so he'd left her to find greener pastures. But there weren't any.

"You're just bitter," Pearl said.

"Damn right," shouted Ben, and everyone shushed him.

It was too late, though, and one of those well-meaning young people came over to the group, smiling and leaning over to "be at their level."

"How's your game going, Mrs. Lowenstien? Mrs. Beck?"

"Just fine, dearie," Beth said too loudly and facing the wrong way.

"Do you need me to show you how to work the controller again?"

"No, no, that's fine," Beth said, so the worker turned and left.

Beth was the best at playing the serene, senile old sweetie, which was the fastest way to get rid of the well-meaning young people. Pearl admired the skill, but hadn't quite mastered it.

"I'm just saying," Ben continued, looking at Pearl directly, "that old people like us are exempt from political action, since we're essentially powerless. So, you can come back to our previous activities," he said as he walked his fingers up Pearl's wheelchair handle.

Pearl plucked his hand from her chair. "Powerless, huh? Weren't you the CEO of some company or other, Ben?"

"Well, yes. It wasn't especially large, you know. I did end up here."

"But you know the current CEO?"

"Yes."

"And you must know a few politicians."

"A few from back in the day, but that's years ago, Pearl."

"Ben, you know as well as I do that you are three phone calls away from the governor. Aren't you?"

Ben's thin lips pressed together into a straight line as he grudgingly admitted, "Two, actually. My nephew married his daughter."

"Humph. 'Powerless,' he says," Pearl jerked her thumb at Ben. "Get a load of them. 'We can't do anything about the war. We're old!'"

The old ladies cackled in glee.

Tom had had enough. He stood up and shook his cane at the old women. "As if we miss sex with you. You're nothing but a bunch of dried up old husks!"

Sheila stood, too and banged her walker on the ground. "That's rich coming from a bunch of old coots who need a pill to tell them which way is 'up!'"

A crowd was beginning to gather around them. The elderly people on the edges of the group were keeping the well-meaning young people occupied while the argument went on.

Teddy stood. "Sheila, you old slut. I don't need you to tell your biddy friends how good I am in bed! My reputation precedes me!"

Sheila giggled. "Sure it does. You're part of the 'Blue Pill Group!'"

Biff laughed. "You old tarts! It's hardly worth getting a woody with you all. You're all so wrinkled, we can't find your twats!"

Beth, stood and cried, "Tom, you're so fat that I never did find your withered old dick!" Then she sat, horrified at herself.

Accounts differ on who threw the first fruit cup, but soon the entire rec room at the Shady Pines Retirement Community was ankle-deep in soft fruit, coffee, tea, and animal crackers. There was a theory that a catheter or two were removed and the collection bags emptied, too, but the rec room had always smelled peculiar, so it was hard to prove.

Once the pandemonium broke out, the well-meaning young people appeared with backup recruits, and the residents were wheeled away, shouting insults that made the well-meaning young people's ears burn in embarrassment and congratulate themselves on convincing their parents to send their own grandparents to a classier facility than this one.

Pearl picked maraschino cherries from her best wig, which lay in her lap. As she was wheeled next to Ben by a well-meaning young person, he grinned at her and waggled his hand near his ear like it was a phone. He mouthed, "Call me," like a desperate high school student.

Pearl rolled her eyes and promised herself that she'd get him to call the governor before he was allowed any misbehavin' at all.

The well-meaning young person scolded her. "Now, Mrs. Miller, do we have to call your granddaughter again?"

Pearl cackled. The thought of her twenty-something granddaughter hearing the details of this row would be something to see. "Oh, please call her," she cried. "In fact, have her come visit and I'll tell her myself." She laughed the rest of the way back to her room.

♥

Here is the gaping calamity I meant:
I cannot shut their ravenous appetites
A moment more now. They are all deserting.
The first I caught was sidling though the postern
Close by the Cave of Pan: the next hoisting herself
With rope and pulley down: a third on the point
Of slipping past: while a fourth malcontent seated
For instant flight to Orsilochus' brother
On bird-back I dragged off by the hair in time…
They are all snatching excuses to sneak home.
From *Lysistrata* by Astrophanes

Amber was against the idea of Liz having her hair done at a random shop in the Midwest because she was very concerned that she'd have to fix Liz's hair afterward. "Just don't let them cut anything or put in highlights," she begged. "God, don't let them do *any* coloring! I'm serious, Liz."

Liz promised. The little hippie chick knew what she was doing when it came to hair, and Liz didn't argue with her anymore. In fact, Liz could swear that Amber was better about yanking since that first day.

The visit was a surprise to the owner of Beauty Quest who was ambushed by the secret service an hour before Liz arrived so they could sweep the area and set up a perimeter. Then the entourage and the press descended on the four-chair shop.

Liz wasn't impressed, but the shop was clean and had three customers in chairs and three waiting, so it was doing okay. The floor was linoleum, the lighting fluorescent, and the pictures of models with haircuts were at least ten years out of date, but the potted plants were dusted and the patrons seemed happy. She shook hands with everyone in the shop and then took a seat in the first chair.

She smiled as the owner wrapped the smock around her. Her name was Maryanne, and she looked like she wrestled alligators in her spare time.

"What would you like today, then, Ms. Stratton?" Maryanne asked, eager to show off her skills. "A little color? A cut? Oh! How about some highlights?"

"Ah, that sounds lovely, Maryanne, but just an up-do today," Liz said.

"Mmm-hmm," she said, pulling Liz's hair down and fluffing it with her hands. "Lovely, lovely. Let's go wash."

Liz thought she could relax a little as the warm water soaked her hair, but Maryanne was a talker. She dove in as if they had been in the middle of a conversation. "So the girls and I were talking about this 'closing the store' business before you came it."

"Really?" Liz said above the sound of rushing water.

"Yeah," said Maryanne as she soaped up Liz's head with her muscular hands. "We're wondering how you cope with it."

"Oh, well—it's—not—hard," Liz grunted between Maryanne's attempts to squeeze her head off or shampoo her hair. Liz couldn't tell which.

"That's what she said," Maryanne cried, and the rest

of the shop squealed in laughter. She rinsed off Liz's hair as she laughed.

Liz tried to laugh as her head was twisted into a towel so tightly that she began to see through time. Maryanne led her back to the chair, still chuckling at her own joke. Liz smiled gamely, knowing that the cameras were still rolling.

"So, are you all on the strike with us, then?" she asked as Maryanne combed her hair. Liz was sure she could hear the last three inches snapping off like guitar strings in the teeth.

"Well, actually, most of us started, right ladies?" There was general assent. "But then most of us fell off of the wagon."

"Oh, why?" asked Liz, turning in her chair imploringly. "Surely you all feel it's important to end the war, right? This is a great way to get their attention."

"We know, we know," said Maryanne, turning Liz back into her chair like a child. "It was just, you know, hard."

"That's what she said," squealed a little old lady in the next chair.

The shop dissolved into the same puerile laughter.

Liz frowned. "So, you all just gave up because you were horny?" She saw the whole shop sheepishly grinning at her in the mirror, though Maryanne had a hold of her head so firmly that she couldn't move. Liz was intensely aware that the cameras were still rolling and recording. She saw Cal in the back of the crowd having a panic attack.

"Did you all get your free goodie pack from our campaign staffers?" Liz asked.

"Oh, yes, dear," said the old lady next to her. "I'm all for self-love, but, well, my husband is—"

"He's hung like a horse," finished Maryanne, who Liz could see could be counted on *not* to be tactful. "Suzie there can't stop bragging about it. Believe me, if I had a cock like that at home, I'd have a hard time giving it up, too!"

Liz, who talked frankly about sex for a living—Liz, who encouraged others to talk about sex frankly on television for a living—found herself blushing. Somehow, thinking about seventy-year-old Suzie's seventy-year-old husband's huge member was too much. She willed herself to go on, and opened her mouth to respond when a voice from the back of the room chimed in.

"Ms. Stratton, I'm with you all the way!" cried a pleasantly plump woman under the driers. "Unless, of course, blowjobs count as sex. Do they?"

All attention was on Liz again. "It counts as sex unless you're president," she said without thinking.

The squeals of laughter tinkled again.

Liz decided to take control of the situation. "Look, ladies. I know it's...difficult to control your urges, much less the urges of your partners. But this is a sacrifice to protest something very serious, and in order for it to work, we need to be diligent. I mean, remember your mothers and grandmothers giving up nylon stockings for the war effort, or gas rationing? If we don't end this war, we'll be sacrificing much, much more than just sex, like sons and daughters. Right?"

"My son is already gone," said a small voice. Liz pulled away from Maryanne's grip and turned to see a large woman with half her hair in curlers slumped in the last chair. Liz stood, walked over to her, and rested a hand on her shoulder.

"Go on."

"He died somewheres on a road with a bomb on it," she said to the floor. "It was a year ago. I haven't done much since then. His daddy and me sleep in different rooms, anyway." She smiled weakly, lifting her gaze to Liz's briefly.

Liz knelt in front of the woman's chair. "What's your name, honey?"

"Doris."

"Do any of you question whether Doris would rather have sex or have her son alive? Anyone?" It was very quiet in the salon. Liz gave Doris a hug. Then she said, "This is why it's important that we see this operation through to the end. Whether I win or lose is not nearly as important as ending this war. We need to do it for Doris and so that there are no more Dorises in the world!"

Liz returned to her chair to a round of applause. She glanced at the mirror as she sat and realized that she had just given one of the most moving speeches of her career with half her hair hanging in her face and wearing a mauve smock.

She now knew why Amber was so concerned, but she was glad she had come.

♥

When Liz emerged from the salon an hour later, she felt pretty good, despite the twisted mess atop her head. Maryanne had really outdone herself: Liz's hair was a mass of ropey loops and goofy little spurts that sprouted from every angle.

Still, Liz tipped her well and posed for photographs with everyone. She gave Doris her contact information so that the campaign could help her find a grief counselor and Liz could have her on the show someday.

Liz dragged herself onto the bus and shooed everyone out of her private bunk. She closed the door and immediately began pulling pins out of her scalp. She reminded herself to be extra nice to Amber and appreciate the luxury of having her own private hairdresser. When her hair was finally free, Liz gave it a good shake so it fell down her shoulders in a coffee-brown cascade.

"Ah," she sighed. "That is so much better."

"I agree," said a very deep voice from behind her.

Liz whipped around. Then she realized that the man in her quarters was Dion Young, the secret serviceman.

"Holy crap, you scared me," she said and grabbed a counter for support.

"I'm sorry," he said, smiling.

"W—why are you in here?"

"Well, I was on my way out, but you closed the door. I'm sorry for watching. That was—wrong of me. I would have said something if you started—if you were—undressing. Shall I go?"

"No, no, stay," Liz said, recovering enough to remember how very cute Dion was with his sandy hair, three-day beard, and green eyes. "No harm, no foul, right?" She smiled in a way she hoped was as disarming and charming as his was.

The bus lurched and sent her sprawling onto the bed and knocked Dion onto the floor. When he sat up, he grinned at her. "Come here often?"

Liz burst into giggles. "That's what she said," she cried and laughed so hard tears rolled down her cheeks.

When she recovered, she was relieved to see Dion still smiling.

"I'm sorry. Were you in that salon with me?"

"No, I was stationed outside."

"Oh my God, Dion! I mean, I've had transsexual strippers on my show before that I thought were frank, but they can't hold a candle to those ladies in there. I thought my ears were going to burn off from embarrassment."

"Wow," he said, sitting on the edge of the bed. "That's wild. I wish I had heard it."

"I'm sure you will," she said. "With all the media there, I'll be surprised if there is anyone in America who *hasn't* seen it by morning." She sat up and hugged her knees to her chest. "I hope I handled that right." Then she glanced at Dion. "Sorry. Moment of weakness."

"Not a problem," he said, leaning back a little.

"I mean, I don't really talk to anyone here on the

road. Zeke and Cal are running things, and the rest of my friends are back in LA—"

"I hear you," he said. "You can talk to me whenever you like."

"Yeah?"

"Yeah. And I can't tell anyone. That's the 'secret' in 'secret service.'"

Liz snorted. "Is that a joke?"

Dion grinned. "Sort of. It was pretty lame, wasn't it?"

"Ye—ah." Liz laughed and bumped him on the shoulder. She was surprised at how familiar she'd gotten with him in such a short amount of time. In fact, she realized that she was dangerously close to kissing him.

She sat up and smoothed her suit. "I should get back out there. I have some briefs to read and stuff."

"Sure thing," he said. "I'll be watching you."

"That would be creepy coming from anyone but you." Liz laughed as she stepped out into the front of the bus.

Dion sat on the bed so he could just see her out the door. He took out his cell phone and pushed a speed dial button. "Yeah, it's me," he said. "I'm finally in. Another day or two, and mission accomplished." He hung up and peeked out at Liz. He caught her eye and she waved. He winked in return and smiled the lopsided grin that always got them.

Chapter 7

Maureen and her girlfriends were in a low-key gay club in Hollywood where the paparazzi rarely lurked. Her friends were there to dance without being molested by handsy heterosexuals. Since the sex strike took effect, it was too risky to go to a straight club. The men were getting more and more desperate, and less and less apt to hear a "no," even when said firmly or loudly. Maureen was there for that reason, too, mostly. She was also taking in the sights.

It was hot inside, and loud, and apparently the bartenders hadn't heard about the smoking ban in bars. The air was thick and heady with smoke of various legalities, and it was pitch dark except for the lights pulsating over the dance floor. Men in all sorts of undress danced everywhere, and they welcomed the girls with gleeful cheers. Contrary to popular opinion, most gay men love women, especially pretty girls. They just didn't *love* women. There was plenty of bumping and grinding going on, but it was more innocent than it would be if they were at a straight club. It was innocent in a childish way, like they were all kids imitating something they saw on television, but had no real interest in actually taking part in.

Maureen made her way to the bar after a long dance session with a gay boy with a rockin' body and a pierced nose. She was slightly afraid he was going to follow her and complain about his boyfriend, so she was relieved when she found herself alone at the bar. She was dressed in tight jeans and a halter-top, so most people didn't recognize her from television: this wasn't really the show's demographic, anyway. She found that she liked the anonymity. She wasn't sure she was cut out to be as famous as Liz.

She waved a twenty over the bar to get the bartender's attention. "Mandarin cosmo, please!" she shouted over the music. He nodded and made her drink in front of her. She had always admired a good bartender. She'd had to mix a few drinks herself back in the day, and a man who could get a curl of orange zest into your drink while dressed in leather pants had her respect.

She accepted her drink and held out her bill when someone pushed her arm down onto the bar.

"Your money's no good here."

Maureen looked up to see a beautiful woman slipping the bartender a fifty-dollar bill. "I'll have the same as her," she said and smiled at Maureen.

"Thank you." Maureen sipped her drink. "This guy's a master at the Cosmo."

"I know." The woman accepted her drink and sipped, not taking her eyes off Maureen. "I thought Cosmos were passé, but I like the orange twist."

Maureen smiled. "They were the rage years ago. I've always liked them, and I don't view cocktails as fashion accessories, anyway."

The woman smiled and set her glass down. "I'm Vanessa," she said, holding out her hand.

"Maureen." She shook Vanessa's hand.

"I know who you are," Vanessa said. "I've seen your show."

"Well, it's hardly mine," Maureen said modestly. "I'm just babysitting for a friend while she's busy." She shifted a little under Vanessa's heavy gaze. Her eyes were taking Maureen in inch by inch, and Maureen realized that she was being undressed in Vanessa's mind. It had been a while since Maureen had had such an overture from a woman, and she found herself blushing.

"Would you like to sit at a booth? I'd love to get to know you better," Vanessa suggested. Maureen nodded, so Vanessa led her to one of the private booths that ran along the sides of the club. As they went, Maureen took Vanessa in: long legs, short dress, cute ass, and short, light hair that Maureen couldn't decide was blonde or light brown. It looked soft, though, and she wanted to feel it in her fingers. Vanessa oozed sex, and it wafted off of her in such waves that even the gay men turned to look appreciatively. Maureen was a little fascinated following her to the booth. She slid into the booth next to Vanessa, who immediately put her hand on Maureen's knee. Maureen gently moved the hand aside. "Getting to know me is first," she said.

"Of course," said Vanessa. "Where are my manners? I like your show." She leaned in close and breathed the last part into Maureen's ear.

"Thank you." Maureen closed her eyes and found herself very attracted to the forward woman. When she opened her eyes, she was looking into Vanessa's very blue ones. "Tell me about yourself, Vanessa."

"I'm just a single gal who works in television, too," she said.

"Oh? Anything I might have seen?"

"Perhaps. I report for one of the local news stations."

Maureen smiled. "I thought I'd seen your face before." She touched Vanessa's chin with her fingertips. "You're the meteorologist on Channel Six."

"Weekends," Vanessa said, smiling. "So, we're mutual fans." She took Maureen's hand in hers and stroked her fingers gently.

"I suppose so." Maureen relaxed and leaned back into the upholstery. "That feels nice, Vanessa."

"Can we go somewhere quieter, Maureen?" Vanessa leaned against the seat back, too, and gazed at her face.

Maureen sighed. "I'd like to, Vanessa," she said. "But there's a sex strike on—"

"I wasn't going to invite you straight to bed," Vanessa protested.

"Maybe not," Maureen said, sitting up. "But I'm

pretty sure in a couple drinks, that's where we'd want to be."

"I want to see more of you," Vanessa said.

"Lunch tomorrow?"

"Lunch? Really, lunch?" Vanessa sat back, pouting.

"I'm only doing lunch dates now because of the strike, honey," Maureen explained. "Believe me, you are a dish I would love to—"

"Lick ice cream out of?"

"—yes. But I'm only doing lunch dates because of what I do. Do you understand?"

Vanessa, who Maureen realized was much younger than she first thought, sulked a moment. Then she pulled a pen out of her tiny purse and wrote her number on a card.

"You can reach me here," she said. "Call when the strike is over."

"Over?"

"Yes, over. I'm not the kind of girl who does lunch. For you, almost."

Vanessa leaned over and kissed Maureen with her full, luscious lips and Maureen felt herself get wet and jiggly.

"Call me when you can fuck." Then Vanessa slid out of the booth and slinked her way out of sight.

Maureen's friends descended on her as soon as Vanessa vanished. "Who the hell was that?"

"Channel Six weather girl," Maureen said, turning the card over in her hands.

"Wow, you got her number? What's she like?"

"She wanted to fuck," Maureen said with a sigh.

"Shitty timing."

"That's the truth," Maureen said.

She wondered if she would ever call the girl who made her so wet. She tucked the card into her bra and stood up to dance with the gay men so she didn't have to think about it anymore.

♥

A week later, Maureen sat at the table in the bus as it barreled along the Missouri highway on the way to somewhere over the rainbow. She had met the bus in St. Louis so she and Liz and Zeke could talk about the show.

She loved being on television, and she loved being the host of *Spare Me!* She was, however, new at this, and had run out of ideas, as had her similarly new producer. They had resorted to "Liz's sexiest shows" re-runs until they could come up with more content. Hence the emergency trip to Missouri.

Liz read the list while leaning against the bus window and flat farmland whizzed behind her head. "Well, this is a good list, Maureen, but I can see how it can get old talking about *not* having sex. It's certainly easier to find material on depravity, etc."

Zeke stroked his chin. "How about interviewing people who are abstaining for the campaign and see how it's affecting them? Like the Greater LA S&M club?"

"Yeah, sure," said Liz, sitting up and scribbling on the list. "You could interview all sorts of weirdoes. And the theme could be, 'If that huge sexual libido can abstain for a good cause, so can you!'"

The three of them bent heads and scribbled lists of the baby-dressers, beastialists, and drag queens that had been on the show recently.

"Oh, oh, how about that woman who could only come if there was a video camera in the room?" said Maureen

"'Video Vicky'? She'd be great," Liz muttered. "You might have to schedule her for next month—she's having a baby in, like, two weeks."

"Aw, that's sweet," Maureen said.

The door to Liz's private room in the back opened and Dion stepped out. Maureen's eyes got wide as she watched him walk to the front of the bus where he sat and began reading the paper.

"Who's that?" she hissed at Liz.

Liz glanced up and smiled. "That's Dion. He's in my security detail."

"Oh, my!" said Maureen, sitting back. "He's delicious. Does he come in any other flavors?"

"Wouldn't know," Liz said quickly.

Maureen leaned forward. "You—ou like him," she sang softly.

To Maureen's glee, Liz blushed. "Do not."

Zeke turned to look at Dion carefully. *Damn his height, his hair, and his perfect vision*, Zeke thought, and flung mental daggers at the secret serviceman's head.

Maureen was suddenly sympathetic. "Oh hell! With the sex strike going on, you couldn't do anything. Shit,

I'd love to have you on the show. Wouldn't this just make the ratings?"

"Shut up," Liz hissed. She wrote *Things to do on initial dates that aren't sex, even though you want to jump his bones* on her list.

"What are you going to do?" Maureen asked.

Liz looked at the back of Dion's head. "Well, obviously, nothing. I can't risk a scandal, and I think fucking a guard while preaching abstinence would pretty much kill the campaign, don't you?"

"Oh, definitely," Zeke said a little too quickly and enthusiastically, causing Liz to look at him queerly.

"Well, thanks for the support," she said unhappily. "Maybe he'll still be around on the first Wednesday in November. There's not much I can do until then, you know?"

"Mmmm, I could just take him off the market for you," Maureen purred. "You know, to make it easier on you."

Liz smiled and rolled her eyes. "Don't you dare. You're on strike, too, you know. We're all the picture of abstinent resolve, don't cha know?"

Maureen pouted sweetly, and then the three of them sighed together and doodled a bit on their lists. Finally, Maureen threw down her pencil.

"Fuck, this is hard," she moaned. "I'm used to…well, you know…at least a couple times a month. That's a lot for a single gal, I know, but I live in LA for chrissakes!"

"I know," Liz said. "I was counting the months on

my fingers earlier, too. Granted, I've hit a dry spell, but still, months?" She shook her head sadly. "I'd love to just wake up next to someone. I miss that kind of intimacy." She looked up across the table at Zeke. "What about you?" she asked.

"Me, what?"

"When was the last time you had sex, Zeke?"

"I don't kiss and tell," he said.

"I thought that's all men ever did," said Maureen. She bumped her shoulder against his. "If you tell yours, I'll tell mine. Mine's good," she promised.

Zeke looked quite uncomfortable. "It was a week or two before the campaign began," he said.

"Who was she? Was she cute? Where did you meet her?" Liz leaned in, hungry for details, even Zeke details.

"Um, I met her at a club. She'd just moved to LA from Virginia, I think she said."

"Oh my God, Zeke. She was an aspiring actress?" Maureen said.

"You didn't have casting couch sex, did you?" Liz asked, grinning like an idiot. "I didn't know that sort of thing still happened."

"It wasn't like that," Zeke said defensively. "I did get her a lead or two on agents, but I liked her. Of course, I haven't heard from her since." He began doodling again.

Liz and Maureen looked at each other. After a moment, Maureen leaned in to Zeke. "She must have been pretty cute, though, huh? Huh?"

"Well, yeah," Zeke admitted. He grinned to himself. "She had this long, dark hair. She could wind it around like a bun and then let it go so it fell all over my face."

"She was on top," Maureen squealed so loud that everyone else on the bus, including Dion, looked up at them. Maureen grinned wickedly at Zeke and leaned back in her chair.

"You little tart," Liz scolded. "Your turn."

She winked at Zeke kindly, and he silently thanked her. He folded his hands in his lap to keep from reaching over and squeezing her knee.

Maureen rolled her eyes and lied. "Well, I met this guy at this party at this house. I forget who was holding the party or why. He was this aspiring actor/waiter who was serving drinks. He recognized me from the show—you know, only working night shifts—and so I took him home." She licked her lips. "He reminded me of someone I had a crush on in high school, except he had much better abs."

"Did you do anything special?" asked Liz.

"Oh, not really," Maureen said. "He made me breakfast to make up for his tiny penis, but that's about all."

"That's sad," Liz said. "It wasn't good at all?"

"Didn't say that," said Maureen. "I mean, pizza's pizza, right?"

"I thought only men said shit like that," Zeke said.

"Nope," said Liz. "You should know that by now, Zeke. You've produced my show since the beginning."

"True."

"Your turn, Liz," Maureen said, leaning on the table, chin in hand, expectantly.

Liz didn't want to have a turn, but it was obvious that Maureen wasn't going to give up. Zeke tried not to look as uncomfortable as he felt as Liz dove in to her story.

"Um, do you guys remember the show we did about six months ago about the hot new yoga trend?"

Maureen gasped. "That yoga guy? The one with the hair? And the arms?"

Liz nodded. "Yeah, Yuri Davidson."

"Yuri the Yogi," Zeke said.

He had taken an instant dislike to the guy when they'd met on set, and now he knew why. He desperately wanted to avoid the rest of this conversation.

But Liz went on. "Yuri invited me out for drinks after the show, which I thought was a little forward, you know, but how many invitations do I get? I work too much." She looked off into space for a moment, completely forgetting that she got at least one invitation a day from Zeke. "Somehow, we ended up back at his hotel." She stopped and smiled coyly.

"More!" Maureen cried. "What's it like having sex with Yuri the Yogi?"

"Surprisingly straightforward and a little boring," Liz said analytically. "He didn't have the tiny penis problem, but he was quite unimaginative, and not limber at all!" She shook her head. "God, what if we die in a crash right now, and those are our last sexual experiences?"

"Sobering thought," said Zeke. Even though he had quite enjoyed little miss Virginia, he'd much rather die in Liz's arms.

After a moment, Maureen grumbled, "They better fucking declare peace soon. I don't know how much longer I can stand it."

Everyone within earshot had to agree wholeheartedly.

♥

Maureen's actual last sexual experience had been just before the strike was called. She had found Grace in a bar on a Tuesday night. The girl had recognized Maureen from the show and had gushed admiration, so they ended up leaving together. Grace's apartment was on the small size, but Maureen spotted the expensive upgrades with a LA resident's skillful eye. Tile floors to help cool the summer heat, stone countertops—though granite was passé, other stone was not—and restaurant-quality appliances. Grace had done well.

"How about a glass of wine?" Grace kicked off her shoes and walked to the oversized refrigerator. "I have a nice white open."

"Sure." Maureen amused herself by admiring the "art" on Grace's walls—mostly framed posters of impressionists.

Grace handed her a glass of too-cold wine and Maureen sipped it. "Nice place."

"Thank you. How about a sit?" Grace arranged herself seductively on the couch.

Maureen joined her and slid her hand between Grace's knees. "Nice dress," she said, and kissed her.

Grace had suitably luscious lips and a firm ass that was the perfect size for Maureen's hands. She hadn't had her breasts done yet—always the probability in this town—but Maureen didn't mind. She liked the asymmetry of natural breasts.

She quickly ascertained that Grace was a relative novice at female-on-female relations, so Maureen gladly directed her. This hand here, that hand there, do this with your mouth, no, let me show you.

Afterward, Maureen pulled one of her own strawberry-blonde hairs from between Grace's teeth as they snuggled under a blanket on the couch—they hadn't made it into the bedroom.

"That's kinda gross," Grace said, licking her lips.

"They don't call it 'flossing' for nothing, sugar," Maureen sat up and stretched. "I'm going to call it a night." She stood and began hunting for her panties.

"You could stay here." Grace's voice had a peculiar note to it, and Maureen glanced back at her. She was sitting up, holding the plush blanket up to her own chest modestly and watching Maureen with hopeful eyes.

"No, I'm going to go home now," Maureen said, pulling on her jeans and stepping into her shoes.

"Will you call me?" Grace asked as Maureen walked to the door, pulling on her shirt as she went.

"Sure, sugar. I'll see you around." Maureen was in such a hurry that she left her panties behind, wadded in a ball under the blanket.

She sat in her car a block away wishing that she were a smoker so she could get a little relief from the thoughts that flew through her head. She thought this pattern of sleeping with girls and then running from them had ended in college, when she had sworn off girls because of Sarah. She didn't like herself this way, but abject admiration was hard for her to resist.

Sarah had been a year behind Maureen in college and followed her around like an adoring fan. She was tall, with short black hair and a cute little nose. She was wickedly funny, and her habit of hanging on Maureen's every word became endearing. Eventually, Maureen gave in to Sarah's amorous advances and a yearlong relationship developed.

A straight girl had once remarked to Maureen that it must be nice going out with a girl because women understood each other. She was dealing with a boyfriend who didn't get her "shoe thing." Maureen tried to inform her that not only did women "get" women, but women knew how to torture each other better than men did.

Sarah was jealous. Maureen was a gregarious person and habitually had a crowd around her. As a ginger-haired kid, she had learned early that she either had to shun the spotlight by hiding or embrace it. If she were going to stick out, anyway, she decided that she'd do it on her terms.

But Sarah was quiet and bookish. She was a devil in bed, but in life she was likely to be railroaded. She was often swept aside by the crowds Maureen attracted with her personality, complexion, and figure. Sarah took every laugh, touch on the arm, and air-kiss as evidence that Maureen was cheating on her.

Maureen wasn't, though not for lack of opportunity.

Sarah was not convinced and left, noisily swearing revenge. She flung Maureen's possessions out on the lawn, even though she had been staying at Maureen's place. She tried to poison Maureen's friends against her. She sat glaring at Maureen at the cafe where Maureen worked so much that the manager finally had Sarah removed by the police. That didn't stop her from parking outside of Maureen's apartment several nights a week with a camera.

Every couple days, Maureen would get an email loaded with pictures of people coming and going out of her apartment building. There was never a message, just the pictures.

Even so, Maureen was devastated when Sarah left, had pleaded with her to stay, and swore her innocence. She dragged herself around campus afterward, and didn't think about Sarah's threats of revenge until her parents phoned a week later. Sarah had called them and outed Maureen.

Maureen swore off girls, partly to appease her parents who were desperate for grandchildren. Her older brother refused to marry any girl he brought home. He found tiny faults with all of them, which he then blew out of proportion and used as an excuse to leave them. Their parents had written him off as a lost cause, and so pinned their hopes on Maureen spreading their genes. A gay daughter was not acceptable, although they did mention artificial insemination every now and then, just to remind her that there was no reason to wait for "Mr. Right." She knew they were hoping that even if she found a "Mrs. Right," she'd still choose to have kids.

Sarah's behavior was the other reason for swearing off girls.

As for leaving girls after sleeping with them, Maureen had had a bit of a reputation for that before the Sarah affair. She wasn't proud of it, but she had slept with several women whom she didn't want to see again. To be frank, since then she'd slept with several men whom she didn't want to see the next morning, either. Oddly, she didn't feel as bad about leaving the naked men in their bedrooms as she did about the girls.

She liked sex, and she did want another serious relationship someday. But until then, she saw sex as a hobby.

Maureen whacked the steering wheel. She felt like calling Grace right away and apologizing, maybe offer to take her to dinner or something, but she couldn't. They had never exchanged numbers, and she wasn't brave enough to go back to Grace's apartment and ask for it.

Maureen threw the car into gear, flipped a U-ee in the middle of the dark street, and drove back to Grace's apartment. She didn't like the girl enough to leave her own number under her doorknocker. But she felt guilty enough to jot an apologetic note and cram it under her windshield wiper. Maureen drove away alleviated of a little guilt. She still felt like a heel when she got home and punished herself by crawling under her sheets without showering so when she woke, she still smelled like cigarettes, alcohol, and Grace.

♥

Liz tapped away at her laptop in her hotel room that night with the news chattering in the background. She had on her silk pajamas with the kittens and her hair was twisted up in a bun held in place with a pencil. She was working on an idea for a new speech when there was a soft tapping at the door. She opened it to find Zeke holding a steaming paper cup with a teabag string draped over the edge. "I saw your light on and thought you might like some herbal tea."

"Thanks," she said, taking the tea. "Want to come in?"

"Oh, uh, no," he said, realizing he was getting a massive erection just seeing her in pajamas again. It was cold and her nipples were making an appearance. "I really need to get some sleep. Good night."

"You sure? Okay, then. Thanks for the tea. Good night." She closed the door softly.

Zeke stood a moment, kicking himself, and then stalked off to his room next door.

Liz had just arranged herself at the computer with her tea when there was another knock. She assumed it was Zeke changing his mind, so she just unlatched the door and said, "Come on in. I just need to finish this thought." She ran back to the computer and finished typing her sentence. She felt the cold night air whoosh as the door opened and closed.

"Thanks again for the tea," she said as she turned around. "That was really thought—" Her heart stopped when she realize that the man standing somewhat awkwardly next to her bed was not Zeke but Dion.

"It's not tea, actually," Dion said. "It's bourbon. Your favorite brand. But I could probably find some tea if you'd prefer." He grinned lopsidedly and his hair fell in his face as if on cue.

"Um, bourbon's great," Liz said. She scrambled to find the glass tumblers from the bathroom. "I…uh…didn't get any ice," she said. "But I don't really want much. I've got a busy day tomorrow."

She watched as Dion poured her two fingers of bourbon and handed her the glass. She wondered what the hell she was doing.

"Aren't you supposed to be protecting me or something?" she asked, inhaling the smoky scent of the liquor.

"I'm off duty tonight," he said. "Besides, how much closer could a protector be?"

Liz didn't answer, but took a sip of bourbon instead. She looked at him over the lip of the glass. He peeked at her from over his, too.

He took her glass from her and set both in front of the television. He put one hand on her hip and the other cupped her face. "I've wanted to do this since the first time I saw you in person," he breathed and pulled her close to him, kissing her with much more restraint than Liz expected.

He tasted of bourbon and somehow smelled of maraschino cherries and starch. She liked how his hand felt on her face and the way his other hand traveled up her hip to her side to her back. She loved how he was holding her and how he was now cupping her breast—

Liz backed away suddenly, panting. "I'm so sorry, Dion, but you have to leave, now." She pointed at the door.

Dion stepped closer to her. "But why? Am I moving too fast?"

"No, no, no—I mean, in June, I would have been all over you," she explained while backing way. "I'm not risking a scandal during the race, though, no matter what you taste like or smell like."

"You taste like strawberries dipped in caramel," he murmured, and he was kissing her again.

Liz pulled away again, more violently this time. "Dammit, Dion, don't make me ask again. We need to *wait*. That's the whole point."

"I'm not sure I can wait," he said. "And I'm not sure you can wait, either." He turned to go. "Just remember: I'm ready anytime you are. You give me a nod and I'll meet you in your room on the bus ten minutes later. Ten minutes." He opened her door and stepped out. Then he leaned back in and looked at her with obvious lust. "Keep the bourbon. Just think of me as you drink it." Then he was gone.

Liz made it to the bed before her knees gave way. She sat shaking with desire and jittery with adrenaline. When she felt a little steadier, she rummaged around in her luggage until she found what she was looking for: a white paper goody bag.

She switched off the television, quaffed both of the

bourbons, and turned off the light. In the morning, the tea was stone cold and untouched when Zeke saw it next to her computer. He wondered in passing where the Maker's Mark bourbon had come from.

♥

Later that day, Liz sat on the edge of her bus bunk and pulled on her stockings. A crowd had gathering in the nearby pavilion, waiting for her to appear and encourage them to vote for her and keep their legs crossed until the war was over.

And Liz had a run in her pantyhose. Dammit.

Cal knocked loudly on the door. "Liz, they're waiting!"

"I know," she called. "I'm nearly ready. I'll meet you outside." She tore open her bag and dug through it. She knew she had a fresh pair of hose in there somewhere.

She heard the door open and click closed. "Cal, do you have any hose on the bus?" she asked. "Oh, wait. Here's a pair." She turned to find Dion smiling at her, again.

"Jesus, do you ever enter a room announced?"

"Last time I knocked," he said. He stepped forward and took her in his arms. "I missed you."

"Stop," Liz protested weakly. "I'm late." With great force of will, she pulled away. "I need to put these on."

She turned away modestly, pulled on the hose, and stepped into her shoes.

When she turned around, she yelped at the sight of Dion, presumably naked, under the covers of her bed.

"How'd you get out of your clothes so fast?"

"Talent," he said. "Practice? Care to join me?" He lifted the covers just enough that she could see a flash of bare hip, but not enough that she could miss the tent.

"If I didn't want you so badly, I'd have you fired for sexual harassment," she said. "I have to go."

She backed out of the room and closed the door behind her. She turned and ran into Maureen who was waiting for her just outside the door.

Maureen smiled lasciviously. "I saw Mr. Handsome go in there. Now I see you come out all flustered two minutes later. Either that was a record-breaking quickie, or you told him no."

"I was a good girl, but it was—difficult," Liz said. "I've got to get out before I go back in there."

"Suit yourself," Maureen said. "I mean, I'm so proud of you."

Maureen watched Liz as she retreated from the bus. When she was sure Liz wasn't coming back, she let herself in to the back room.

Dion was surprised to see her. He looked up as he sat on the edge of the bed in his boxers. "Hello. This isn't what it looks like—" he began.

"Of course it is," Maureen said. "I was just curious. I can see how Liz would be tempted." She bit her lip coyly.

Dion smiled. "I'll take that as a compliment. Would you care to sit?"

"All right," Maureen said, perching coquettishly on the bed next to Dion.

"I'm sorry, I don't know your name…"

"Maureen."

"Maureen. You're a piece of work, aren't you?"

"Yes, I am," she said leaning in a little closer to Dion. "I suspect you are, too."

"Perhaps so," he said and leaned in for a kiss, but his phone rang. "Damn. Need to get that," he murmured and reached for his pants.

"No worries." She dove for his trousers first. "I'll get it for you." She seized the pants and pulled out the phone, answering it before Dion could take it away.

"Young? Is that you? Have you compromised Stratton yet?" barked a voice that was Southern and authoritative.

"No," Maureen said in a deep voice.

"Well, get on it. We need that bitch out of the race." The Southerner hung up.

"It was your mommy," Maureen purred. "She says to be good." She tossed the phone into the corner of the room and took off her shirt. "I say we be bad."

"I'll apologize to Mom later," he said, reaching for her. He buried his face in her cleavage and moaned.

"Has it been a while, honey?" she cooed.

"God, yes. This strike is killing me. I used to get it every week at least." He pulled down her bra straps.

"Wait, let me close the curtains!" Maureen pulled away and minced around the tiny room, pulling the curtains over the already one-way windows.

As she passed him, Dion slapped her on the ass. "You like it in the dark, eh?" he asked when he got his hands on her again.

"You're right, I do," she said, pulling away again to switch off the lights.

When she got back, Dion had shimmied out of his boxers and was laying on his back on the bed, socks only. Maureen climbed up next to him and removed his socks painfully slowly. "I have some 'stuff' in a goody bag in the other room," she whispered in his ear as she tickled the hairs on his belly.

"Forget it," he moaned. "Just come here."

Maureen allowed her hand to trace larger and larger circles on his body until she fingered his balls and his cock. Dion shivered and moaned as she took his whole penis in her hand, but then went rigid when she hissed, "That was Ostrem on the phone, wasn't it? Wasn't it?"

"Who?" Dion said too casually.

Maureen squeezed just a little too hard. Dion yelped, "Yes, yes, it was!"

"What is he paying you to do? How were you supposed to compromise Liz?" She tugged in what she knew to be the wrong direction.

"Ah—ah—ah—Just sex, seduce her, spill the beans. Ow-ow-ow!" he whimpered.

Maureen grinned wickedly. "Ever heard of a purple nurple?" she asked.

Dion dissolved into tears and begged her to let him go. She stood and put her shirt on as he curled in a ball and watched her with wide, horrified eyes.

"I'm sending Big Sam back here now. You've got two minutes to clear out. If we ever hear anything about a relationship between you and Liz, I'm going to invite every girl you went to high school with to come on the show for a free paternity test." She fluffed her hair and left him without looking back. She had to find Liz.

♥

Liz peeked from behind the curtain. In front of her stood a crowd of thousands of horny women who had given up sex to show support for her effort to end the war. They expected her to say something that could keep them from going to bed with their husbands or lovers—or both—until the war was over. But Liz kept thinking about that…that…man who was currently in her room on the bus waiting for her—as she'd left him, she supposed—naked and half-crazy with desire. Honestly, she didn't know whether she was going back to him once she was done with the crowd. What could she say to those women to keep them on track if she wasn't able to even contain herself?

She slumped on a folding chair and flipped through the note cards, not reading them. She was thinking of Dion's floppy hair, his sexy sunglasses, his lopsided grin, what his cock must look like. She sighed and swore.

Maureen walked up looking more smug and coy than usual. "I've got something to tell you that might solve your problem," she said.

"Oh? Which problem?"

"The—secret problem."

"What is it?"

"He tried to seduce me," Maureen said.

"What?" Liz was surprised at the emotion she felt at this news. "Why you...you little slut," she hissed.

Maureen tried not to look hurt, but she was. "That's neither here nor there," she said, pouting. "*He* tried to seduce *me*, remember? But there's more."

"What?" Liz snapped in rising fury.

"He's working for Ostrem," Maureen said.

Liz sat back. "Wh—what?"

Maureen knelt beside her friend. "At first, I just wanted to show what a slime ball Dion is, but then his phone rang and I answered it. It was Ostrem on the other end. I heard him tell Dion to hurry up and finish 'compromising' you. Then I...coerced...a confession out of Dion. His job was to seduce you and then tell everyone that you'd reneged on the sex strike." She patted Liz's hand. "I'm sorry. I know you liked him."

Liz sat stricken for a moment. "Wow," she said finally. "That would have really ruined us. That son of a bitch. Those sons of bitches." She looked at Maureen. "Thank you."

"You're the one who was sticking to her principles."

"He came to me in my room last night. Tried to get me drunk. Oh, God, I've been so naive and stupid!"

"No, no, you've been strong! You stuck to your guns! I'm proud of you. Really. I mean it."

"I might have, though, after the rally. I was thinking about it."

"No harm in thinking. They can't hang you for that," Maureen said. "Now, you need to go out there and wow them. Can you use that anger? Can you channel it to fire up that horny multitude? Channel all that sexual energy into positive work?"

"I can," Liz said. "I'm so angry I could spit fire. It's time I take off the gloves and fight like a girl—with teeth and nails."

"Attagirl," Maureen said as Liz strode onto the stage.

♥

Liz wasn't one for drinking herself into a stupor, but she felt so stupid for falling for Dion Young's tactics. He was the same kind of asshole that her longtime boyfriend Evan had been.

That jackass had cheated on her so many times that she lost count. She had expected him to be that way, and tolerated it until she realized that she had wasted years on him.

She could have had three kids in that span of time. In fact, a friend of hers did, and that realization had been the reason she threw him out.

She had begun dating Evan because he was so forward and charming, just like Dion. She poured herself another neat Maker's Mark from Dion's bottle and let the aroma waft up and bathe her face. She felt like hell.

There was a tap at the door of her room on the bus and then Cal let herself in. She sat next to Liz on the bed and put an arm around her.

They sat quietly for a moment.

Finally, Cal said, "You gave a fine speech today. I've never seen you so fired up."

"I was livid," Liz mumbled. She glanced at Cal. "You know what happened? Maureen told you?"

Cal nodded. "We left Dion at the Greyhound station. I wanted to leave him in a bad neighborhood without his cell phone, but I was outvoted."

Liz groaned and lay back on the bed. "How could I be so stupid? I was just thinking how much he was like Evan. Remember Evan?"

Cal nodded. "He treated you like shit, but he was beautiful."

"I was such a fool, Cal," Liz said.

Cal snorted. "Pooh. How could you have known your own secret service guy was working for the other side? I mean, that's dirty pool."

She poured herself a drink and leaned back on the bed next to Liz.

"They really have it in for me, don't they?" Liz asked.

"It looks like it," Cal said.

"I mean, to find someone like Dion and then plant him. That was a lot of trouble to go to."

"True," said Cal, swirling her bourbon. Then she sat up a little. "Actually, this might be a good sign."

"How could it be a good sign?" Liz groaned. "I nearly succumbed to the wiles of a cheap whoring spy. How could it be a good thing?"

"Well," Cal said, tucking her legs under her and

leaning in. "It was a lot of trouble to go to, and it took a lot of pull from way high up, right?"

"Yeah?"

Cal's eyes gleamed. "Liz, they're worried about you. I mean, they think you're a threat!"

"So, you think that means we have a chance?"

"Probably! What's more, I think we need to do something spectacular to show them that we aren't afraid of them, and we're not going anywhere."

"Like what?"

"Let's get the team together and figure it out!"

♥

Later that night in Liz's hotel room Cal, Zeke, and Maureen were finishing up the plans for "Operation October Surprise."

"That's all we can do tonight, team," Cal said, gathering up her things. "Let's get out of Liz's hair."

"Oh, look, she's out," Maureen whispered.

Sure enough, Liz had nodded off, leaning against her headboard. Her chin rested on her chest and she snored softly. The combination of the late hour, bourbon, and her Dion-inspired shame spiral had put her out completely.

"I'll take care of her," Cal said, stifling a yawn. "You guys go on."

Maureen picked up her bag and staggered a little on her way to the door. She mumbled, "G'night," and left.

When the door clicked shut, Cal took off Liz's shoes and tried to pull off her jeans, but had trouble until Zeke

stepped up and lifted Liz a bit off the bed. A look passed
between the two of them. Then Cal got to work peeling
off Liz's clothes and slipping her into a tee-shirt to sleep
in—her pajamas were far too much trouble—as if she
were a small child who had fallen asleep in the car. Zeke
turned away when modesty required, but he helped move
Liz's deeply somnolent body the rest of the time. When
she was safely tucked into bed, Cal picked up her things
and took a step toward the door. Zeke did not. Cal paused
a moment and then left the two of them alone, holding the
door so it closed with only a soft "click."

Zeke turned off all the lights in the room, except for
one small lamp in the far corner. Then he sat in the
armchair nearest the bed and watched Liz sleep. He
didn't know what he was going to say when she woke up.
He wasn't sure what she might think, or if he'd be brave
enough to admit that he didn't intend to let her out of his
sight long enough for her to get hurt again. He hunkered
down in the soft chair, propping his feet up on another
chair and tried to sleep, but his head was swirling with
images of Liz being magnificent on stage and then
dissolving into the puddle of hurt and shame that he'd
seen today. He wished again that he'd had a chance to say
a few words to Mr. Dion Young, or better yet, beat the
shit out of every one of his seventy-three inches.

Instead, the event the team had planned tonight
would be a triumph of publicity, but Zeke wondered
whether it might completely wreck Liz's chances of
being president.

On the other hand, it might catapult her straight to

the White House. He might be watching the next president snore, he thought. He smiled fondly and tried to doze off.

♥

Liz opened her eyes when her wake-up call rang at 6:30 a.m. Her head hurt, and she moaned in protest to the world at large.

"Why do they put bourbon in such big bottles?" she asked and tried to silence the phone by whacking it.

It stopped suddenly, so Liz rolled over and was instantly asleep again.

"I'm sorry, honey. I can't let you do that," a gentle voice said, and a warm hand shook her shoulder.

"Dad, I can totally sleep five more minute and still get to school—" Liz murmured. Then she sat up. "Crap. It's been a million years since I was in high school." She fumbled for her glasses and peered into the face attached to the warm hand. "Zeke?"

"Good morning."

"God, you look like hell. When did you get here? I didn't hear the door, I'm sorry."

"I—actually, I never left." Zeke nodded at the chair he'd eventually slept in.

Liz's lovely brow furrowed. "Why?" she asked.

Zeke willed himself not to redden. "We—I—didn't feel like leaving you alone last night."

"Why not? I was asleep, it's not like I was in danger. One of our guys is outside, right?"

"Yes," Zeke said.

Liz shook her aching head, but managed a smile. "So, you're going to sleep in the same room with me from now on, just in case?"

A peculiar look crossed Zeke's face, but all he said was, "If at all possible."

"Fine," Liz said. "But let's just get a room with two beds from now on." She groaned quietly. "I need an aspirin," she said and staggered to the bathroom in her T-shirt and panties.

Zeke stood stunned for a moment. He felt as if he'd just won the lottery or climbed Mt. Everest. He allowed himself a shit-eating grin.

Cal marched in, saw it, and smiled in response. Things were going to work out. She could tell.

Chapter 8

This is the craziest thing I've ever done," Liz said as she balanced on impossibly high heels.

"I can think of crazier things," Cal said, pinning a bit of Liz's costume back.

"Not fair, you knew me in college," Liz said. "Nothing I did before age twenty-five should be held against me."

"It's just a good thing none of it hit the papers, or we wouldn't be here," Cal said, tugging on a strap. "Damn thing won't stay up," she growled.

"What kinds of things did you do in college?" Zeke asked.

Liz grinned at him. "Well, what do you think girls who go to a women's college do on the weekend?"

"UMASS and fraternity row were just up the road, you know," Cal said. "And the busses were free on the weekends."

"Why?" asked Zeke.

Liz giggled. "Too keep the drunks off the road between the schools. We called it the 'love bus.'"

"That all sounds pretty tame to me," Zeke said. "Rather typical, especially compared to the current administration."

"Oh, pooh," Cal said. "He can't have had as much fun as they say he did. He's such a stick-in-the-mud now." She gave Liz a knowing wink. "We had our fun, didn't we, Liz?"

Liz smiled. "Those were some times, weren't they?"

"Oh, come one," Zeke pleaded. "You can't tease me like that. Give me some details."

"Not here, Zeke," Cal said. "It's silliness, anyway. We'll get together at Thanksgiving and have some drinks and tell all."

Zeke looked at both of them. "Promise?"

"Promise," Cal and Liz said, crossing their hearts.

"As long as you deliver some goods, too," Liz added, smiling.

Zeke sat back and watched as they finished Liz's outfit. He had counted himself among the luckiest bastards in the world because Liz allowed him to sleep in the same room with her since the "Dion incident." Granted, Zeke was still dying to sleep with Liz, in the same bed, but one thing at a time. To offset any wild rumors about Liz sleeping in a room with a man, they were careful to announce that Liz was taking enhanced security precautions, including a plain-clothes officer stationed in her room at night.

No one seemed to give it a second thought—to their immense relief.

Those nights, he watched her sleep and amused himself by creating little vignettes of a home life with her. He knew it wasn't healthy, so he promised himself that he'd tell Liz how he felt after the election. He couldn't do it before. That would really screw things up.

Liz finally stood up and turned to him. "So, how do I look?" She wore a gold lamé bathing suit with strategically placed sequins. She also wore a headdress of feathers and eye makeup that made Cleopatra seem conservative.

"You look like an understudy for *Showgirls*," Zeke said. "Pretty damn hot."

"Is that any way to talk to Madam President?" Cal said, scolding, as she applied more kohl to Liz's face.

"Well, it's true," Zeke said. "I mean, her legs go on forever in that getup."

"Hmm, so it doesn't scream 'Leader of the Free World' to you?" Liz asked.

"Not the poi-nt!" Cal sang, as she handed Liz her note cards. "Now, just don't trip on those stripper heels, and we'll be golden."

Liz clicked her ridiculously high heels together in a salute. "Yes, ma'am! Or madam!"

Elektra walked in to say, "It's time, honey. You ready?"

Zeke did a double-take when he saw the petite black woman in the shimmery sheath with the plunging neckline. She had on opera length black gloves and somehow projected sex, class, and authority all at the same time.

"Damn, girl," Cal said. "Look at you!"

Elektra smiled and did a little spin. "I have to say, that girl Amber of yours is a genius. Mr. Sampson is going to have a heart attack when he sees this!"

"What do you think of Liz?" Cal asked.

Liz suddenly felt shy, but did a careful spin for Elektra.

"Hmmm," Elektra said, appraisingly. "I think if we covered her in whipped cream, we'd even have the homos standing at attention!"

Liz almost forgot to laugh because she was too surprised. "I'll take that as a compliment," she said.

♥

Zeke traveled down a corridor to a side entrance of conference room. The campaign hadn't given any details on the conference, but they had requested male correspondents by name. The room was full of frustrated male energy.

Zeke slipped into the edge of the crowd where he had a good view of the stage. The people with these seats didn't know who he was, so he could watch with relative anonymity.

The stage was set up with a short row of chairs and a podium with a jumbo-tron screen set up behind. There was a plant or two in front of a blue curtain. It looked as boring and official as could be.

"I tried to get out of this assignment," Zeke heard one reporter tell another. "I hate this bitch with every inch of me."

"I hear ya," said his friend. "My girlfriend cut me off a month ago, and me, and righty just don't get along the way we used to."

"What's worse is that my cable is broke."

"Hey, mine, too! None of the pay-per-view comes in right."

"Yeah, none of my premium channels have any good stuff on at night. I'm going through porn withdrawal."

Zeke grinned privately. The bribes to the cable companies and premium channels had been his idea. It just took a couple key people to lean on a switch or two, and suddenly there was no soft-core porn on television.

"You know, I wonder if there isn't a conspiracy. 'Cause I can't get my porn sites to load anymore, either."

"Mine, either!"

The reporters looked at each other and began scribbling notes.

Zeke hadn't heard about any plans to curb Internet porn, but he'd take credit for it if anyone asked. He just didn't think it was possible. He suspected these two idiots just didn't know how to optimize their downloads. Or their significant others had wiped the caches clean on their browsers.

Zeke made a mental note to post directions on how to do that to the campaign blog.

Music swelled and the crowd shifted its attention to the stage. Cal's voice announced over the loudspeaker,

"And now, ladies and gentlemen, please put your hands together for Elizabeth Stratton, Elektra Sampson, and introducing the WAP drill team!"

The crowd clapped until Liz and Elektra strode onto the stage in all their glimmery sexiness, waving and smiling just as any politician would, only with much less on. The clapping staggered and fell over like a surprised drunk. The sight of Liz's long, lean body in the shiny golden suit was enough to make Zeke's pants a little tighter, even though he'd seen her just hours ago padding around in satin pajamas. That thought made his pants even tighter so he had to shift a little.

The crowd continued to clap in confusion as the "drill team" made its entrance. They'd bussed the girls in from a Vegas show, which had allowed them to use their costumes for the event. The stage was filled with girls, feathers, and sequins, but not much else. It took about three seconds for the crowd to recover from this shock and show its enthusiastic appreciation.

"Holy shit!" Zeke heard the reporter say to his friend. "I'm going to have to write my editor a thank-you note!"

"Hell, yeah," his friend said. "This is more T and A than I've seen in a month!"

Every man in the room was whooping with joy at the sight, and it took Liz a good long time to calm them down enough that she could talk. "So, you like my 'drill team'?" she asked, which renewed the cheering. "You all should see their routine sometime. Now that I have your attention," she began, but a cry of "Take it off!" pleaded from the front of the room.

"Not yet, eager beaver," Liz said coyly. "Be patient. We have some things to talk about first."

This was the cue for the lights to dim and the jumbotron to switch on. As Liz began to speak about ending the war and the draft, a classic stag film flickered above her head with the sound off. The showgirls moved slowly behind her, striking poses as they made a stately march back and forth. The crowd was enraptured.

"Gentlemen and ladies," Liz said. "As you can see, there is so much more to life than fighting and winning. There is love and sex. In order to attain peace, each side must concede something, must sacrifice. In order to gain peace, my supporters have sacrificed sex." She gestured to the film, which showed two people having enthusiastic relations. "Look at that. Look at what we're willing to live without while the war goes on." She looked up at the screen. "I don't know about you guys, but I really, really miss that. Don't you?" The crowd roared. "Wouldn't you all like that to happen again? I sure would. Don't you want to know how we can all start doing that again?"

When the cheering and jeering quieted, Liz went on. "In order to gain peace, this country is going to have to concede some things to Mesopotamianstan that we won't like. Such as promising to keep our fingers out of their oil fields and not interfering with the natural order of their government. That's going to be very difficult for us to do because we like oil, and we seem to think that everyone would be happier in a democracy. We're democracy missionaries, and it's made us the unwelcome neighbor who pushes his 'religion' onto others of the world.

"That's not to say that Mesopotamianstan won't have to concede some things, too. They'll have to promise to nip terrorism in the bud and to follow basic human rights conventions used by the rest of the world. They won't want to, but in a compromise, no one leaves completely happy."

At this point, the showgirls began to descend the stairs and mingle with the audience. They glided up the aisles smiling at the men and stopping to give kisses and have their pictures taken.

But Liz continued to speak. "Aren't they nice, boys? Wouldn't you give anything to have them available again? Or any woman?" There was a general rumbling of assent. "Well, you know what to do, gentlemen and ladies of the press. Tell the world what must be done to end the sex strike. End the war. Tell the world how we can do it so that it will be done! We can close this door on history and open other doors at the same time. Thank you!"

Pandemonium would have broken out had they not had so many security personnel. The men were straining to have some contact with the showgirls who were patient and obliging. "Look but don't touch" rules were enforced. The crowd hung around for ninety minutes after Liz and Elektra left the stage, and the girls were good and tired when they got back to the dressing room, but all went peacefully enough.

Liz took them all out to dinner that night at a local Japanese restaurant. Without their feathers and glitter, the girls looked thin but average. Their sex-goddess appeal lay in their costumes, more for some than others, but Liz was glad to see that they were just regular girls underneath. Since they had all volunteered their time and the show had donated the use of the costumes, as stunts went, this one had been cheap.

♥

After dinner, the staff and showgirls commandeered the big-screen television in the lounge of the hotel to watch the news. It was the first time most of the girls had been on national television, so all of them hovered by the TV waiting for Stone Phillips to appear. They could tell that they were going to be the lead story just by looking at him.

Stone struggled to keep his normally placid face from twisting into a wry grin as he introduced the story. "This unusual presidential race took another…interesting turn today," he began, lip twitching. "Elizabeth Stratton and her running mate Elektra Sampson took to the stage of a press conference wearing provocative outfits and flanked by…supporters in very ornate dress. I must warn you, this clip may offend some viewers."

Liz couldn't have asked for better footage. Although the stag film was understandably blurred out, the television screen was filled with tits and ass and feathers galore. The editors at the news program had tried to do her speech justice, but the footage was so provocative that Liz even had trouble concentrating on her own words. She was very pleased with how good she looked in her outfit, too.

Stone Phillips reappeared on the screen, still struggling to keep a serious face. "We have with us three commentators to help us understand this press conference."

"Here come the pundits," Cal whispered, squeezing Liz's hand.

"First is conservative think-tank leader Reverend Mitchell Mennen."

The bearded pundit appeared on screen.

"One guess what his position will be," Zeke said.

Cal giggled. "Missionary, I'd guess."

"Next is Gretchen Lund, political advisor to Senator Mary Kelly during her successful Congressional race."

A prim woman in her forties appeared, hair in a bun.

"I'm curious about what she'll say," Liz said.

"And finally, Dr. Marjorie Green of the Women's Studies Department at Mt. Holyoke College."

Both women gasped.

"Professor Green!"

She hadn't aged much in the fifteen years since they had taken women's studies from her in college. Her long gray hair was pulled back in a loose ponytail and her granny glasses rested on the bridge of her nose. She wore her customary flowing cotton dress with a tailored suit jacket over top.

Cal had had lunch with her a couple years back—as president of WAP, she was in contact with many Women's Studies departments.

Liz hadn't had any contact with Dr. Green since she graduated, but she remembered the highly intellectual professor very clearly. "I think I'm going to die of shame on this spot," she moaned.

"I don't think it's going to be that bad," Cal said, but the color had drained from her face and she gripped Liz's hand harder.

Stone began the commentary with the Reverend Mennen, who, naturally, took a dim view to their shenanigans. "Stone, I was outraged to see this behavior from a serious contender for the highest office in the land. Such puerile tactics are better suited to...well, I can't think of a single instance where they would be appropriate. Displaying themselves like that, like commodities, it was just sickening."

"Don't you think they were trying to make a point about—" Stone began.

"I don't care what her point was, I was too offended to care what the devil they were talking about," the reverend huffed.

"Looks like his wife is striking, too," Cal said, clearly enjoying herself.

"Ms. Lund? What do you think of tonight's spectacle?"

"Well," Ms. Lund said in her straightforward suit and Washington-sized pearls. "I don't know if I would have suggested to Ms. Stratton to appear like this so close to the election, if ever. I am very concerned about her credibility eroding, and I wonder if this stunt hasn't lost her the vote of every man in the country. I mean, she is antagonizing half of the voting population."

"Dr. Green?"

Liz and Cal leaned in and squeezed their hands.

"How do you interpret tonight's event?"

Dr. Green smiled at Stone Phillips charmingly. "Stone, this is a turning point in this campaign. This may affect the way all campaigns in the future are run. Here is what has happened: Stratton and Sampson are responding to the negative ads and dirty politics of the Democrats and Republicans. These campaigns have been especially nasty in the last weeks, insinuating all sorts of things about the WAP candidates and flat-out stating that neither of them is fit for office. Instead of responding in kind, the WAP campaign has re-invigorated its position of representing women by showing in gaudy glory the power that women everywhere have. Instead of trying to convince us that Ostrem is in the back pocket of the oil companies, or that Beckinger is a puppet to the union bosses, Stratton and Sampson have shown us that they are perfectly in command of one of the true powers women have: sex. Their efforts with the sex strike have propelled the peace process faster than any other impetus. Any thinking person will see that women who have the kind of power that Liz and Elektra do are the kind of people we want in office."

"That's ridiculous," Reverend Mennen huffed through his fluffy beard. "What are they going to do about Iran? Show up to a nuke negotiation in Wonder bras and three-inch heels?"

Dr. Green laughed. "If they thought it would be

effective, they might, Reverend. The point is that they are open to all of the negotiation options available to women, even those traditionally taboo. The paradigm has shifted. Women can use sexuality as a tool of negotiation. If the men can play dirty pool in the political arena, so can women."

"Doesn't that put men at a disadvantage, Marjorie?" Gretchen asked. "I mean, when Senator Clinton got choked up in 2008, it was suggested that she faked crying, and it hurt her in the polls because it was seen as a tool men couldn't use, giving her an unfair advantage."

"Gretchen, Beckinger and Ostrem drew the line in the sand with their behavior. I don't lose any sleep over their being at a disadvantage."

"Do you have anything to add, Reverend?" asked Stone.

The Reverend had been turning purple and huffing like a steam train in his little box in the corner. When Stone addressed him, he was so angry that he could only spit out single words. "Lewd. Disgusting. Display. Female. Parts. Unseemly. Sinful!" he cried at the top of his crescendo.

"Thank you all for your comments," Stone said in conclusion and then moved on to the other, far more boring, stories of the day.

A cheer went up in the hotel lounge, and Liz and Cal began to breathe again.

"I have to write Dr. Green a thank you note," said Liz.

"Better yet, give her a cabinet position," Cal said.

"She deserves something juicy like Secretary of State or Chief of Staff."

"Do you think she remembers us?" Liz asked, sipping her Manhattan thoughtfully.

"Well, she remembered me with a little jog of her memory when we had lunch at the WAP conference last year," said Cal. "I'm sure someone at MHC has figured out who you are. The Alumnae Association doesn't miss much. Neither does the student newspaper."

"That would be a fun stop on the campaign," Liz said. "I haven't been back, not even for a reunion."

Cal grinned. "That can be arranged."

♥

October in central Massachusetts was a picture postcard with a brisk breeze. The air was crisp, the water sparkled, and the leaves set the trees aflame. Bits of fire, little leaf-embers, floated down from the canopy of the grand maples and elms of the college campus. Liz and Cal snuck off the bus as soon as they could wearing jeans and old MHC hooded sweatshirts and took a walk around the grand brick buildings of their alma mater. They would have gone more slowly, but they wanted to stay ahead of the secret service detail that was not nearly as discrete as it thought it was.

"Wow, it feels so natural to be back here," Liz said. "I feel like we're just hurrying to class, trying to beat the bell."

Cal smiled. "I don't feel that young, but I know what

you mean." She pointed at a building in the distance. "There's Wilder. Let's go visit our old room."

They stood by the door of the squat dormitory with its Dutch gables, waiting for someone to let them in. Finally, a student appeared with a key fob.

"Hi," Cal said. "We're alums. Could you let us in so we can see our old room?"

The student eyed them, looking at their old sweatshirts carefully. "Sing a verse of the school song," she challenged them.

Liz grinned. "Nobody sings that," she said. "We only ever sang the alternate version.

> "Oh, Mount Holyoke, we pay thee tuition,
> In the fervor of youth that's gone wrong,
> Each year it gets higher and higher,
> My God, alma mater, how long?"

Cal joined in here.

> "So from barroom to bedroom we stagger,
> And united in free love for all,
> Our drinks are too strong and our morals gone,
> Mount Holyoke what's happening to me?
> Mount Holyoke what's happening to me?"

The student grinned and held the door open for them. "Welcome home, ladies," she said.

They ducked in before the secret service guys could follow. The men stood outside, sulking.

The dorm had been given another coat of paint, yet Liz knew the clanking radiators would flake and peel by winter's end. Dark overstuffed furniture lined the walls of the parlor they stood in, and she could smell dinner cooking in the kitchen. A young woman sat at the bell desk, reading a thick text. She looked up at them. "Can I call someone for you?"

"Oh, we're alums," Cal said. "We wondered if we could go up to the second floor and see our old room?"

The girl looked at them more closely. A smile leapt to her face as she recognized them. "Liz? Cal? Is it really you?"

"Shh," Liz said. "We're incognito." She plucked at her sweatshirt.

"We'll get you and the girls in our room backstage tonight if we can go in without causing a huge stir," Cal bargained.

"No sweat," said the girl, picking up the phone. "Lemme see if they're in."

A moment later, Liz and Cal met Trisha and Robin, the current residents of 201 Wilder Hall. They stepped into the corner room, which boasted two windows and a view of the green and the student center.

"I used to sit on my bed here and watch the whole world go by," Liz said, pointing to a window.

Robin bounced in glee. "That's my bed! Liz Stratton slept in my bed!"

Trisha was equally star-struck with Cal. "What did you major in, Ms. Talmadge?" she asked shyly.

"Boys, mostly," Cal answered with a wicked grin.

"Then that subject got too hard, so I switched to Women's Studies."

"Did you see Dr. Green on the TV last week?" Robin asked.

Liz and Cal looked at each other. "Yes, we did. She's the reason we're here. We're going to see her next."

"She's my hero—and so are you," Trisha said to the both of them.

"She's probably the main reason we are where we are today," Cal said. "She inspired us when we took her class."

"Really?" Robin and Trisha were wide-eyed. "She was teaching here when you were here?"

"It wasn't that long ago," said Liz, who had suddenly grown weary of talking to nineteen-year-olds. They were worse than twenty-five-year-olds.

♥

"Were we that...chipper when we were nineteen?" Cal asked once they'd left the dorm.

The secret service was following much more closely now, but they didn't care.

The crisp air made Liz feel giddy. "I think we might have been worse, honey," she said. "Let's go find Dr. Green. I want to thank her for the other night."

They marched past the student union and the lakes on the way to the tall old building that housed the Humanities. Dr. Green's office was exactly where it had been fifteen years ago, but she wasn't there. The excited department secretary told them she was teaching a class down the hall, so they went to wait by the door until class was over.

The door was open, so Liz and Cal slipped into the back of the lecture room and stood behind the last row of seats. Dr. Green was leading a discussion about women and politics, answering a question posed by a student: why aren't there more female politicians?

"Women are underrepresented in politics for the same reasons they are underrepresented in all professions: first, they have children and are expected to be the primary caregivers. Next, they have been conditioned to think that competing with men in the professions is unseemly." At this point she looked up and saw Liz and Cal at the back of the room. "Oh, my," she said. "It seems we've attracted a couple of visitors. Class, may I present former students Liz Stratton and Cal Talmadge!"

Forty heads swung around, and then the class cheered for them as they walked to the front of the class.

"I'm sorry for just dropping in, Dr. Green," Liz said. "We just wanted to stop in and say 'hi.' The secretary suggested we come by your classroom."

"I think it's wonderful that you've come to see all of us," Dr. Green said. "These ladies have oodles of questions for you, I'm sure, and I'm happy to devote the rest of the class time to you."

♥

Official faculty events could actually be fun, Cal

decided, if you were faculty. She watched tables of them chatting with each other, cliquishly sitting at tables divided by mostly by department. Tablecloths and cloth napkins notwithstanding, this was just like any other school cafeteria.

She and Liz were circulating, shaking hands, and schmoozing in general. They were both good at this. They smiled, hovered, chatted lightly, and talked seriously, depending on what the current audience demanded. The faculty were flattered to meet Liz, but most were intelligent enough to have serious questions, too. They also got endless razzing about being alumnae.

It was hard work that took all of Cal's concentration. Almost all of her concentration, anyway. Most of the evening, she had been half aware of someone watching her. This wasn't unlikely as she and Liz were the stars of the evening, but something was different about this pair of eyes that made the back of her neck itch in a peculiar way.

She tried to surreptitiously glance around to locate the source, but she couldn't focus long enough to find it.

Eventually, the two women got to the table that held the source of Cal's itch. A pair of cool brown eyes latched onto hers as she and Liz approached a table of English faculty. The intensity in those eyes made Cal's breath catch in her throat and she coughed.

"Hello!" Liz said, placing her hands on the backs of two chairs. The old men occupying them smiled up at her. "Is everyone having a good time?"

Cal went to stand next to her friend amidst a chorus

of "Oh, yes—es," and smiled at everyone at the table. "Liz will answer questions, if you have any," she said, as she had to every table, but she was staring at the bespectacled man with the brown eyes.

He was in his late thirties, with one of those not-tall-but-perfectly-proportioned bodies that some men under five feet, nine inches possessed. He looked far too athletic to be an academic, and too smart to be a jock. His mop of dark, loose curls gave him a boyish look, but the way he locked her with his gaze was not at all childish. She wished suddenly that he had been her teacher.

"I have a question," he said. "I'm Dr. Nicolas Brown, Poet in Residence. Whom would you appoint as Poet Laureate?"

Liz thought a moment. "Fantasy or living?"

"I like the fantasy idea," Dr. Brown answered. "How about both?"

"Let's see...I think Plath as my fantasy Poet Laureate and, living...I don't know. What are you doing for the next four years?" The table chuckled. "Honestly, I'd have to appoint a council to pick one. I haven't been keeping up with modern poets. I'd hate to pick someone based on what Oprah says, although she's a dear friend and I owe her so much."

There were other questions, and Cal tried to pay attention, but her gaze kept going back to Dr. Nicolas Brown's. She determined that there was no ring on his left hand, and that she liked his hands a lot. The fingers were not long, but looked powerful, like baker's hands that kneaded lots of bread. She tore herself away when it was time to move on to the next table, but she couldn't help throwing a glance over her shoulder.

He was watching her and caught her glance. He smiled.

The dinner wrapped up so that they had just enough time to get everyone over to the auditorium for the rally. Liz, Cal, and the entourage walked out of the building chatting and in high spirits, and Cal didn't even notice the English professor standing by the door as she passed it. But she did feel his gaze on the back of her neck, so she stopped and turned around.

"Hello, Dr. Brown" she said.

"Hello, Ms. Talmadge," he said. "Please call me Nicolas." He held out his gloved hand and Cal shook it, cursing the snap in the air.

"Call me Cal," she said. "Are you coming to the rally?"

"Yes. May I walk with you?"

"Of course," she said. "Chapin Auditorium hasn't moved since I was here last, has it?"

"Naw," he said. "The dorms get shuffled every decade or so just to keep the students on their toes, but the main buildings stay pretty much as they are."

They were quiet a moment as they had to negotiate a press of people crossing the bridge to the main part of the campus. The October leaves on the maple trees were barely hanging on, and the creek below was littered with a thin crust of red and gold. A pair of ducks and an impossibly large trout watched the crowd negotiate the bridge.

Cal sighed appreciatively. "I forgot how pretty it is here in the fall," she said.

"Yes, it's my favorite season," Nicolas said. "And this campus is probably the prettiest I've ever been to."

"I remember one day I was so overwhelmed by mid-terms that I just struck out on a walk. I walked around the perimeter of the whole campus, golf course and stables included."

"That must have taken all day," Nicolas said.

"Nearly. I was so energized by the end that I studied for hours afterward." She grinned at the memory and then looked at Nicolas. "That was a while ago, I guess."

"I was a student once, too," he said. "I don't have quite the nostalgia for University of Florida that you do for MHC, but I understand."

They had been walking ever so slightly slower than the group, and now they had a modicum of privacy. Cal found herself blushing for no reason. Then she felt his hand on her elbow pull her to a stop.

"Cal, I don't normally do this. Correct me if I'm wrong, dammit..." Nicolas stammered for words. "Is there something here?"

"Here?" Cal said weakly.

"You know. I'm feeling...I don't know...is this chemistry I feel? Here? Between us?"

Cal broke into a big smile. "Perhaps," she said.

"But you feel it, too?"

"Yes. I do," she admitted. "It seemed wrong to point it out. Silly, huh?"

"How about if I ask you for a drink after the...what

is this? A 'show'? Anyway, a drink after?"

"Yes, okay," she said. "Meet me outside the door we just came out of at ten."

"Done," Nicolas said. "Until then, we have this very long walk to the auditorium to enjoy." He slid her arm through his, and they walked the rest of the way across campus just like that, unnoticed.

♥

The noise coming from the auditorium had the particular high-pitched hum that only a huge group of young women has. Women from two women's colleges plus plenty of co-eds from other local colleges packed Skinner Hall, chattering with excitement. Liz could feel the pulsing hormones wafting through the curtain. She wondered how well the young ladies out there were abstaining.

"Do you think we'd have been able to give up sex for a whole campaign when we were twenty?" she whispered to Cal.

Cal grinned her wicked grin. "Maybe. But not when I was twenty-one."

Liz smiled back. "I remember Rory. I don't blame you." She looked out over the crowd again. "What do you think about them?"

"They look pretty determined," Cal said. "I wouldn't put it past them. They're capable of anything. Remind them of that."

"Right-o."

Liz parted the curtain and a moment later the

auditorium reverberated with glee-filled screams of young-adult females.

"All right, enough," Liz said finally. "It's not like I'm one of the Beatles or Duran Duran. I want to do something a little different tonight. Normally, I'd stand up here and pontificate, listing our platform ideas and hyping you up. Instead, I want questions from you. I'll answer them to the best of my ability, and I'll tell you honestly when I can't answer a question and why. Does that sound good?"

"Yes!" came the answer.

"Great. There's the microphone in front of the stage. Form a nice line and go to town!"

There was some rustling as a spot was turned on to the mike and an orderly line formed. The first woman at the microphone was typical, from her sweatshirt to her flip-flops.

"Ms. Stratton," she said. "My name is Lauren Bierce. I'm unclear on how not having sex with my boyfriend is going to stop the war in Mesopotamianstan. Could you explain?"

Liz smiled. "Wow. We didn't waste any time getting to the issue, did we? Okay, it works like a union. Unions work to improve working conditions for its members by stopping work, right? All of the workers stop, even if the things the union wants changed doesn't affect them. So, for example, let's say at an envelope factory, the folders work fifteen-hour shifts, but the gluers only work eight-hour shifts. In order to get eight-hour shifts for the folders, the gluers stop working, too, even though they already have that kind of shift. They do it because they know that if they need support in the future, the folders will help.

"So, to our situation. I know that your boyfriend probably has little individual power to stop a foreign war. However, if he were to band together with all of his friends, and they all went to their fathers who went to their bosses, well, you get the idea. It won't take long before the people at the top feel the pressure, not only of their own needs, but also of those of the people they represent. So, tell your boyfriend that if he wants to see your delicates again, he needs to do his part and start pressuring the people he knows to do something about ending the war, just like you are."

The next person in line looked older than a typical student. "Ms. Stratton," she said. "Don't you think that this sex strike is a silly diversion to the campaign? Shouldn't you be focusing on trying to get into the White House instead?"

"Well," Liz sighed. "I do admit that this campaign has taken a riskier track than I thought it would when I began. However, when I began, WAP was little more than an outside irritant to the Democrats and the Republicans. But last week we polled at an astounding twenty-four percent! Think about that. That means that one in three people are thinking of voting for us. Registered Democrats and Republicans and Independents have said they'd vote for us. Before the sex strike, WAP polled at something like two percent. So, to answer your question, no, I don't think the sex strike is a silly diversion. I think it is a legitimate way to make our concerns take center stage. So even if we don't get to the White House, our concerns are front and center because the strike doesn't have to end on the first Tuesday in November. We can hold out until the war is over. Can't we?"

The crowd broke out in applause.

♥

Zeke rubbed Liz's feet in their room at the small hotel on campus. The rally had gone on much later than even Liz had estimated. The questions had kept coming, and she had worked really hard to answer each one honestly. She had been spectacular, but she was completely worn out and looked somewhat deflated in her satin pajamas.

"You looked like you were having fun out there," Zeke said as he squeezed her left heel.

"Oh, it was a blast. The whole day was wonderful," she said, her head propped up against the headboard. "That's wonderful. Please don't stop."

"As you wish."

"I had forgotten what a magical place this is," Liz said, staring at the ceiling. "If we're elected, we should do something to charter more women's colleges or something."

"That would be fun," Zeke said, moving on to her arch.

"Yeah." Then Liz groaned as Zeke pressed his

thumbs into the ball of her foot. "That's the spot. Jesus, that feels nice."

Zeke laughed and shushed her. "You sound like you are having too much fun," he said. "You don't want any rumors flying around just because of a foot rub."

She laughed, too. "You're right. I'll be quiet as a church mouse. Squeak! Squeak!"

They laughed a bit, and then Liz relaxed into the pillows with a sigh. "You're too good to me, Zeke," she murmured.

"I know," Zeke said and moved on to her other foot.

He continued to work the foot for a while. When he was done, he set her foot down on the bedspread but left his hand on it as he looked up at her face. She was smiling, and possibly dozing. Without thinking, he slid his fingers slowly up her foot to her ankle and then pulled them back down, caressing her.

Liz didn't react, so he did it again. Slowly trace fingers up, slowly drag them down. He didn't breathe.

He closed his eyes and let his fingers trace their way up her calf under her pajama leg to the soft spot behind her knee and back again.

She sighed and moved a little, so he did it again, so slowly.

Liz started and sat up. She met Zeke's eyes and held him there with her stare. He couldn't stand it and looked away, pulling his hands into his lap.

"Oh, Zeke," she said softly and put her hand over his.

"I'm sorry," he said. "I can be out of here in five

seconds." He tried to pull away, but Liz held his hand fast. He looked up at her.

"How long have you felt this way?" she asked.

"Oh, probably since that first lunch in Arizona," he said.

"So, all those times you asked me to dinner?"

"I hoped each time you'd say 'yes,'" he admitted. "Liz, let go. Let me go."

She bit her lip. "No," she said, "Dammit. You've got a helluva sense of timing."

"Really?" Zeke took her hands in his. "Really, Liz? You could, we could—really?"

"Well, we can't now, Zeke," she said. "We can't risk a scandal. You just said so five minutes ago."

"Liz, I can hold out if I can hope. Shit. I've wanted you for ten years. I can wait a bit, if you'll just tell me you'll give me a chance."

"Of course," she said. Then after a moment, "Why did you wait until now, Zeke?"

Zeke laughed sadly. "Liz, I've asked you to dinner every day for ten years. How is that waiting?"

"I'm sorry to have put you through that," she said. "Let me make it up to you." She sat next to him and kissed him.

Zeke smiled. "I thought we couldn't do this."

"Silly, it's a sex strike. No one said anything about kissing." She kissed him again. "You are going to have to find another place to sleep tonight, though."

"Kiss me again, and I'll do anything you ask."

Chapter 9

The air had a distinctive frosty bite to it that brought Cal back to dates when she was still a student at Mt. Holyoke. The meeting at the door was the same.

The dash in the cold to the car was the same, and so was the anticipation of the dry air from the heaters finally warming them up enough for a smile.

"So, where to?" Cal asked.

"Well, I was wondering if you had a suggestion. Having been a student here, you must have a favorite," Nicolas said, pulling out of the parking lot.

Cal laughed. "You don't really want to go where I went," she said.

"Yes, I do," he insisted. "I'm very curious, especially now."

"I'm embarrassed to say," she said. "But I'll show

you. If it's too terrible, we can just go on and find something else."

"Agreed."

Cal directed him out of campus and down the highway, which found its way to one of the few traffic lights in the college town. As they idled at the light, she pointed across the street at a squat building with a tiki torch burning weakly in front.

"No," Nicolas said in disbelief. "The Huki-Lau? Really? You and your friends used to go to the Huki-Lau? On purpose?"

"I told you it was terrible," Cal said.

"You better hope this never gets out to the press," Nicolas said as he turned into the lot.

"Oh, we can't go in there!" Cal said. "It's too embarrassing!"

"Can, will, and are," he said triumphantly as he switched off the engine. "Here we go."

The Huki-Lau was pretty much as Cal remembered it: Chinese buffet along one wall, tiki torches, grass skirts, and palm fronds everywhere and booths circling a stage and tiny dance floor. Two nights a week a trio played music that some people danced to. The other five nights was karaoke.

For booths that didn't have a clear view of the stage, televisions bolted to the wall showed the stage and the singers.

A tiny redheaded woman was on the screen hollering out something like a U2 song. Cal felt like slinking away, but Nicolas was grinning in glee. "I've never been here," he whispered conspiratorially. "I've always wondered what it was like!"

A tired-looking waitress led them to a stage-view booth and handed them thick menus with pictures of drinks. Cal smiled when she realized that the pictures were the same as the last time she was there.

"Liz will be so jealous that I'm here without her," she said.

"Really?" Nicolas said. "I can't imagine you two here."

"There'd always be at least four of us."

"Why?"

"Oh, neither Liz or I had a car," she explained. "We always had to have a friend drive us, and if a car left campus, it was always full of girls. We traveled in packs."

"So, four co-eds giggling away in a car on their way to a tiki bar for a Friday night, huh?" Nicolas said. "That's a fun picture."

Cal grinned. "Well, we'd start here," she said. "But, as you can see, this isn't a great place to meet people, so we'd usually move on after a drink and bad Chinese."

The waitress showed up to take their orders. Nicolas ordered a G&T, but Cal ordered by pointing to the menu and smiling. The waitress, though tired, smiled too, and left.

"What was that?"

"My usual," Cal said. "Regulars get it. You'll see."

Nicolas leaned forward on the table. "My, you're interesting," he said. "Why are you so interesting?"

"I don't know," Cal said. "You're forward. Why are you so forward?"

Nicolas sat back, flustered. "Oh, Jesus. I'm sorry. I do that. I just say what's in my head. I don't have much of a filter. It can get me into trouble—you know, with women."

Cal reached across the table and patted his hand reassuringly. "It's refreshing, believe me," she said, leaving her hand on his.

Nicolas put his other hand on top of hers and grinned again. "So, how did you go from Mt. Holyoke to WAP?" he asked.

"That seems like a pretty straight line to me," she said.

"But you're so…approachable," he said. "Many of my colleagues in the Women's Studies department are— if you'll forgive me—a little prickly."

Cal rolled her eyes. "Just a different approach, or maybe a different reason for studying women's issues." She smiled. "Not all of us are shrill harpies lobbying for male castration."

"So you saw that, too." Nicolas chuckled. "I wasn't worried about that," he said, stroking her fingers with his thumb.

They had to sit back when their drinks arrived because, although Nicolas's G&T sat neatly on a bar napkin, the scorpion that Cal ordered took up most of the table. Purple and sporting straws and umbrellas as "legs," the drink came in a stemmed contraption that more resembled a punchbowl than a cocktail glass.

"It's for sharing," Cal answered Nicolas's raised eyebrows. "Lean back," she warned. The waitress stepped up and lit the drink on fire. "Now *blow!*"

After the flames were out, they sat giggling over it, making a show of slurping up the fruity slush.

Finally, Nicolas pushed back. "No more," he moaned. "I have to drive us back tonight!"

"Wuss," Cal chided him. "We can get a cab."

"No, no," he said. "That would have worked on me ten years ago, but I'm an adult now, really," he hiccupped. "No, really."

Cal was tipsy, but she was having a really, really good time. "Well, then, what should we do now?"

Just then, the music changed and they both looked up at the stage where a very fat man began to sing "My Way!" Nicolas grinned at Cal and raised his mischievous eyebrows.

"Oh, no," she said. "I'm not in college anymore. And I'm so not drunk enough."

"Oh, please," he said. "Together!"

Cal began to protest again, but soon found herself with a microphone in her hand as Nicolas spoke to the DJ. Then Nicolas was next to her in front of the very sparse late-Thursday-night crowd.

The music came up and the words to "Jackson" blinked to life on the screen. Cal couldn't help grinning at the duet choice. Nicolas had a passable voice, but Cal was able to show off a little as her training in the campus a cappella group came back.

They collapsed back in their booth laughing. "I

didn't know you liked country music," she told him.

"I didn't know you could actually sing," he said. He took both her hands in his and gazed at her. Suddenly—he seemed to say everything suddenly—he said, "I'm finding this booth…confining. Let's get out of here."

Cal nodded and stood before she could change her mind.

She hadn't necked in a car since school, but she had seen it coming. She hadn't said anything when Nicolas parked his car in a picturesque spot next to the river and tuned the radio to jazz. But it was just as delicious as she remembered it: the thrill of being semi-in-public, kissing someone new, and being out past curfew—she was going to be dead tired tomorrow.

Finally, she came up for air. "Nicolas, I hate to be a wet blanket here, but I really do have to be up early tomorrow—"

"But you're leaving tomorrow," he said earnestly. He took off his glasses and looked seventeen. "Oh, please, just come home with me. Please!"

Cal closed her eyes and tried not to show how badly she wanted to do exactly that. "We're adults," she said. "We're old enough to know better, Nicolas."

He turned on the car. "I live near campus. I'll just drive by and, if it's too terrible, we'll just pass by on the way to the hotel, okay?" He grinned at her.

Cal bit her lip. "You're bad," she said.

"Oh, no," he said. "I'm very, very good. You'll see."

♥

If asked, Dr. Brown would quickly explain he wasn't from the South. He claimed no Southern connection at all besides graduate school at UF. He had discovered that his spider specialist hero taught there, so he applied, packed his bags, and left the cold Northeast for the balmy extreme South.

It was the Southerners who taught him that he was not one of them, nor would he ever be. That was fine with him. He missed the passage of time reflected in the seasons of the North. He missed Northern punctuality. He missed apple cider.

He couldn't argue with seventy degrees in January, though. His closet poet side wrote poems about manatees and the Bermuda Triangle and Hemingway. His spider-hunter side was in heaven.

After graduation, Nicolas bounced around from job to job. There wasn't a lot of call for spider specialists outside of academia and pesticide companies, and he couldn't bring himself to study how to kill the most fascinating critters on earth. He spent a little time teaching high school biology to support his writing habit, but throwing poems into the ether to have them frequently rejected disheartened him. He kept writing, but eventually applied for academic positions. Mount Holyoke welcomed him with a tenure-track position teaching young women biology. Research was part of the deal, which meant less time to write. The writer in him recognized it as a compromise and a cop-out, but he was comfortable with it for now.

Then one magazine decided to publish a poem and

sent him some money. Then another did, and another. On a lark, Nicolas put five poems into an envelope and sent them to *The New Yorker*, and damned if two of them didn't show up there, too!

Finally, a national publisher bought a collection of his poems. He found himself one day a year later staring at his book *Florida Gales* in a bookstore windows. *Florida Gales* was a best-selling poetry book for several months, though he was hardly a house-hold name. Poets rarely are.

Now, he was publishing a couple poems and spider articles a year. Not fast, but acceptable. And MHC offered him a Poet in Residence Position, which took Nicolas by complete surprise. He accepted the position, deciding that he could forsake the spiders for a couple years to write. They'd be there when he was done.

But in the back of his mind, he felt complacent in a dangerous way. He was beginning to feel lazy, and that made him nervous. He needed a little more hunger in his life to keep him working.

His house wasn't as dark or cold as before, but it was just as empty. For a man as attractive as he thought he was, he was lonely. He had lots of female friends, but he was rarely able to close the deal. Like many nice guys, he found himself relegated to the "friend" column so quickly it made his head spin. Part of this was due to his earnestness and thoughtfulness. Honestly, many of his female friends started out thinking he was gay because he was so neat and polite, and his name was "Nicolas," not "Nick."

Cal knew for sure that Nicolas wasn't gay. He was every ounce a man, and a very eager one at that. She was enjoying their necking session on his couch in his neat living room. When she came up for air, he plunged his face into her bosom and moaned with pleasure.

"Oh, God," she said. "Nicolas, honey. It's two a.m. I have to leave."

"No, no, no," he murmured from her chest. "Don't go."

"No choice," she said. "I have to get up and get Liz elected."

"No," he said, looking up at her from her lap. "I won't let you go. This is too good. For both of us. I think."

"Oh, I would give anything to stay," she said. Suddenly a thought popped into her head. "Oh, shit."

He sat up, surprised by her vehemence. "What?"

"I may as well go," she said, sitting up straight. "We have this fucking sex-strike going on!"

"Fuck, no!" Nicolas said, sitting back on the couch, slapping his hand to his forehead. "I totally forgot!"

"Weirdly, I did, too," she said, staring into space. "I didn't remember until this second. We were so close to— Shit, I would have ruined it all!"

Nicolas took her into his arms again. "No, it wouldn't have been ruined. I can keep a secret. It would have been fine." He kissed her again and looked deep into her eyes. "Damn your little sex-strike," he groaned. "I would have done unspeakable things to you tonight."

"You're not mad?" she asked, surprised.

"Why would I be?"

"Well, haven't I given you the equivalent of blue-balls or something? I thought that was a sin."

Nicolas shifted uncomfortably. "Well, this isn't how I planned to end the evening," he said. "Not that I had any of this planned, so to speak. I was hoping that I would wake up in your arms and watch the morning sun play with your golden hair, but perhaps another time." He drew a finger across her forehead and tucked a wisp of hair behind her ear.

Cal looked him directly in the eye. "If you promise no hanky-panky and that I'll be back at the hotel by six a.m., I'll stay here tonight."

"You're kidding. Really? But won't that look…I don't know…bad?" Nicolas asked.

"I'm not the important one," Cal said. "I doubt anyone will notice. But on the principle of the thing, here are the ground rules: nothing below the waist, 'no' is instantly obeyed, and I'm not late in the morning. Agreed?"

Nicolas cupped her face in both his hands and said, "Agreed." He kissed her. "Bedroom's that way. Race you!"

♥

Cal stood under the water in the shower in her hotel room trying to replace sleep with hot water. It was six a.m., which is when she would have rolled out of bed—had she ever gone to sleep, that is.

She didn't really have to worry about people noticing her as she walked in in the same clothes she wore the night before, because neither the hotel staff nor the secret service cared, and they were the only ones up. Still, she hurried to her room with her eyes on the floor.

It had been very hard to leave Nicolas in the car, but it had been harder still to leave his warm bed for the cold dark that morning. As she had dictated, only hanky and no panky had taken place that night, but Cal found herself wishing on more than one occasion that night that one of them would "lose control," and they'd finish the deed. Alas, they were both mature enough to stop before any silly sex strike rules were broken. However, this didn't mean that they didn't have a marvelous time.

They drove in relative silence on the way to the campus hotel, drunk on each other and lack of sleep, but also very aware that this was the end of the night. But it was also the end of what? How were they to handle this...whatever this was?

Nicolas pulled into an empty parking lot a few blocks from campus and put the car into park. He swiveled in his seat so he was facing her and took one of her gloved hands into his. He stroked the back of her hand with his thumb and said nothing for a moment, letting the engine run and a plume of exhaust puff around the outside of the car.

Finally, he swallowed. "I don't know what you may be feeling," he began, "but I know what I'm feeling. I want to see you again." He looked up at her like a brave, frightened teenager.

Cal realized she was grinning. "Of course, silly," she said. "I really want to see you again."

"So, when?"

Cal sighed. "That is the difficulty. I don't think the campaign has plans to come through here again."

"That means…"

"That means that I couldn't make it back here until November at the earliest."

"After the election," Nicolas said. "No, that won't do. How about if I come out to see you?"

"On the campaign trail? Really?"

"Sure. Is there a rule against it?"

"No, there isn't, not against you coming to a campaign stop," Cal said. "But, you realize that the other rule will still be in effect."

"Nuts, really?"

"Really, really."

Nicolas looked down at Cal's hand long enough that Cal began to panic. Then he looked up at her again.

"It usually takes me five or six dates for me to get to third base, so I figure I owe you at least that many dinners. Sound fair?"

She leaned in and kissed him. "More than fair."

They sealed the deal with a good five minutes of necking before they remembered themselves and headed to the hotel.

Cal scrubbed her head with shampoo in an effort to massage energy into her feeble, hormone-scrambled brain. She could still feel Nicolas's hands and lips burning everywhere. She was so wound up that she felt like a balloon about to pop. Then she brightened. Without even rinsing the shampoo from her hair, she leapt from the shower and dug through the promotion materials in her room, dripping shamelessly on them. She found what she wanted, one of the campaign "goody bags," and returned to the shower with a smile on her face.

♥

When Nicolas got home, he emailed the Department secretary to cancel his classes that day. He then took off all his clothes and fell into the bed where he and Cal so recently lay. He wiggled over to the spot where her perfume lingered most strongly and fell asleep, breathing her scent.

When he awoke the autumn sun glowed warmly on the bed. He opened his eyes and they fell first on a golden hair shining in the sun. He smiled and stoked the strand like a pet. His eyes flashed. He leapt from the bed and raced to his desk. He tore through the piles of papers and books until he found a blank sheet and a pencil. He sat his naked ass down on the cold wooden chair and penned the poem that so urgently presented itself in his head.

> *Rosy-Golden, light*
> *Muse of*
> *music and fear.*
> *Desire and denial,*
> *A mirrored goddess:*
> *Amazonian,*

Sex kitten,
And a door both open and closed.
Hours separate us,
And principle.

Nicolas did manage a meal and a shower that day, but mostly he sat in that chair and wrote poem after poem. Not all of them were about Cal. Actually, most of them weren't about her, but once the gates were open, the words gushed from the reservoir.

He fell into bed late that night, exhausted but awake. His brain felt so drained that he actually turned on the television normally only used for the morning news and caught the middle of a black-and-white movie. It was a romance involving characters he didn't know, but instantly cared about because they were tangled in a no-win romantic situation. He wept in befuddled relief at the end when it all turned out all right. He fell asleep in the spot that smelled like Cal without realizing that he hadn't spoken a single word since he and Cal parted that morning.

Chapter 10

Even though Cal was cross-eyed from her never-ending date with Nicolas, she recognized a fellow non-sleeper with a "glow" about her.

"You slept with him, didn't you?" Cal whispered from across the table. Not seeing an instant denial, she squealed quietly, "Oh, you did! You did!"

"No, no, no," Liz insisted. "It's not like that." Then coyly, she asked, "Who do you mean?"

Cal grinned. "You know who."

"Yes, but I'm surprised you do."

"Oh, please," Cal said. "Anyone within ten feet of you two can feel the chemistry."

"I'm the last one to notice?" Liz said with a sigh.

"You always are," Cal said with a smile. Then she leaned forward. "So our—um—sex strike is still intact, correct?"

Liz smiled. "Of course. We're adults. Not that it was easy."

"I want a blow-by-blow."

"For starters, I don't kiss and tell—"

"Yes, you do, honey."

"—and second, there was none of that anyway."

Liz sat back with a smile and a sigh. Without thinking, Cal did, too. Liz's sharp ears recognized the same happy note.

"Cal, is there something you want to tell me?" she asked.

"Hmm? About what?"

Liz sat forward. "That self-satisfied sigh of a woman in—Cal, where'd you go last night after the rally?"

Liz was stunned when Cal blushed. "You had a date?"

"The Poetry Professor with the brown eyes," Cal admitted.

"Wow! That was quick." Liz peered more closely at her friend. "Wait a minute. You didn't get any sleep last night, either."

"No, I didn't. But we were good, too!" Cal added quickly. "Though it was hard."

"That's what she said," Zeke said, walking up to the table and sitting down. "What? Is that joke passé now?"

Liz and Cal giggled. "I can see by Cal's face that last night's adventures have been discussed and given approval."

"Yes," Cal said. "But none of this can be out in the open yet, kids."

"Right," Liz said.

"I've been waiting years. A couple more weeks will be okay," he said.

Elektra joined them. "Good morning, team," she said. She took one look at the faces around the table and said, "Okay, what's going on here?"

Cal jumped in. "We've had a breakthrough. Liz and Zeke have admitted their feelings for each other."

"'Bout damn time," Elektra said. "It was like a sauna standing near the two of you."

"And Cal had a date last night!" Liz said.

"Really?" Zeke asked. "Who?"

"Professor here. I'll fill you in later," Liz said.

"I see," Elektra said carefully. "We're still go for the strike, though, right?"

"Oh, yes," Liz said.

"I believe you, but no one else will," Elektra said.

"We know, Elektra," Zeke said. "We're all keeping it under our hats for now."

"Good plan," she said, shaking out her napkin. "'Specially since they want to see us tonight."

"Who?" asked Liz.

"Haven't checked your email yet?"

Three mobile email devices suddenly appeared and thumbs flew. All of them read the email from the office of the President at the same time.

To: Elizabeth Stratton and Elektra Sampson
From: The Office of the President of the United States

Subject: Meeting Tonight
Ladies:

Your presence is requested at a meeting of upper-level officials tonight. Subject to be announced at the meeting. A car will pick you up at 7:30 p.m. outside of your hotel to take you to the meeting place.

Melvin Bernstrom
President of the United States

"Oh, my God," Liz said. "Is this for real?"

"I'll check this out. I'll call the White House and make them confirm or deny it. I'm not letting either of you in a car without confirmation," Cal said, punching a speed-dial number in her phone.

"You have the White House number in speed-dial?" Liz asked.

"Yeah. The switchboard operator, Madge, and I go way back," Cal said. "Hey, Madge. Cal. I need someone to confirm an email we received...uh, huh. Really? Can you confirm the car, too? Wow. Okay. No, they'll be there. Thanks again, Madge. Bye."

"Where do you know Madge from?"

Cal smiled. "She's a charter member of WAP. Plus, when you call the White House to protest as often as I do, it's best to make friends where you can. Madge says this is on the up and up. She was even left instructions for when I called by the chief of staff himself."

Liz leaned back in her chair. "What the hell do they want?"

Zeke put a reassuring hand on her knee under the table.

"We should be prepared for anything," Elektra said. "Maybe they've dug up some dirt, or maybe they made up some dirt."

"You think the president would stoop to fictional blackmail?" Liz asked.

"You are way too nice to be president," said Cal. "This is the same man who is continuing a war just so his buddies can make a buck. He'd like to make a buck now, so he would love his friend Ostrem to win the election."

"I see," Liz said. "Then let's be prepared. Let's put our heads together and come up with a plan."

♥

The black sedan pulled up to their Boston hotel's front door right on time. Liz and Elektra walked to the car with only a pocketbook and an overcoat each.

"Ladies," the driver said in greeting as he held the door for them.

Liz smiled at him. "As long as we're back by curfew, there won't be any trouble."

The driver smiled and closed the door after them.

The drive was far shorter than Liz had anticipated. She'd hoped to compose herself a little more since her nap on the bus didn't really replace a night of sleep. But in twenty minutes, the driver pulled behind a large building and stepped out to open the door for them. Then he led them up a flight of carpeted stairs. Finally, he opened a door to a small meeting room in what looked like a hotel.

Seated at the table in the center of the room was, in fact, the president—Liz had doubted Bernstrom would actually show—and astonishingly, beside him sat both Bill Ostrem and Oscar Beckinger.

They stood as Liz and Elektra entered. The president shook hands with them enthusiastically. "Ms. Stratton, Mrs. Sampson. So good to finally meet you. Someone get their coats. Sit, sit."

"It's a pleasure, Mr. President," Elektra said as she sat and crossed her ankles. "I never thought I'd see the day when I got to shake the hand of a sitting president."

"I never thought I'd see this day, either," Ostrem grumbled. He yelped as Beckinger kicked him under the table.

"So, I'm dying of curiosity, Mr. President. Why did you ask us here?" Liz asked.

The president rubbed his face. "Well, it's like this," he said. "We're sick of this sex strike thingy, and we want it to stop."

Liz and Elektra glanced at each other.

"Oh, really?" Liz said.

"Sure, sure we are," President Berntrom said. "Aren't you sick of it, too?"

"Naturally," Elektra said. "You can imagine how hard Mr. Sampson is to handle these days."

"No, but I mean you miss it, too, don't you?"

"We're only human, Mr. President," Liz said. "Are you going somewhere with this?"

"I just want to establish that we all want the sex strike to end."

"Mr. President," Liz said carefully. "We want the war to end. The sex strike will end once the war is over, and we are prepared to stick to our guns until then."

"I told you this wouldn't work," Ostrem grumbled and yelped again, as he was kicked from two sides this time.

Beckinger leaned across the table and smiled winningly, all confidence and teeth. "You know you're losing impetus, don't you? You've heard the reports about women giving in? You've heard about the preachers telling women that it's their wifely duty to lie with their husbands? Why not end it now while you've still got some people following you? We can arrange a bit of a cease-fire that will appease your constituency. How would that be?"

Liz was amazed that she ever thought him attractive. "That would be a start," she said.

"All you'd have to do is call off the strike and drop out of the race," said the president. "We'll call a cease-fire before the election and we'll all be back to normal relations before we know it. That was easier than I thought it would be."

"Hold up," Elektra said, in a voice that had stopped seventeen-year-old felons in their tracks. "We haven't agreed to anything yet. I'm not dropping out of the race, and neither is Ms. Stratton. We're not settling for a cease-fire, either, because in a cease-fire, guns are still pointed both ways, we just save on ammunition."

"That's right," Liz said. "We are committed to ending the war, not delaying it or stalling it so that one of you can be elected just to start it up again."

Governor Ostrem had had enough. He and stood and glowered at the women from across the table. "Listen here, ladies," he hissed. "If you don't drop out of this race, if you don't call off this strike, we will make sure that you don't win, by any means at our disposal. Any means, do you hear?"

Liz locked him with a steely gaze she usually reserved for weasely show guests who were trying to avoid answering a direct question. "Governor Ostrem," she said, pronouncing each syllable of his name. "And the rest of you. Listen to me carefully: We realize that we may not win this race. We realize that you may do your damnedest to ruin our reputations to ensure that we don't win. We also realize, however, that we have the nation's undivided attention; we have the spotlight. We are shining that spotlight onto our cause, ending the war, and we don't intend to give up as long as we have America's attention. We may not win the election, gentlemen, but we are already two of the most powerful people in America because we have the backing of half of the populace, and we control the one thing you want more than anything else: the female body."

Liz and Elektra stood and picked up their pocketbooks.

"Unless there is anything else, gentlemen, we'll be on our way," Elektra said. "Good night."

And they left.

♥

"How'd it go in there, ladies?" the driver asked politely as he held the door for them.

"Surprisingly well," said Liz. "What is your name?"

"Ed."

"Well, Ed," Liz said. "There's a $100 tip in it for you if you can find us some Veuve Cliquot and Ben and Jerry's Phish Phood in this town."

"Yes, ma'am!"

Elektra and Liz giggled as they sat in the back of the car.

"I have to say, Elektra. You have brass balls," Liz said.

"Same to ya," replied Elektra. "I cannot believe that just happened. Some nerve they have."

"I'm amazed they let us just march out of there with the last word and everything."

"I think they're amazed we just marched out of there with the last word," Elektra said. "I bet Ostrem went apoplectic after we left. I've never seen a man so purple."

They gave Ed his $100 and then toted the pints of ice cream and bottles of champagne into the hotel where Cal and Zeke awaited them. None of the other staff knew of the meeting, but Cal and Zeke were waiting and hugely relieved to see them.

"What's the ice-cream for?" asked Zeke.

"We're celebrating," Elektra said.

"They're afraid of us," Liz said. "Running scared. Ready to offer us anything to call off the dogs."

"It was fun," Elektra said. "I wouldn't be surprised if Ostrem were dead of a stroke by now."

"Ostrem was there?" Cal asked.

"Ostrem, the president and Beckinger. The whole lot of them," Liz said, digging in to a pint of ice cream.

"They're working together? Oh, that's bad," Zeke said.

"They wouldn't have offered us anything if we weren't hurting them badly," Liz said, mouth full of mocha and nuts.

"You should have seen your girl, there tonight," Elektra said as she opened the champagne. "She was on fire and steely."

"Nothing intimidates Elektra," Liz said. "We make a great team."

"Well, then, a toast," Cal said, raising her glass. "To having them on the run."

"On the run!"

They clinked glasses and tossed back the first of many toasts that night.

After three glasses, Zeke put his arm around Liz's waist and whispered, "I worship you, you know."

Liz smiled. "I did not know. Thank you for telling me."

"I adore everything about you."

"Go on. Tell me more about my eyes."

Instead, he pulled her to him and kissed her.

"You," Liz said. "I've thought back over the years, and I don't know what I would have done without you. You have always been there for me."

"I know," he said. "Pathetic."

"Heroic," she corrected. "I really couldn't have done any of this without you. Thank you."

"Oh, don't do that. Don't thank me. I had to. I loved you."

"I know that now. Thank you for loving me. Obtuse me."

"You're more than welcome."

Two bottles into the celebration, Liz had an idea.

"It's not enough to simply deny them sex anymore," Liz said. "It is now time to taunt them. I want revenge. I want to see them squirm."

"What do you propose?" Zeke asked, emptying his glass.

"I'm thinking, bikini days," Liz began.

"Oh! Oh! And girl-on-girl massage-a-thons," Cal jumped in.

"And lingerie lunches!" Elektra said. "Mr. Sampson really likes those."

"So the idea is to get as much naked female flesh into the public sphere as possible?" Zeke asked.

"Yes. Unavailable female flesh," Liz said. "Porn is one thing. A girl in a tube-top on the street is another."

"But it's fall. Won't it be too cold in most places for fleshy bits?" Cal wondered.

"Improvisation. Black lacy bra under a white shirt. Too short skirt at work. Skin, skin, skin. Women should be as naked as possible before the election."

"I thought torture was illegal," Zeke said.

"Poor boy," Cal said, patting his knee. "In every war there are innocent casualties."

"I like the idea," Elektra said. "I would like to show those old men that we can fight dirty, too."

♥

Esther watched the evening news with her cat while her live-in boyfriend Mark pouted in the bedroom. She had cut him off after a particularly derisive remark about a woman being president, but she found later that she did want the war to end enough to give up sex with the whiny misogynistic shit in the other room. She knew she would make up with him later, but at the moment she was enjoying the perks her anger had given her. Like watching the ten o'clock news with Powder and a pint of ice cream unmolested by "Randy McHandsy."

Her favorite local anchor, a pert blonde named Blaire Sanders, was wearing a shirt Esther didn't approve of. It was eggplant, which clashed with her skin tone, and hung off her shoulders like a flour sack. The way it was gathered completely erased her waist, too. Esther wondered if the wardrobe mistress was getting even for something.

Esther snapped out of her critique when she heard the words "bikini days." This was intriguing enough that Esther hit the reverse button on the DVR to the beginning of the story. It annoyed the hell out of Mark when she did this, but it amused her to see people talking backwards.

"In election news," purple-blonde Blaire said. "WAP

candidate Liz Stratton is encouraging women everywhere to don their skimpiest outfits. She has called 'bikini days' until the election. Ms. Stratton says that the feedback from the press conference that is now being called 'The Spectacle' was so positive, that she believes more skin is called for."

The picture changed to a shot of Liz Stratton standing at a podium, smiling to a group of reporters, wearing a conservative white blouse unbuttoned to mid-chest and a lacy lavender bra showing through. "It is imperative that we keep the attention of the country on our cause. To that end, I want everyone who believes that the war in Mesopotaminastan should end to wear as little as is legal in her geographic area. I don't want to hear about anyone getting frostbite, now, but I want men's eyes popping out of their heads, ladies!"

The anchorwoman came back on screen, grinning from ear to ear. "The campaign has set up a page on the website on ideas for 'bikini days.'" Still grinning, she turned to her male co-anchor. "It should be an interesting couple weeks, huh, George?"

George shifted a little in his seat and smiled bravely. "Yes, yes, interesting, Blaire."

"Heck, bikinis sell coffee, why not politics?" the weather guy/comic relief said from the edge of the desk. It was rumored that he was gay, and his glee at George's discomfort was palpable.

George cleared his throat and began a story about yet another convenience store being robbed.

Esther turned off the TV and stroked Powder for a

moment. In her head, she went through the outfits in her closet and pictured herself going to work in the skirt she reserved for third dates, or the shoes she wore when she needed to feel good about herself. Her boss, a dangerously fat man who sweated as he ate lunch, might have a coronary when he saw her, but Esther decided she would risk it. It was for a good cause, after all.

The next morning Mark watched with widening eyes as Esther dressed for work. She put on each of his favorite articles of clothing, and primped and pranced in front of the mirror until she looked as good as he'd ever seen her. When she turned to leave, she found Mark kneeling in the bedroom doorway blocking her way.

"Please," he said in a funny, growly voice. "Please, Esther. Just once. You're killing me."

Esther drew her fingertips along his handsome jaw-line, rough with stubble, and kissed his forehead. "You're a dear, Mark, but no." Using the extra height her favorite attention-getting heels gave her, she stepped over her boyfriend and left for work.

The office she worked at was full of ladies who had seen the same news segment Esther had. Every woman there was dolled up in her most revealing outfit. They ranged in taste from vamp-ish to subtle, but they all had basically the same effect. Every woman who showed her skin, from three-hundred-pound Vera to pixie-like Angie, reduced the men in the office to staring, drooling mannequins. Productivity was reduced by precisely two-thirds: Esther's company hadn't yet achieved an equal man-woman ratio.

Esther, however, found that she was getting more work done. What men who were still functional sheepishly scurried along the hallways with their eyes averted. If they had to speak to a woman in person, they kept the conversation as short as possible. If something had to be worked out in detail, telephones or emails were used. Best of all, even Creepy Dan was too overwhelmed to come sniffing around Esther's door. Before Bikini Days, Esther could count on Dan to interrupt her at least ten times a day so he could rake his lascivious eyes over her body. Ironically, now that she and every other woman were dressed as he had only fantasized, he couldn't stand to look at them. Esther was in heaven.

♥

Maureen sat on the stage of *Spare Me!* feeling hot under the lights and angry. The smug bitch in the navy pantsuit seated across from her was an executive of a major "energy development company," which everyone knew was just an oil company that dabbled in wind on the side.

She had just finished telling Maureen and the audience that her company supported ending the war in Mesopotamianstan.

"I'm sorry," Maureen said. "Could you explain why to me again? I'm fuzzy on the details."

"Well, naturally, war isn't good for the economy—" the executive, Ms. Jackson, began.

Maureen cut in. "That's bull. Wars are great for the

economy. They've pulled this country out of at least two recessions. Give me a better reason."

Ms. Jackson re-crossed her legs. "This war hasn't been good for the economy of our company," she said. "We've been cut out of Mesopotamianstan exploration for years as a result of the war."

"But the price of oil has doubled since then," Maureen said. "You're telling me that hasn't helped your company? Plus, *The Times* reported that your company has had exclusive development rights there for the last three years."

Ms. Jackson glared at Maureen. "We develop other kinds of energy, too, you know," she snapped. "We've spent millions of dollars on our West Texas wind farms."

"Hardly anyone lives in West Texas, so what good is that?" Maureen said. "Ms. Jackson, it comes down to this: I don't believe what you or your company says. I think that you are profiting hugely from this war. What's more, I think that your company is an example of the rampant war profiteering that has been going on since this 'operation' began. And I think it's shameful."

"I didn't come on this show to be abused in this way," Ms. Jackson huffed.

"You're welcome to leave," Maureen said. "I'm tired of your lies."

Ms. Jackson stood and pulled the microphone off of her lapel. She stomped off of the set to the jeers of the audience.

Maureen sat back in her chair and crossed her arms, glaring after her.

In her head, however, she was thinking, *Shit. Now how am I going to fill time on the show?*

She glanced at her producer, Kevin. He shrugged. Then he signaled a commercial break. Thank heaven this wasn't a live show. They'd have some time to scramble.

Kevin stepped up and sat in the chair the oil executive had just vacated. "That was cute," he said, smiling. Maureen wished again that he weren't a flaming homosexual. He was tasty.

"I know, I know," she moaned. "I got fed up. I also got the feeling that she wasn't up for another ten minutes of interview." She sighed. "Do we have any emergency filler hiding in the back?"

Kevin flipped though the sheets on his clipboard. "Nope. Maybe it's time to interview the audience again."

Maureen shook her head. "I hate that. Let me think." She looked up at the lights and wished that Liz were there. "Wait. We can link a phone call to the speakers, right?"

"Ya-huh. What are you thinking?"

"Let's get Liz on the phone. But don't tell the audience."

Kevin grinned and scampered off. Maureen wondered again if he had a straight brother with a similar button-cute ass.

♥

"And now, we have a surprise for you!" Maureen said when the intro music and applause quieted. "We've got the most famous woman in the world on the phone!"

An excited murmur rippled through the crowd.

"She is super-popular, super-cute, and knows how to whup ass. Are you there, mystery guest?" Maureen asked the ether.

"Yes, I am," Liz said from the speakers. The audience cheered. "Thank you, thank you." Liz's voice was a little tinny and scratchy from the cell phone, and Maureen could tell that she was weary. She hoped that the audience didn't pick up on it.

"So, where are you, Liz?"

"Ah, good question. Let me look," Liz said. Maureen could hear her shift her seat on the bus. "Well, we're somewhere where there's lots of fall color on the trees and rolling hills. What's that?" There was a muffled murmur on the line. "My handler, Zeke, has told me that we're in Massachusetts on the turnpike on our way out of Boston. Silly me."

The audience chuckled.

"I'm not surprised you're having trouble keeping track," said Maureen. "You've been everywhere since you started the campaign."

"It's true," Liz said. "I couldn't have done it without my support staff, and all of you in the audience." They clapped. "That's right," she said. "I'm like Tinkerbelle in Peter Pan. I'll go away if you stop believing, so keep believing, keep clapping!"

The crowd cheered.

Maureen had to grin. "Liz, a few audience members had some questions for you. Will you answer them?"

"Sure thing."

"Okay, our first question is from Beverly from Orange County."

Beverly stood awkwardly at the microphone, a housewife who had had her hair done especially for this outing. "Hi, Liz," she said.

"Orange County is a big place. Which town, Beverly?"

"Oh, Irvine."

"Nice. I like to have lunch downtown near the college. What's your question?"

"Oh, um, I was wondering if you had any advice on how to keep my husband happy during the sex strike?"

"Well, the point is kind of to keep him *un*happy, Beverly," Liz said to the amusement of the crowd. "However, I don't want any divorces occurring here. Remember, this is a sex strike. Without getting too Bill Clinton here, there are things that are sex, and things that are not. I'll let you draw the lines, but maybe your man needs to know that while you still love him and want him to be happy, you are giving up something special in order to show solidarity to something that's important to you. Then make him his favorite dinner."

The next woman at the microphone was very young and Orange-County. "Liz, I wondered if there was a man in your life right now?"

Maureen heard the half-moment extra that Liz took before she answered, though she didn't think the audience noticed. "No," she said. "I've been on the road so much that I haven't met anyone new, not that I'd have had time to start a romance, even if I had."

"So this sex-strike is kinda easy for you, then, isn't it?" the woman said.

"Well, it's as easy as any dry-spell is for any girl, I guess," Liz admitted to laughter. "I'm not finding it easy, myself, but I guess I don't have the daily temptation that a woman with a husband faces."

A new woman stepped to the mic. "I heard rumors that you had a man sleeping in your room with you, Liz. Is it true?"

Liz laughed. "It's true. I had a plain-clothes secret service agent posted in my room at night when we had a minor security scare. It was only temporary, and it was purely innocent."

"Why not have a female agent in your room? Wouldn't that be less suspicious?"

"Our best agent happened to be a man, and I decided not to hold it against him."

The audience laughed a bit.

A woman of a certain age and a certain seriousness stepped up. "Liz, if you get elected, whose going to be your Foreign Affairs secretary?"

"We haven't filled that position yet," Liz said. "We're looking for someone with experience, naturally, but also someone who is passionate about ending this war while keeping the country secure."

"What will be your first priority if you're elected to office?"

"Ending the war, naturally, but my second would be to eliminate the glass ceiling in this country. If we can't legislate it out, then we'll culture it out."

"Where are you going to be on election night?"

"I'll be at home, since I have to cast my ballot in California. After that, we're going to Camp Pendleton to watch the results with some military wives. We're having an election night bash, and everyone in the audience gets to go!"

The audience cheered at Liz's generosity.

♥

Liz was over the moon. She was in love with Zeke Rowan. Two days ago, when she'd snapped out of her snooze to find his fingers tickling the tender spot behind her knee, her first feeling was of shock, but then she realized how turned on she was. In fact, his hand cupping her calf made her very excited, indeed. She surprised herself by wanting to jump him right then and there.

She sat back in her seat and watched Zeke at work, bent over his laptop, furiously typing by punching the keyboard with only his index fingers. He felt her looking at him, so he peeked at her over his glasses and gave her a wink.

Though they were able to eat together and saw each other nearly every minute during the day, since they had decided to keep the relationship quiet until after the election, they couldn't be affectionate, even in the relative privacy of the bus. Most of the staffers were aware of the change in relationship, though most of them had figured out that Zeke had the hots for Liz long ago.

That much had been common knowledge.

Liz closed her eyes and played a game she'd started two days ago: *when did I realize that I loved Zeke?* That night in her room, Liz wasn't exactly shocked by her feelings for Zeke. The feelings were familiar and comfortable; what had been surprising was that they hadn't hit her prior to this. It was like realizing that your mom's spaghetti was your favorite food without having missed it before.

She went back in her memory day-by-day, trying to pinpoint the exact time she began to rely on Zeke in a way that wasn't just professional. She went back years before she realized that it had been a long time indeed since she had become so connected to Zeke.

She kicked herself again for being so blind and not recognizing her feelings for him sooner. So much time gone. Worse, so much energy spent on space wasters like Dion and Evan. She moaned inwardly at the thought of "Agent" Dion Young. She hoped he was miserable somewhere. She still hadn't recovered fully from the shame of that event.

Liz stole a peek at Zeke again. He had waxed his head that morning, so it was especially shiny. His dark-rimmed glasses framed his round face and made his brown eyes stand out. He was dressed in his customary dark colors, but he was a little casual today in jeans— dark washed—and a tee shirt—black. She squinted at the printing on the shirt and made out the words *Runs with Scissors*.

She found herself wishing she hadn't called the sex

strike so she could pull that shirt off and wrap his thin frame around her.

Cal slid into the seat next to her. "I know what you're thinking," she whispered.

"How?"

"'Cause I'm thinking it, too."

"I doubt it."

"You're thinking about jumping him."

"You are, too?" Liz grinned. "I think we might have a problem, here."

"Not him," Cal said. "I've got my own libido, you know."

"True. You still need to tell me more about Nicolas."

"Fine. But you're going to laugh." Cal pulled out her smart phone and brought up a picture of a man in a corduroy jacket with suede patches on the elbows drinking from an enormous purple glass.

"Cute," Liz said. "Wait. That's a scorpion. He took you to the Huki Lau?"

"Other way around."

"Nice," Liz said. "You like him?"

"I want to nibble his ears off and keep locks of his hair in my bra."

"Isn't that what you once said about George Michael?"

"Oh, he's British and gay," Cal said. "Don't hold my teenage crushes against me, Ms. I-Want-to-Have-Luke-Perry's-Babies.'"

"Okay, fair enough." Liz laughed. "Seriously, I'm happy for you, Cal. When do you see him again?"

"Friday."

"Really? Aren't we in…Ohio on Friday?"

"He's flying out."

"Really? Isn't that far to go for a date? I mean, I know guys who'd go to those lengths for sex, but a date?"

Cal's face twitched ever so slightly, but Liz caught it.

"Cal, no!" Liz hissed. "You didn't promise him something!"

Cal dropped her gaze to her lap. "No, I didn't. But, Liz, he's sooo yummy. I'm not sure I can hold out."

"Calliope Anne Talmadge." Liz pointed at Zeke. "You see that adorable man over there? I am going out of my mind because I've been in love with him without realizing it for at least five years, if not ten, and all we can do now is kiss in secret. If I can hold out, so can you, Madam President of the Women's Achievement Party."

Cal pouted. "I'm not some sort of saint just because I work for a women's organization."

"I know," Liz said. "I'm not a saint, either. But if I have to do it, so do you." She threw her arm over her friend's shoulders. "You should make sure Mr. Brown knows he's not getting past second base in Ohio."

"Yeah, I'll call him. I'm sorry."

"Pshaw," Liz said. "You didn't do anything wrong. I can't wait to meet him. What's he like?"

Cal grinned. "Besides sexy in that young-professor way, he's devastatingly intelligent. He's not intimidated by me, either."

"I know how that is," Liz said. "It's really hard to find men that aren't afraid of my brain or think that they have to prove something because of it."

"He's funny, and sweet, and so earnest. I'm charmed, Lizzy. I haven't felt this way since...well, since Jerry."

Liz nodded. She remembered the hell Jerry had put Cal through, but she knew how Cal had loved him. "I'm sure Nicolas will be a far better man than Jerry."

Liz thought later that it was remarkable that intelligent and powerful women like them could be reduced to giggling schoolgirls by men. She supposed that men went through similar transformations, too, but a powerful man compromising himself to have sex was cliché. However, strong women were somehow expected to be steely and perhaps made of stone below the waist. She suspected that most of the country assumed that Cal was a lesbian since she wasn't married and headed a pro-women's organization. She supposed that a portion of America assumed Liz was also batting for the other team for similar reasons. America would be surprised to hear the two of them chattering like teenagers about boys.

Liz thought it was unfortunate that people believed it was impossible for a woman to play a man's game and still be a woman. Hillary had not been able to convince people that a little girl lived under her smart pantsuits, much less a sexual being. It was a shame, because recognizing such things would make powerful women more human, and thereby more relatable to people.

That would make my job easier.

Chapter 11

How was it possible that Liz Stratton, queen of all that is daytime television, was, at this moment, nibbling his ear?

They had locked the greenroom door under the pretenses of hacking out a new speech before the rally, but they were actually trying to set a land-speed record for necking. Liz had his earlobe in her teeth, and Zeke had his hands up her skirt, kneading her ass.

"Goddamn sex strike," she hissed through her teeth softly into his ear. "I so want you to nail me to the wall."

"Don't say things like that, or I won't be able to stop, Liz."

"Sorry," she said, nuzzling his neck with her nose.

"I hope I live up to all this."

She sat back and looked at him. "What do you mean?"

"Only that, with all this waiting, aren't you afraid that we'll fall short of each other's expectations?" he asked.

She grinned. "You won't disappoint me," she purred. "And no one's ever told me that he's been disappointed."

"Come here," he said, pulling her to him.

Someone rapped loudly on the door. "It's Cal!"

Liz pulled her skirt down and opened the door. Cal took one look at Liz and closed the door behind her quickly. "Jesus, Liz! Zeke! Aren't you pushing the risky business stuff too far?" She grabbed Liz's chin. "I can't believe I have to check my presidential candidate for hickeys."

"I know that I'd be castrated if I left any marks," he said. "Relax, Cal."

"I'll relax when you two behave like adults and not over-hormoned teenagers."

"What crawled up your pantyhose?" Liz asked, not unkindly.

"Nothing," Cal snapped and slammed a stack of papers onto the table.

"Wait. Isn't that professor of yours supposed to be here tonight?" Liz asked.

"Nicolas can't make it," Cal sniffed.

"Oh, Cal. I'm sorry." Liz gave Cal a hug. "You don't think it's because of the strike, do you?"

"I hope not. Because then he'd be an asshole instead of just a lame-o who has papers to grade."

"Oh, sweetie. You don't deserve this," Liz cooed, rubbing Cal's back.

"Nicolas was coming?" he asked. He was more annoyed now when they forgot he was in the room.

"Yes, he was supposed to fly out here for a date," Liz explained.

"A 'date'?" Zeke asked. "He was going to fly out to Ohio from Massachusetts for a no-sex date? Does he carry his halo around with him, or is it in the saint bank?"

"It's not too good to be true," Cal said, pouting. "You're waiting."

"I'm the exception, remember? There are guys all over America trying every trick in the book to get back in bed with their women. I'll bet stock in jewelry companies has tripled since this began."

Cal sniffed again and sat down. "Well, I'm still disappointed. I thought he might be different."

"Maybe he is, Cal," Liz said.

"I'm not going to hold my breath anymore," Cal said. "Ever onward. Just do me a favor and don't flaunt it anymore, okay?"

"Will do," Zeke said. "I could go kick the guy's ass, too. Would that help?"

Cal laughed. "I guess I sound like a little girl, sitting by the phone, wondering if some dick is going to call me back, don't I?"

"We've all been through it, Cal. It doesn't get easier, does it, Zeke?"

"Living proof, right here," Zeke said, thumping his chest. "Ten years of sitting by the phone, she finally calls back, and we can't have sex for who knows how long?"

"You're right. It could be worse," Cal agreed. "I am

really happy for you two, you know that?"

"Thanks," Liz said. "Persistence and luck."

"Persistence and luck. That should have been our campaign slogan," Cal mused.

"'Luck' is too close to 'fuck,'" Zeke said. "We'd have had to change it."

The lights blinked on and off. "Two minute warning," Cal said. "You ready?"

"Sure thing, chief," Liz said. "What are we doing today?"

"Well," Cal said, all business again. "This is an elementary school, and there's a school carnival today. We're going to be rallying in the gym before the festivities and then we're going to mingle with the crowd."

"Should be fun," Zeke said. "Security must be going mad, huh?"

"Yeah. At least we're inside."

Liz, Zeke, and Cal emerged from the greenroom and walked to the stage. Liz parted the curtain and peeked at the crowd of parents and little kids. Way in the back on some bleachers were the television cameras and reporters. She called Cal over.

"Hey. There are little kids out there."

"This is an elementary school."

"I—I mean, I'm not supposed to talk about sex with little kids out there, am I?"

Cal took Liz's cards from her. "Here," she said, handing one back. "Do this." The card read "education."

"I can't talk for the whole time on this."

"So don't. Do what you can and then we'll go to the carnival. The parents will be relieved that you didn't talk until the kids melted down."

Reassured, Liz stepped through the curtain to applause.

Her spiel on education only lasted fifteen minutes, but that seemed to be plenty for the eight-year-olds in the audience who were jittery with desire for the blow-up trampoline humming in the corner of the gym. After the speech, Liz walked down the steps on the side of the stage and shook hands. Finally, the principal of the school stepped up to show her around.

"I'm Mr. Duval," said the pleasantly plump man who was losing his curly black hair. "What say we start at this end an make our way around?"

The various television crews followed them as they wandered around the carnival along the perimeter of the gym. They visited the fishing booth where a clothespin was lowered into a "lake" where someone would clip a prize to it. Liz caught a happy-face sticker that she stuck to her lapel. There was a horseshoe pitch where Liz failed miserably. At the face-painting booth, she let someone paint a wiggly American flag on her right cheek. She was having a really good time.

A loud fan-fare blared over the loudspeakers and everyone in the crowd pushed back toward the stage.

"What's happening, Mr. Duval?" Liz asked.

"It's the big event," he said. "It's the hotdog eating contest." He led her to the front of the crowd. "It's always fun to watch."

Long tables had been set up where Liz had just been speaking and piles of hotdogs, sans buns, were stacked in front of six seats. Five people ranging in age from seven to eighty stood behind the table variously readying themselves for the task at hand.

"Why is that seat empty?" asked Liz.

"I don't know," Mr. Duval said.

Someone official looking stepped forward to introduce the contestants.

"First is Angie from fourth grade, and her Dad, Francis. Parker from the fifth grade and his granddad Abe." Cheers from their classmates rose from the audience.

"Last is Benny from the second grade. Benny's dad was going to eat with him, but he's home sick with the flu." Benny looked around a bit worried.

"So, no one else is on his team?" asked Liz.

"Well, no. He wanted to go on, anyway," Mr. Duval said.

"Can I go up there with him?" Liz asked.

Mr. Duval peered at Liz over his half-glasses. She was wearing a slim suit that showed off her trim figure.

"Are you sure you want to do that?"

Liz smiled. "Sure." She made her way through the crowd and mounted the stairs. She spoke to the announcer and then stood by Benny.

"We have a late contestant," said the announcer in surprise. "Ms. Liz Stratton is going to be on Benny's team in place of his father!"

A cheer rose up. Liz could see the cameramen

shaking with excitement. Here's a scoop that would be played all over America.

She leaned over to Benny and whispered, "Hey Benny. I'm Liz. Do you like hot dogs?"

The little boy grinned and nodded yes.

"Do you have any tips for me?"

"Eat fast."

A buzzer went off and the contest began. Liz leaned over the table, snatched a hotdog off the pile, and shoved it into her mouth. Blech. It was the cheapest, nastiest little hot dog she'd ever eaten. Suddenly, this didn't seem like such a good idea.

She looked down to see Benny chewing the ends off of three hot dogs at once. As he chewed, he looked at her and waved one hand in encouragement. The crowd cheered.

Liz swallowed and shoved another dog in her mouth. She cursed the egg-white omelet she'd had for breakfast. After the next one, she cursed the Caesar salad she'd had for dinner the night before. Before long, Liz was cursing every cappuccino she'd ever drunk. She cursed the zipper on her skirt.

She cursed the German town of Frankfurt. By the time the end buzzer indicated the end of the contest three minutes later, Liz, who normally lived on espresso drinks and salads, had eaten six hot dogs.

Benny had eaten ten.

The winner ate fifteen. Angela was a healthy girl.

♥

Liz watched footage on the news from her hotel bed with Zeke and Cal perched on the edge.

"You look like a pro," Cal said. "Look at that. Not a speck on your outfit. How did you do that?"

"I like your technique," Zeke said. Cal swatted him. "No, really. One at a time, end first, sucking them in like spaghetti. It works for me."

Liz laughed at a close-up shot of her inhaling a hotdog. "It does look like I'm blowing a chain of wieners."

"The fake news shows are going to love this," Zeke said. "I'll see if I can't get Steven Clarkson to give us an interview."

Liz smiled. "Let's be sure to bring him a pound of wieners if I go."

♥

A few days later, Liz stood in the wings of *Too Late with Steven Clarkson* awaiting her cue, marveling at Zeke's connections. She held a small pail of wieners.

"Ladies and gentlemen," Steven Clarkson said when the music bringing him in from commercial stopped. "Ladies and gentlemen, we are honored tonight to have an actual presidential candidate in our studios tonight. She is one of the first women to run for the highest office of the land—and have a chance at winning it. She's also the force behind the second most popular talk show on daytime television, *Spare Me!* Now she's here to explain to me why I can't stand up to shake her hand on air. Ms. Liz Stratton!"

The music rose and Liz strode onto the stage smiling to very loud cheers. Steven did stand and shake her hand, and she gave an extra wave as she sat, placing the pail on the desk before her. Several women in the crowd kept cheering even after the music stopped.

After a moment, Steven said, "Ms. Stratton, can you make them stop that, too?" The crowd laughed. "How are you?"

"Just fine, Steven. Call me Liz. Thanks for having me on the show."

"Thanks for being here," he said. "Now, I was going to start off by asking, why?" The crowd chuckled as he cringed a little. "Why a sex strike? But...um...you seem to have brought something on stage with you."

"Just a little present," Liz said with a smile, sliding the pail toward him.

He peeked into it and sat back in mock shock. He peeked again. "Uh, this appears to be a bucket of...wieners."

"It is. It's the exact number of wieners I ate during the contest. This show broadcast the clip earlier this week."

"Did we?" He gingerly tipped the pail over and the hot dogs slid out. "Gee, that's not as many as I thought."

"What do you mean?"

"Uh, well, I mean—"

"I know. A ball-buster like me should be able to eat more than six wieners in one sitting, right?"

"Sure."

"By that logic, the little girl who won should run for president. She ate fifteen."

"Fifteen? Oh, my God."

"I know. Look out for Angie Olson in 2036!"

The crowd laughed.

Steven tried to regain control. "Okay, Ms. Stratton. Why a sex strike? I mean, why not a shoe strike? Or a PMS strike?"

"Steven, I think you're missing the point," she said. "Men want those kinds of strikes. If we had a, say, leftover casserole strike, no one would do anything to end it, right?"

"Tell me how this particular strike came about," he said, leaning forward over his desk. "I mean, have you used it before? Like on a boyfriend or anything?"

Liz laughed. "Well, to be honest, what woman hasn't? Think about it. Let's say you had a fight with your wife."

"Oh, that never happens," he said with a straight face.

"Really?" Liz grinned. "Okay, pretend you had a fight with Jon Stewart's wife." He laughed in spite of himself. "How often do you get to have sex if you are in the middle of an argument?"

"All the time," he said. "And it's fabulous!"

"I imagine so," Liz said through her chuckles. "Most of us, however, suffer a dry spell if we're angry with each other. Eventually, one party apologizes and then there's the make-up sex."

"So, this is all a ploy for national make-up sex?"

"Doesn't that sound wonderful?" Liz asked.

"That does sound wonderful," he admitted. "I want them to declare peace tomorrow. You know the whole country would call in sick the next day, though, don't you?"

"I'm willing to endure a day of lost productivity for this cause," Liz said.

"So, tell me, Liz. How did you get from hosting a talk show to running for president?"

"Well, my friend Calliope Talmadge ambushed me."

"Really? So you didn't know what she was going to propose when she came onto your set that day?"

"No. Actually, she wasn't even scheduled that day."

"No?"

"No, it was supposed to be Ethan Falconwright, but his son fell and broke his arm that morning, and he had to cancel."

"So, if Ethan Falconwright's son hadn't broken his arm, I'd be able to go home and get it wrong ways from Mrs. Clarkson tonight? Damn you, Falconwright spawn!" Steven shook his fist at the camera.

"I'm sure Ethan will write you a letter of apology."

"Do you know who he is voting for, incidentally?"

"Nope."

"Harvey Birdman."

Liz laughed again. This was fun.

"Another thing: Why are your news conferences so…entertaining?"

Liz couldn't help grinning. "Why, what do you mean?"

"I think the media is referring to your notorious news conference as 'The Spectacle.' Do you have any idea why?"

"Why, no, Steven. Whatever do you mean?" she said, batting innocent eyelashes.

"Well, we just happen to have a clip that might explain it."

The clip showed Liz in her shiny suit, flanked by showgirls and Elektra.

When it was over, Steven sat silently a moment while the audience hooted. "You know," he said. "I think I need to see that again, just to get the full effect."

She laughed, but the ten-second clip did roll again.

"So, that woman standing next to you is your running mate?"

"Elektra Sampson. Toughest, smartest woman you'll ever meet."

"She's hot."

Liz laughed. "She's sixty and married."

"Was this just an attention-getting mechanism? This Spectacle?"

"Did it work?"

"Yes. Yes, it did."

"Steven, we want to focus attention on our issues, so we're using every tool in our repertoire. I'm sure if Bill Ostrem looked good in a two-piece, he'd be out flaunting it, too."

"Thank you for the image in my head," he said with a shiver. "So, Liz, when I introduced you, I said you actually have a chance at winning the presidency. Was I lying?"

"Actually, no, Steven. The last time I checked, the race was neck-in-neck. We're at twenty-nine percent, and the others are in the thirty to thirty-five percent range. It's anybody's guess what will happen come Election Day."

"Amazing. And you're not worried that you might be a spoiler for one of the other candidates like Nader or Perot were?"

"I wouldn't be running if I wanted either of the other guys to win," Liz said. "I agree with some positions of each party, but I'd vote third party this election if I weren't voting for myself."

"Is that because you are a woman and just can't commit to one guy?" he asked. He winked at her as the crowd laughed.

"No. It's because I'm a woman who's seen her share of losers and doesn't want to be associated with them anymore," she said. "I'd go to a party alone before I went with either of them."

"So, why is the war such a big issue for you and your constituents?"

"As good as the war has been for the comedy industry," she began, "it's been devastating to the families and economy of this country. We're running out of young men and money. We're sick of it, and we are willing to give up the best thing in life until it's done."

"So, you admit you like sex?" Steven asked, with interest.

Liz grinned. "Sex is my favorite thing, ever. I like it better than chocolate ice-cream or week-long trips to Hawaii."

"How about chocolate ice-cream on the beach in Hawaii?" he asked.

"Um…nope. Sex is better."

"So, why a sex strike?" he asked again. "If you like it so much?"

"Steven, I love sex. But I can live without it until we end this war. My guess is that the people in charge of ending the war will have less resolve than I will or the people following my lead."

"So, you're counting on old men want to have sex in a worse way than the women who follow you."

"Throwing in the odd gay couple, yes."

"Do you think it'll work?"

"Has anything else worked?"

"Do you think you'll win the election?"

"Maybe," Liz said. "But I'm sure we'll end the war. I have shown that I don't need an oval office to represent a large portion of the country and incite them to action, or inaction, as the case may be."

The crowd cheered, and Steven smiled at her. "Ms. Liz Stratton, everybody!" The music rose and carried them out to commercial.

Later in the dressing room, Liz was surprised when Steven Clarkson came back to see her. After she let him in, he sat in a chair across from her, leaned his elbows on his knees, and looked into her eyes with that earnest gaze.

"What you're doing is great," he said. "I wanted you to know that my wife and I support what you're doing one hundred percent."

"Really?"

"Yeah. You know I have a lot of politicians on the show."

"Sure. I've been envious of your guest list for a long time."

"Right. You've had your share on your show, too."

"Yes."

"So you know that ninety percent of them are total sleazebags."

"Yes!" Liz sat back in her chair and put her hands over her eyes. "They talk out of both sides of their faces. It's so weird."

"Liz, I don't get that from you."

"Thanks?"

"No, I'm serious." Steven said, still earnest. "I wasn't sure about you before you came on the show. I mean, for research, I watched about five year's worth of your show."

"Well, 2006 wasn't my best year."

"I don't know, I thought the 'Tranny Grannies' episode was gold." He laughed. "But the point is that I wasn't sure you were the real thing until I met you tonight. You're serious about this. You're not in it for the power. You're not here for the glory. You don't tell people what they want to hear. You're here because you think you can make things better."

"Thanks, Steven," Liz said. "I—I'm so flattered."

"It's the truth," he said. "I've met so many politicians that I can see them, you know? In all their glory. It's why it's my job to make fun of them. People need to see them as they are. You do it, too, on your show."

"They're afraid of us, you and me, Steven."

"And they should be."

"Thank you," Liz said. "This really means the world to me. It's been brutal lately, you know? I can't watch TV anymore because the ads are so mean."

"You hang in there," he said. "You do good work. Ignore the ads and stuff. That's where I come in."

"What do you mean?"

"We're starting a new segment attacking attack ads. It's going to be fun. And since your campaign is the only one that doesn't run such garbage—"

"You'll basically be helping us out on the sly."

"Well, not officially," he said. "We'll just not ridicule those running noble campaigns." He stood. "I'll let you go now. It was a real honor to have you on, Liz."

Liz stood and gave him a hug. "If this presidency thing doesn't work out, will you come to LA and be on *Spare Me!*?"

"Sure."

"Oh, and Steven? I do, you know?"

"Do what?"

"Miss sex. A lot. I want this war and strike to be over more than you know."

He looked at her face carefully. "Oh," he said. "Something, or someone new has happened, hasn't it?"

Liz looked down before she could catch herself.

"Don't worry. It's a secret," Steven said, smiling. "Goodnight, Liz."

Liz sat a moment after the door closed behind him, basking in the high praise. It felt good coming from someone in her industry who actually understood where she was coming from professionally. Plus, she knew that Steven Clarkson was as smart as they come. He understood politics better than most politicians ever would, but the two of them were on similar missions. And he supported her. That was something she could hang her hat on.

♥

Liz was still in revelry from her conversation with Steven Clarkson that night as she sat in bed with the TV on to some old movie as she killed time before *Too Late* came on at 11:35 p.m. She heard a familiar tap on the door, so she stood and let in Zeke and his bowl of popcorn.

They curled up on the bed and watched the film together, but Liz wasn't paying attention to it at all. Finally she put it on mute and turned to Zeke.

"Do you think we're going to win?"

"The election?" He sat up a little. "I don't know." He reached out and traced her lovely jaw with his fingertips. "You should win, if there were justice in the world."

"I'm serious," she said, smiling and taking his wrist in both her hands.

"So am I. You're the best candidate, especially given the scum you're running against."

"I'm better than scum, thanks."

"Much better," Zeke said, kissing her. "God, the things I could do to you—"

"Mustn't even talk about it, or we'll lose control," Liz said. "Remember the rules."

"First rule of secret affair: Don't talk about secret affair."

"Second rule: Don't talk about sex re: the secret affair."

"Third rule: Don't have sex re: secret affair."

"Last rule: Don't break rules one through three."

She rested her ear on his chest and let his heartbeat fill her head.

Finally, Zeke said, "Are you afraid of winning, honey?"

"Yes," Liz said quietly.

"What are you afraid of?"

"That I'll fuck up. I mean, if I fucked up at my old job, someone turned off the TV and I didn't get a paycheck. If I fuck up as president, people could die. Lots of people."

"Do you want one of the other guys to win instead?"

"No, because I *know* they'll fuck up."

"Then you're kind of stuck," he said. "If you can't trust someone else to do a better job, then you have to do it yourself, right?" He stroked her hair and kissed the top of her head. He did find it ironic that he could be comforting the future leader of the free world, but he assumed that first ladies had always done this kind of thing.

Liz sighed deeply and looked at the clock. "It's 11:35," she said. Zeke picked up the remote and changed the channel. The theme music for *Too Late with Steven Clarkson* filled the room and Steven's face flashed on screen. Liz smiled and so did Zeke.

"I think we might do it," she said.

"I hope we do," he said, pride and love swelling him beyond what he thought possible.

♥

"I don't know what you paid Steven Clarkson to give you that kind of interview, but it was worth it!" Cal sang as Liz sat down at breakfast.

"Hmm?"

"Here." Cal thrust the morning paper in front of her. She read "*Too Late* Bump Hits Stratton and Sex Strike."

"How can they know that already? It's only been a day."

"All they need, apparently."

The article reported that polls since Liz's appearance on the show had raised her numbers to over thirty percent.

"That's amazing." Liz shook her head. "That comedy talk shows could have this much clout."

"Well, between you and Oprah, you have the book, diet, and pop-psychology markets cornered," Cal said. "Just try to get on the *New York Times* bestseller list without O's approval."

"This is different than a book club, but I see where you're coming from," Liz said. "I'm not sure I like why it happens, but I'm glad for the bump."

"You are?" Cal asked. When Liz looked at her curiously, she added, "Zeke told me he was concerned about you the other night."

Liz rubbed her forehead. "I'm glad for the bump," she repeated. "Winning...we'll cross that bridge when we get there."

Zeke sat next to Liz and squeezed her knee in greeting. "How are you this morning, kiddo?"

"Just fine, thanks. Here's the paper."

"Wow. I don't know what you did to Colbert before the show, but I hope you saved some for me later."

Liz laughed and squeezed his hand. "Be good, or you'll pay for it."

"Promise?"

"Promise."

Chapter 12

Cal sat in her room wrapped in a comforter as tears left trails of anger behind them. How could he? How could he not understand? Hadn't she been up front with him? What right did he have to be angry with her?

But, like many women in her predicament, the weak little voice in the back of her head said quietly, "But are you sure it's not your fault?" She bit her lip and replayed the day in her head carefully, analyzing the minutia.

Nicolas and Cal had been playing phone tag and missing appointments with each other for days. Cal was bitterly disappointed when Nicolas had to cancel the trip to Ohio at the last minute. His excuse of grading papers had sounded suspect, and it had been, in fact, a lie. He had sent poems to her email as tiny gifts, but they were little comfort.

She had tried not to take out her frustrations on the campaign staff, but she did snap at them over the next couple of days. Most people chalked it up to the same tension and frustration that everyone on the tour was feeling.

Cal expected Nicolas to bail out on their next try in Chicago, too. That is, she tried to tell herself to expect it so that she wouldn't be disappointed if he blew her off again. She was doubly delighted, then, when she got a text message from Nicolas saying that he had landed at the airport and found the driver she had sent for him. He was on his way! She was over the moon.

The campaign had arrived in Chicago two days prior and had done all the campaigning yesterday. Today was a little break, a reward so tired campaigners could go to a museum or a zoo or shop or sleep in late. Cal had left her day wide open and had two plans: Plan A included touring the city with Nicolas followed by dinner and snuggling. Plan B involved trying not to eat more than one gallon of ice cream by herself as she dove into unnecessary busy work to keep from feeling rejected and depressed.

Cal waited for Nicolas in the hotel lounge, watching each car as it rolled to the curb. Finally, his dark head emerged from a black SUV. Cal leapt from her chair and nearly ran to the door. It took all her composure to greet him with a discrete kiss.

She felt like jumping and squealing like a cheerleader on the fifty-yard line.

Nicolas took Cal into his arms and held her tightly

for a moment. "I am so glad to see you," he said.

"Me, too," she said. "Let's get you checked in so that we can go have some fun."

"Okay. I could use a shower."

Upstairs, Cal stood next to Nicolas as he opened his room. She took one of his bags and followed him into the room. "Where do you want thi—is," she yelped as he grabbed her and tossed her onto the bed.

He laughed, kissing her. "Right here will do."

Cal laughed, too, and ran her hands through his hair. "I've got a whole day planned, Nicolas," she protested mildly.

"Me, too," he said. "First, I'm going to ravish you, then I'm going to make sweet love to you, then we're going to cuddle and order room service until we're sick of hotel food." He stripped off his shirt and gnawed on Cal's neck.

"Ooh," Cal groaned. "Sounds lovely, Nicolas. But the rules from before still apply. Nicolas, did you hear me? The same rules—apply?"

"Are you sure?" He nibbled on her collarbone. "You really want to—miss this?"

"No, I mean, yes—I mean, Nicolas!" Cal sat upright when Nicolas's hand slid up the inside of her thigh. "It's not what I want, Nicolas. I want you with every inch of me. But it's not happening today, or tonight. You understand, right? We have to be strong because we want the war to end. Right?"

Nicolas knelt surprised and shirtless on the bed, looking at the mildly disheveled and wild-eyed Cal. He shook his head. "Oh, God, I want you so badly," he said softly.

"But you understand?"

"Yeah," he said. He threw his legs over the edge of the bed and looked out the window at the grey city. "This isn't going to be easy."

Cal wrapped her arms around him and rested her chin on his shoulder. His skin tingled. "You said you owed me five or six dinners before we tried this again," she reminded him. "I'm going to hold you to that."

"Can I at least expect the cuddling and room service part tonight?" Nicolas asked hopefully.

"Let's think about it," Cal said. "We're a little more...public here than we were in South Hadley, Massachusetts."

♥

For all the exciting things to do that Chicago had to offer, Cal and Nicolas ended up sitting in a cafe, sipping warm drinks, and talking. They had a strong second-date aura around them, and people smiled to see two people so obviously in the first stages of love. Nicolas stroked Cal's hand, and she idly caressed his shirt cuff as they chatted about philosophy, politics, poetry, and past pets.

A local artist, who spent his time loitering in the cafe when his paintings weren't going well, sketched them in profile and thought they might make an interesting study if he could only capture the glow of their giddiness and restraint.

They moved from the cafe to a dim private little restaurant and had wine and cheese and all those foodstuffs poets and lovers indulge in by candlelight. Nicolas was nothing if not a romantic. Cal was normally far more pragmatic, but something about Nicolas made her forget herself and her past wounds. She even forgot about Ohio.

So, when they found themselves back at his hotel room, ordering movies on the television and room service, Cal was relaxed and happy. She even changed into her pajamas and crawled into bed with Nicolas. An action flick boomed on the TV, greasy finger food balanced on their knees, and the wine flowed. Eventually, however, the wine and heavy food caught up with Cal and she drifted off during a plot-heavy portion of the film.

When she woke up, the room was dark, the TV was still on, but the noise that she had heard in her sleep didn't match what was happening on screen. She propped herself up on one elbow and squinted at the pictures flickering across the room and realized that the TV was muted. What was that sound? There was a grunt and a little whine and—the bed jiggled a little.

Cal turned around. There was Nicolas, lying beside her, curled in a "C," and he was—

"Oh, my God!" Cal shrieked, leaping off the bed and clutching her pajama shirt to herself.

"Jesus, Cal," Nicolas moaned. "I'm so sorry!"

"What are you doing?" she asked and immediately felt stupid.

"What does it look like I'm doing?" Nicolas snapped. He sat up and yanked the sheet over himself. "Don't tell me you're surprised," he said, not meeting her eyes.

Cal plunked down in a chair next to the bed. "I'm surprised—to see you—" She couldn't finish for a moment. "I mean," she began again, "I'm sorry to react like that. I was just not expecting—in bed next to me, I mean, of course—" She staggered to a stop again.

They sat together in mortified silence as the television flickered ghastly blue light over them. Cal felt like there was something that could be done here. One of them could say something to make light of this, or make it into a good thing, but she was so befuddled that her brain only came up with one solution.

"Maybe I should go," she said very quietly.

"Maybe you should." Nicolas's voice cracked as he spoke, and he looked away as she padded out the door in her bare feet.

This time when Cal stood under the hot water of her shower, she was trying to stop shaking and feel as warm as she was while in bed with Nicolas. She never did and slid between her own cold sheets too stunned still even to weep.

♥

Cal lay on her bed in agony all night, knowing that Nicolas was less than fifty feet away thinking God-knows-what about her. She stood up at least three times determined to knock on his door and apologize, or kiss him, or something, but each time she scurried back to her bed in fear, shame, and defeat. She watched the colorless dawn ease into the day wrapped in her comforter seated in an uncomfortable chair by the window.

All Nicolas wanted to do was escape. He crawled out of bed when it was light enough to see. He was too cowardly to go to Cal's room and apologize, or kiss her, or something. Anything. He began to pull on the clothes he wore the day before, but they reminded him of her, so he put on a fresh shirt from his suitcase. He didn't bother to comb his hair or brush his teeth. He just dragged his suitcase into the hall and let the door close behind him.

Liz rounded the corner on the last leg of her early-morning jog, secret service detail trotting along behind her. She had been going crazy with the demanding campaign schedule until she realized that no one wanted her before seven a.m. For a week, she had been running for an hour a day beginning at five-thirty a.m. and she felt great. She even had a whole thirty minutes to get a shower before her breakfast meeting. She had never felt so perky at breakfast.

Liz checked her stopwatch/pedometer as she stepped into the hotel lobby. She wasn't the runner she'd been in college, but she was pleased with her improvement over the past week. She was wiping her brow and making her way to the elevator when she saw Nicolas at the check-in desk. She smiled and walked over to him.

"Hi, Nicolas," she said, still breathing a little hard. "I'm surprised to see you up this early. I had it from Cal that a late night of pay-per-view was the order of the day."

"Oh, Ms. S—Stratton. H—hello," Nicolas stammered. He looked terrible. Dark circles sagged under his eyes and he was hunched over. He looked cold and pained.

Liz furrowed her brow. "What's up, Nicolas? Where's Cal?"

"I expect she's still in her room," he said.

The clerk handed Nicolas his credit card back and said, "I've credited your account for the remaining nights, Dr. Brown," she said. "I'm sorry your plans have changed, but remember us in the future. Can I call you a cab?"

"Yes," he said.

"No," Liz said, taking Nicolas by the elbow and dragging him to a seating area in the lobby where she sat him down on a couch. "Your 'plans have changed'?" she said in a hushed voice. "What does that mean?"

Nicolas looked as if he might become indignant for being dragged around like that, but then he withered into his coat. "Ms. Stratton," he said. "Cal hates me and she has good reason to."

"Cal does not hate you," Liz said. "What makes you think she hates you?"

"She left me in my room last night."

"And? Come on, just going to her own room doesn't mean she hates you. What else happened?"

Nicolas shrank more into his coat. "She, uh, caught me—" he muttered.

"Caught you? Caught you doing what?" Nicolas was turning a purply-red before her eyes. "Oh, Jesus," she said before she could stop herself. "But Cal knows that all men do that. Why would that make her leave?"

If possible, Nicolas blushed even more deeply. "Maybe it was where she c—caught me."

Liz sat back in her seat and pondered what she would have done if she'd caught Zeke masturbating in bed beside her while she slept. She knew that not much bothered Cal, but given enough of a shock, even cool-as-a-cucumber Cal might stumble through something like this.

Liz put her hand on Nicolas's knee. "Honey, do you really want to break off this thing with Cal, or do you just want to crawl into a hole and die?"

Nicolas smiled weakly. "If it were a deep enough hole…"

"Good." Liz stood up. "Don't move. I mean it." She turned on her heel and marched to the elevators, secret service detail trailing.

Liz found Cal still wrapped in her comforter. After opening the door, Cal went back to her chair and looked out at the ever-lightening sky. Liz sat next to her and stared out the window, too.

After a moment, Cal asked, "What's the most embarrassing thing you've ever done, Liz?"

"Before or after the event with the showgirls?"

"No, I mean really mortifying."

Liz thought back. "The second time I got my period, I was in seventh grade and I didn't know it had happened.

I bled through some of those acid-washed jeans. I didn't have any other clothes. Even though I begged her, the school nurse wouldn't let me go home, so I had to spend the rest of the day in those stained pants. I eventually borrowed a sweater to tie around my waist, but it was too late by then. The whole school knew. I faked sick for three days after that."

Cal nodded. "That's what this feels like." She turned to her friend. "I don't know how you know, but you know what happened last night, don't you?"

"I caught Nicolas trying to check out downstairs."

Cal began crying. "Oh, Liz, I couldn't think of what to do! I mean, he was so embarrassed, and I just ran!"

Liz hugged her friend. "I know. I probably would have, too."

"And now I've lost him forever! I was too chicken-shit to go and, and…"

"And what?"

"Well, that's what stopped me. I don't know what to do. I could apologize, but I don't know what I did wrong, if I did anything wrong."

"No, you didn't."

"But then, what else could I do?" Cal began crying anew. "Look at me! I've been reduced to a blubbering fourteen-year-old! I hate myself like this."

"Let's get you dressed," Liz said. "Nicolas is waiting downstairs. I've put Nelson on him so he won't try escaping before we get down."

"Oh, I couldn't face him again, Liz!" Cal said.

"You will. Go brush your teeth. I'll find something for you to wear."

Fifteen minutes later, Liz and Cal emerged from the elevator, Liz still in her running outfit and Cal wearing a clean suit. Liz waved for Nicolas to follow them into the restaurant where she got a waitress to bring them coffee. They sat, and Cal and Nicolas stared at the table. Finally, with three steaming cups in front of them, Liz began negotiations.

"First of all," Liz said. "Let's establish that what happened is not anyone's fault, all right? Second, no one has been injured, correct?" Small nods answered her. "All right then. I want both of you to sit up and look into each other's eyes. Now."

Slowly, Cal and Nicolas raised their gazes. Almost at once, the both began to talk.

"I'm so, so sorry," Nicolas said as Cal said, "I didn't mean to run out like that, I was just surprised—"

It didn't take long after that for the two of them to be holding hands and whispering sweet nothings again. They didn't even notice when Liz stood up and left to take the world's quickest shower and deal with less sticky issues with the state's senators.

♥

Governor Bill Ostrem rode in the back of a town car in his favorite part of town—the part with all the tittie bars. He fancied himself a connoisseur of tittie bars since he'd been to at least one in every state. There was always one near the airport for those long layovers. He favored a certain kind, the kind with steaks and "chili night" promotions.

Nothing like steak and tittie, he thought, peering out of the window as the neon-lit buildings rolled past. He hated private escorts because every one of them reminded him of his wife when she was young, glamorous and rich, even though he knew the girls were faking the rich part. He liked unpretentious pussy. That's why he liked real strip clubs.

"Jim, where's this place at?" he hollered up to the driver.

"Just down a piece."

"They got steaks and big guns, right?"

"Sure do," Jim answered. "Plus a champagne room, if you know what I mean."

Ostrem did know what Jim meant and sat back in satisfaction. He loved a good driver who knew where the best attractions were. He passed his tongue over his teeth and tried to remember where he was. It had been tough to keep track as he found all small Midwestern towns as indistinguishable as the backwater towns of his own state. All auditoriums looked the same to begin with, but all the towns did, too. He missed the charming little places of his childhood. He blamed McDonald's, but they had contributed a million dollars or something, so he kept his mouth shut. He decided that wherever he was, was fine.

He was glad that there were tittie bars everywhere. The damned sex strike had made the choices somewhat more limited, but most strippers and prostitutes couldn't afford to pay attention to politics, so they continued working. They worked because they needed money. Ostrem smiled. He had money.

Jim pulled the car into the lot of a particularly squat building painted inexplicably to look like an English pub: red and black with a shingle hanging over the door bearing a coat of arms adorned with naked girls in outline. *Ye Olde Countryside Inn* read the sign. Ostrem was impressed.

He stepped out, peeled a $100 off of his wad, and handed it to Jim. "Well done, sir," he said as he patted him on the shoulder and walked in.

The bouncer may not have recognized Ostrem, but he knew an expensive suit when he saw it, and led Ostrem to the premier seat near the stage. A waitress in far too much clothing for Ostrem's taste instantly produced a dirty martini and received a smack on the bottom for her trouble. He settled back with his drink as the DJ announced the next girl: Amber Waves.

The young blonde strode on stage in a red-white-and-blue sequined tailcoat and panties sporting an eagle. A dance mix of "America the Beautiful" blared on the sound system. Ostrem liked her style and clapped enthusiastically, though with some difficulty since his arms had recently become too short to reach across the widening expanse of his belly.

She saw him and also recognized the expensive suit and the premier seat. She stalked over to give him a jiggle. "Hi, honey," she purred. "Are you a patriot?"

"Darlin', I am tonight!" roared the governor.

She smiled and threw herself at a pole in the center of the stage. Ostrem had tried to convince his mistress to take a pole exercise class, but she'd been "too busy," so he still had no idea how dancers defied gravity like Amber did, hanging upside down and flicking her heels at him. He liked it, though, and threw some more money onto the stage.

Amber's coat came off and she had on a bikini top with nice big titties that jiggled like they were mostly real. Ostrem didn't mind fake ones, mind you. He had a taste for some silicone, but he respected natural beauty, you see.

Amber slithered her way back to Ostrem to pick up the $50 from the table with her teeth. She looked in his face and said, "Thank you, darlin'," and slithered back. He put another $50 in front of him.

Amber's top came off and Ostrem took time to admire her. He loved young, creamy skin, and Amber glistened like ripe fruit. He peeled off a hundred dollar bill, but kept his paw on it. When she ambled over to him again, he wiggled it. "You wanna date, young lady?"

She opened her green eyes wide at the sight of the money. "I like dancin', sweet-pea," she said.

Ostrem peeled off another hundred and set it down beside its brother. "Are you sure you don't wanna dance with me?"

Amber stared at the money with obvious interest. Then she looked Ostrem in the eye. "What's your name, darlin'?"

"Bill," he said.

"Are you somebody famous, Bill?"

"Me? Nah. Just a rich fucker on a business trip."

"You look famous," Amber said and danced away.

She came to his table when her song was over and she had replaced her coat and panties, bikini top in her hand. "Are you sure you're not somebody I know?" she asked, sitting very close to him. "I swear I've seen your face somewhere."

Ostrem slung a fat arm around her tiny waist. "I ain't nobody important." He chuckled, pulling her close. She smelled like a stripper should: coconut oil.

"No touching, sweetie," she said, slithering from his grasp. "Not here. Would you like a dance in the Champagne room?"

"Would I!" Ostrem chortled. He pulled his bulk from his chair and followed her to the back of the place, through a beaded curtain.

A bottle of cheap bubbly sat on a table in the room already, and though it was cloyingly sweet, it was also properly chilled, so Ostrem drank the glass Amber offered him when he sat down. She turned on some music, shed her clothes, and began to dance on the other side of the room, out of reach.

"C'mere, baby," he said.

"No touching," Amber repeated, staying just beyond his fingertips.

"I'm dyin' here," he moaned. "My wife, my mistress, they've cut me off."

"Poor baby," she purred. "What did you do to deserve that?"

"Nothing!" he cried. "It's this fucking sex strike. I can't catch a break anywhere."

"Poor thing," Amber pouted as she gyrated.

"Couldn't you help relieve an old man?" Ostrem pleaded, grabbing her wrist roughly. "Please?"

"I don't know…"

"I'll give you $500."

"How much?" Amber asked, amazed.

"$500," he repeated.

"For a dance?"

"No, no, no, you stupid cunt. I need to have sex. I want you bouncing on me like a puppet on a popsicle stick."

"I don't do that," she said carefully.

"I'd give $250 for a blowjob right now," he grumbled.

"I don't do that, either," Amber said. "Could you let go of my arm please?"

"Fuck if I will," he said and pulled her into his lap. He was strong for a fat guy.

"Let go of me!" Her eyes were wide. "Let go!"

"Shut up, cunt. I'm tired of you talking. I know you need the money, and I need your little twat." His other hand made a grab for her breast, but she swatted him away as best she could. "Stop that!" he hissed, snatching her arm out of the air, and then holding her two thin wrists in one meaty paw.

"How do you like that, honey?" he said, pulling her face next to his.

"Danny!" Amber shrieked.

The bouncer appeared in the doorway instantly, but he wasn't exactly as Ostrem remembered. His outfit was the same, but there was something different about it…perhaps it was the shining star on the breast pocket.

Yes, Ostrem decided that was it.

He let go of Amber. "Why, hello, Officer," he said in as syrupy a drawl as he could muster. "I was just having a little chat with this kitten here. She's feisty, isn't she?"

"Sir, could you stand up, please?" said the officer/bouncer.

"I'd rather not," Ostrem said. "I have a bit of a condition."

"Stand up, sir."

Ostrem stood, but he needn't have worried about his erection showing. His belly fat more than disguised it.

Amber re-clad herself and stood behind Danny the officer/bouncer. "Did you get any of that?" she asked him.

"Yes. It's all on tape," he answered.

"Tape?" Ostrem was suddenly interested, and the wad of bills he had been pulling out of his pants to bribe his way out to his car suddenly disappeared into his pocket. "Tape? Of what?"

"Tape of you first soliciting sex from a legal dancer and then, when she refused, of you attempting to force yourself on her."

"Oh, that," Ostrem said. "That was just a little misunderstanding, wasn't it, darlin'?" He looked desperately at Amber. "You knew I was just kidding around, right?"

Amber was still rubbing her wrists. "Governor Ostrem, I don't know how or why you walked into our sting tonight, but I am so very glad you did. You are a legendary asshole, and I'm glad we caught you."

"Amber, darlin'!" Ostrem cried as Officer Danny stepped behind him and tried to get cuffs on his chubby wrists. "Don't be so cruel!"

"Won't work," Danny said, resorting to using two pairs of cuffs on his perp. "She's working for us."

"She's a—a—"

"An officer, yup. Plus, she a she-devil in the sack."

"How—"

"She's my wife, fucker," Officer Danny said, cinching the cuffs very tight until Ostrem yelped. "Oh, too loose? I'll fix that."

Ostrem yelped again.

Jim saw the cruisers with the flashing lights arrive and put two and two together even before he saw Ostrem led from the back of the building to a police car. He put out his cigarette and started the drive back to the garage. He was glad that Ostrem had tipped him in advance. It was nice when things worked out that way.

♥

Liz was laughing so hard that tears streaked down her cheeks. "He did what to a who?" she asked Zeke.

"No, he didn't really," Cal said, still in disbelief.

"No, no, that's what my source in Sioux City says," Zeke said. "Bill Ostrem was caught on video tape trying to rape an undercover police woman who was posing as a stripper."

"In Sioux City?" Liz hooted. "Really? Sioux City?"

"What a scumbag." Cal shook her head. "I mean, I knew he was a lech, but a rapist?"

"Sioux City has, what, four strip clubs? And he picks the one with the stakeout?" Liz put her head on the table and laughed more.

"This is great news!" Zeke said. "Ostrem is out of the race! His vice president pick doesn't have the recognition or name-power that Ostrem had. He's not really a threat. We've got a week to the election, and one opponent is G-O-N-E, gone!"

Cal smiled. "You're right. And probably the best part about it is that that scumbag is never winning another office in his life."

"And she was a cop!" Liz couldn't stop laughing, so Zeke and Cal began adjusting their strategy while Liz hiccupped with glee in her chair.

Chapter 13

Election night two days away, and the last minute plans of attack had been set into motion. Liz and Cal had been in agreement from the beginning that attack ads were not going to be part of the plan, even though Ostrem's stripper stunt and current incarceration gave them more ammunition than they had ever dreamed of. There were lots of other options to get media attention.

"We need to think of a way to get our supporters to the polls while discouraging our dissenters," Cal mused.

"How do we get angry, horny men to stay home on Election Day?" Liz asked while gnawing on a pencil eraser.

Zeke yearned to be that eraser, so he wasn't really thinking when he muttered, "Sex."

Both women looked at him. "What?"

"Well—I mean, I'd stay home from just about anything if someone offered me sex. Or porn. Or a good football game."

Cal sat back in her chair. "You might have something there, Zeke," she said. "The girls at the playboy channel, they could 'fix' the switches that were broken, couldn't they?"

"I'm sure they'd be happy to," Liz said. "I don't think we have much control over the quality of football on a Tuesday, though."

"You do have control of the sex, though," Zeke said.

"What do you mean?"

Cal laughed. "You horn-dog, Zeke. You want a moratorium on the strike so you can get into Liz's pants!"

"Zeke!" Liz was shocked, or mock-shocked, Zeke couldn't tell. "That's brilliant!" Mock-shocked. "Let's say that anyone who votes gets one 'buy' from the sex-strike. And, let's turn the porn on for the guys."

"So, why would any man leave his house on Tuesday?" finished Zeke. "Porn all day and his girl at night?"

"Are you sure this is wise?" a worried Cal said. "I mean, isn't that like falling off the wagon?"

"Maybe," Liz said. "Or maybe it is just a nip to help the troops through the long haul in front of them."

"Liz, really—" Cal began, but she stopped. Liz and Zeke were gazing into each other's eyes, and it was plain that she was not only ignored, but that she was going to be out-voted by the raging hormones. "I think it's risky, you two," she said instead. "Just remember that this is about ending a war, not about satisfying urges!"

She stood and stormed out of the room.

Liz stood and went after her. "Cal!" she said as she took her friend's arm. "I'm sorry. If you really think it's a bad idea, we don't have to do it."

"I think it's risky, but I don't think it's a bad idea, necessarily," Cal said. She turned to her friend. "I'm a little overwhelmed by the electricity between you two is all. That would probably be better if you actually did it, I suppose."

"So, any word from Heir Professor Nicolas?"

Cal smiled. "Yeah. He called last night. He'd be happy to hear about a moratorium."

"Good." Liz gave her friend a squeeze and brought her back to the table.

Elektra had arrived since they had been gone, and she was deep in conversation with Zeke about the moratorium.

"Hmm. That's a good idea," she pronounced. "I like it. Gets our girls out to the polling stations, keeps the horny slobs at home."

"I was going to put it more delicately," said Liz.

"Sure, sure," Elektra said. "What it amounts to is an orgy on Election Night and a baby boom in August next year."

"I think I can live with that," Liz said.

"I'll bet you can," Elektra said. "You and Zeke are going to have to be careful, you know. There can't be any other reasons behind this other than rewarding your voters."

"You're right," Zeke said. "It would be disastrous if people thought we were changing the rules just because we were weak."

"Right, and we need to keep pushing the idea that no matter who wins election day, the strike needs to keep going until the war is over," Cal said.

Zeke's hand slid over to Liz's thigh again. He squeezed it gently, and she covered his hand with hers. They were about to break rules two and three. They had to keep rule one or everything would fall apart.

♥

Since the "Spectacle," male reporters had been falling over themselves to get assignments covering the Stratton-Sampson campaign. Liz and Elektra never failed to excite the male press corps with their outfits, although they never went as far as wearing gold lamé again. This time, lacy bra peeking out from under her demure shirt, Liz flashed them a little extra thigh and received a couple of grateful whoops for her trouble.

"I bring good news," she said. "Two items: first, I have it on good authority that regular programming may return to certain premium cable channels on Tuesday." The crowd murmured excitedly, and most of the men looked at their watches, wondering how many minutes were between them and Tuesday.

"Second, the WAP campaign is happy to announce a little reward for our supporters. Anyone who is participating in the sex strike may have one day of sex after they vote on Tuesday." There was shocked silence.

Finally a hand went up. "Ms. Stratton, are-are you saying the strike is over on Tuesday?" asked a hopeful reporter.

"Not at all, not at all. What we are saying is that there will be a brief lifting of the strike as a reward for voting. Think of it as a little shore leave before we launch into the main battle. Because, you see, no matter who wins the election on Tuesday, the sex strike will go on until the war is over. Peace may be declared more quickly if certain people are elected, but it won't be immediate. This is just a little thank-you present for everyone who has been with us so far. And a little taste of what's been missing for those who stand in our way. That's all, folks. Have a nice Sunday."

As she stepped away from the podium, Liz heard all manner of cell phones and blackberries clicking and beeping as the reporters called home base and chattered excitedly. She had to hand it to Zeke. Sex would make even bigger news than no sex did.

♥

Election Day was going to be long and hard. Liz giggled every time she heard that. It was going to be many hours awake and difficult. The first thing they did was fly to LA on Monday night so that they could vote in their home districts. Liz slept in her own bed for the first time in months. Her cats piled on top of her and purred the whole night. She noted a couple of orchids hadn't thrived under the house-sitter's care, but otherwise, it was good to be home.

After a very early alarm and a typical breakfast of toast and coffee eaten over her sink, Liz went to her precinct and voted for herself in front of all the television cameras in the state. Then she joined Cal and Zeke on a bus headed to Camp Pendleton.

Watching election results with the crowd of army wives that helped begin their campaign was Liz's idea. Their faces had kept her resolve up. It was the grandmotherly woman who had first said that she'd sacrifice anything to end the war who had haunted her most.

The drive was only an hour, so Liz re-read the two speeches in front of her: the conceding speech, and the winner's speech. Both consisted of as few words as she thought she could get away with because she knew that either way, she would be too emotional to trust herself on stage for long. Finally, she shoved them both into her bag and stared out the window.

She looked up when Zeke slid into the seat beside her. "Hi."

She smiled at him and leaned in to his chest. "Hi."

"How are you holding up?" he asked.

"I'm a bunch of jangled nerves."

After a moment he asked, "So, did you vote?"

"Don't you want television?" She laughed. "Yeah, I voted."

"So did I," Zeke said. "Um, don't we get a prize or something?"

Liz sat up and kissed him. "How was that?"

"Lovely, but I was kinda hoping…"

"What?"

"You ever hear of the 'mile-high club'?" Zeke asked with a lascivious grin.

Liz wrinkled her cute brow. "We're on a bus."

"How about the 'sixty-miles-an-hour' club?"

Liz shook her head and rolled her eyes. "You men are all the same. Our first time will not be in the bathroom of a moving bus. What kind of girl do you think I am?"

"Fair enough," Zeke said. "Can't blame a guy for trying."

"You do realize that, because of your lust, you've helped orchestrate a nationwide orgy, don't you?"

"For everyone except me," Zeke said.

"I will make it up to you," Liz whispered in his ear. "Believe, me, I want to."

♥

The gym was the same except that someone had taken it upon herself to decorate the pulled-up basketball hoops with red, white and blue banners. Chairs were set up in front of the stage where a very large screen was set up and a twenty-four-hour news channel was projected. A very happy, relaxed crowd chattered as it waited.

Cheers greeted Liz and Elektra, who had flown in from voting in New York, as they entered the gym and began shaking hands.

They mingled and Liz reconnected with the women from that first rally.

"Ladies, you know you were the inspiration for all this," Liz told them.

A smiling army wife giggled. "Gosh, don't tell my husband that!"

The first couple hours were spent chatting with the people from the base and the dignitaries who had come to support the campaign. A game evolved where anytime someone on the television said "sex strike," everyone had to yell "moratorium!" and kiss the nearest person. It was a lot of fun, actually, Liz thought.

By the five o'clock, polls began closing around the country. Liz sat in a chair watching the screen, nervously nibbling whatever was on her plate. Zeke kept her plate supplied with food from the catering table. He switched her from wine to sparkling water after her third chardonnay, however. She didn't really notice.

He sat next to her when they started calling the first counties. "It'll be fine," he whispered. "We were polling at forty-two percent yesterday. It'll be fine."

Liz began picking the polish off of her manicured nails. "I don't know how much of this tension I can take," she whispered. "I mean, it's going to be hours before we know anything for sure."

Zeke began to answer when a whoop came from the front of the room. "Jackson County Virginia! We've won a county!"

Everyone was cheering and someone gave Liz a glass of champagne. Zeke hugged her. "See?"

Liz drank her champagne and smiled at everyone. She was terrified.

♥

The night wore on and more states reported in. The first state they won was Maryland, which Cal thought appropriate because it had a girl's name, followed by Virginia and Georgia. Liz was surprised because she hadn't figured they'd carry the South at all. Sure enough, though, they carried the other girl states: the Carolinas, both North and South, as well as West Virginia.

Some of the supporters broke open the champagne at the reports of the first counties they'd carried presumably because they were afraid Liz and Elektra would only carry a few. They were drunk by the time all the Eastern polls had closed, and were having a very, very good time by the time the South finished reporting in.

"What are they going to be like in three hours when the West starts reporting?" Liz asked. "Get someone to hide the booze for an hour at least."

For the next couple hours, Liz sat in her hard, cold folding chair, chatting with whomever stopped by, but mostly watching the election coverage closely. She was waiting for the other shoe to drop, but it wasn't. The exit polls and the official counts put her and Elektra a solid second in most places, and the winner in others. As the night wore on, she became less and less responsive to people wanting to talk, and Zeke began shooing people away.

"What's happening?" Liz asked when Zeke sat next to her at the beginning of hour two. "We're not losing."

"Well, the early reports that I've heard have been that there was a record turnout of female voters and a bit of a lag in male voters."

Liz looked at him. "You mean, the porn worked?"

Zeke shrugged. "Maybe. Or maybe you excited your base while the other candidates didn't."

A cheer rose from the crowd as another state was called in their favor. "Which one?" asked Liz.

"Looks like Massachusetts. Way to take that from the Dems, Liz," Cal said, walking up. "You look totally stressed out. Why don't you have a drink and relax?"

"I've had too much already," Liz said. "Any more and I might throw up or pass out."

"That would be unseemly," Cal said. "How about a back rub?"

"I'd take one of those," Liz said gratefully.

♥

The Midwest did not like Liz the way the South or Northeast did. For a couple hours, the votes were mostly Democratic and Liz's name was hardly mentioned. Blue states dotted the map while pink, the color chosen for WAP by the networks, remained segregated in the South and East. The mood in the gym was dampened like a hat left in the rain.

Liz felt a little bit of relief. *It isn't that I don't want the job*, she told herself. *But...*

Once the polls started to close on the other side of the Rockies, things started to pick up. The less populous states were in her favor, which caused the party to kick into high gear. Soon, pink states seemed to be everywhere, partly because the Western states were so much larger than the others. Someone turned music on to the PA speakers, and there was actual dancing.

"How many does that make?" she asked Zeke.

"You're just a bit ahead Beckinger," he said. "It's anyone's race."

A scream pierced the air and everyone jumped up expecting a knife-wielding maniac. Instead, a staffer shrieked, "We took California!"

Liz missed her chair on the way down and sat on the floor, blinking. "Jesus, Zeke. That, that puts us ahead, doesn't it?"

Zeke was laughing. "Yes, yes, it does!"

Liz found herself laughing, too. She felt really good about winning and wondered briefly at the change. Now that she was ahead, she desperately wanted to win, desperately wanted to be the next president. The fear was gone.

Very soon it was clear that the popular vote and the electoral votes did not exactly synch. Liz groaned when she realized how close the votes actually were. The talking heads on the big screen babbled incoherently, not wanting to call close states too early. They had learned from previous elections when the scoop-mad media announced winners before the votes had been tallied. Instead, no one said anything definite.

"We're so close," Liz said, watching a pulsating map of pink and blue on the television.

Zeke wrapped his arm around her waist and said nothing. He had heard from one of the consultants that theirs was a lost cause: California had actually gone to Beckinger. Zeke couldn't bring himself to tell Liz. The thought of disappointing her killed him.

Soon, it was obvious to everyone, including the television pundits, that Liz had not actually carried California. A relieved-looking male anchor announced that Beckinger was the new president of the United States of America.

Liz wanted to slump against Zeke's shoulder and sob. She wanted to howl in anger. She wanted to rally the troops and demand a re-count. She wanted to crawl into a hole and die.

Instead, she took a deep breath, smoothed her hair down, and stood smiling at her supporters. She walked to the little room behind the stage where her two speeches were. She needed one of them.

♥

"Ladies and gentlemen," Liz began, standing at the lectern with every television camera trained in a close-up on her face. "Ladies and gentlemen, we have not won the White House." The crowd groaned, and a few boos and hisses wafted up from the back. "I know, I know," Liz said to calm them. "I'm as disappointed as you are. However, we must not forget the original purpose for the campaign: ending the war in Mesopotamianstan."

The crowd of mostly military wives cheered with some enthusiasm.

"It was here, in this building, that the idea for the sex strike was born. It was your pain and suffering that prompted the outrageous notion that withholding sex could change foreign policy. Well, it has. The fact that forty-three percent of the nation voted for us must tell the world that we are sick of the war. Our 'leaders' must reckon with the millions upon millions of us that are sacrificing right now to protest the war. Some of them might be suffering as we are, unwillingly.

"But let's not forget our purpose—the sex strike continues until the war is over!" Liz waited for the cheers to subside and smiled into the camera. "It is even more important that the strike continues now, now that someone else is destined for the White House—someone whose priority is not on ending the war, but on keeping campaign promises he made to certain rich people he knows. It is vitally important that we keep applying this pressure until the war is over. We need to make them realize that we weren't joking. We don't care if Stratton and Sampson lost the White House: we want the war to end, now!

"We've taken the one thing they can't replace and the one thing we have total legal control over: ourselves. Let them know we're prepared to keep using this tool until they give us what we want. Thank you!"

Liz stepped away from the podium and waved as the crowd cheered. Her tired heart was lifted by their enthusiasm, but once she was behind the curtain, she was spent.

♥

Liz was brushing her teeth when she heard Zeke's familiar knock. She opened the door and let him to come in on his own as she went back to spit in the sink. When she stood up from rinsing her mouth, she saw flowers. Beautiful red roses tied with a huge yellow ribbon that read "Victory!" Behind them stood Zeke looking sheepish.

"Oh my God, these are beautiful, Zeke. Who sent them?"

"Me, silly," he said.

"But we didn't win!"

"Who cares?" Zeke said.

"Oh, they're beautiful." She took them into her arms. "Thank you." She kissed him gently from behind the thorns.

"Come out here," he said.

She stepped out of the bathroom to see that Zeke had also lit candles and turned down the bed. When she looked at him, he pushed a button and started soft music. He gestured her to sit and took the flowers from her, replacing them with a glass of champagne.

"How did you do all this while I was brushing my teeth?"

"Magic elves." He leaned in and kissed her.

"What is this?" she asked.

"What do you think? You're the one who called the moratorium."

"Zeke, it's so late, I'm exhausted—" she began.

"No you're not," he whispered and kissed her again. "It's perfect."

"It's certainly better than the back of a bus." She giggled, drank some champagne, and smiled at him over her glass. "How long have you been planning this?"

"Ten years," he said. "Originally, there was a choir to sing 'Halleluiah,' but you caught me off guard."

"The moratorium was your idea," she reminded him.

"I know. It was a very good idea, don't you agree?"

"Very, very good."

Zeke was looking at Liz appreciatively, which made her giggle again. "Zeke, these pajamas haven't been washed in a week!"

"All the better," he said, spinning her slowly. "Maybe you should take them off."

"You first," she said and sat demurely on the edge of the bed.

"All right," he said. He set down his glass and slipped off his jacket.

"Very nice," Liz said.

"Stop it, you little minx," Zeke scolded. He unbuttoned his oxford and slid out of the sleeves. Though he was not very tall, Zeke's shoulders tapered nicely to a trim waist. Liz smiled.

"Your turn," he said.

"Okay." She stood and shimmied out of her pajama bottoms, revealing her long legs. Her panties peeked out from under her kitten pajama top. She leaned back across the bed and crossed her legs. "How's that?"

"Ooh," Zeke sighed. In two strides he had Liz in his arms, laying her back gently. "You are too much, Liz," he said. Then he kissed her.

Zeke's back was warm and alive under Liz's hands, and she marveled how good his skin felt. They hadn't allowed themselves to get past second base so far, so the way her skin tingled next to his was all new. So was his intoxicating scent. Liz realized in a rush that she could press more of her skin against his if she took her top off, too. She began pulling at the buttons, but Zeke stopped her.

"What are you doing?" he asked, propping himself up on one elbow. "That's my job." He drew one finger down her jaw-line, past her neck, down her breastbone to the first button, which he fiddled with for an excruciatingly long time. When Liz reached up to hurry him along, he pushed her hand down and pinned it under his body. "My job," he repeated, finally working the button loose.

Once he had unfastened the buttons, Zeke drew her top open just so her belly was exposed, allowing the fabric to hang on her breasts. He leaned over her belly, and Liz shivered under his warm breath. He kissed her just above the navel and then kissed again and again in a circle. Each time his lips brushed her, Liz felt a shock that made her jump. She moaned a little, and put her hand on his head.

Zeke took that hand and pinned it to the bed, too. He

moved up so he looked her in the eye and said, "Please, Liz. This—this time, it's my job." He kissed her again, but held each of her hands firmly as he worked his way down to her chest.

He took a corner of fabric in his teeth and let it fall to the bed. He nudged the other side off with his nose. Then he sat back a little and just admired Liz's breasts, smiling.

"I like the way you look at me," she said.

"I like looking," he said. "But I like this more." He kissed her breasts. Then he took a nipple in his mouth and nibbled and sucked until Liz was panting.

"I want to hold you," Liz said finally.

"Not yet," Zeke said.

He inched his way down.

Liz felt him remove her underwear with his teeth, and she kicked them the rest of the way off. Then she felt him kissing his way up her thighs, still holding her wrists firmly.

His warm tongue introduced itself to her wetness. She yelped and tried to mash his face with her hips.

"Careful," he said, grinning. "I don't want to chip a tooth."

"Stop talking," she moaned. "Get on with it!"

"My, you're impatient," Zeke said. "I've been waiting for years. I can wait a little longer for you to calm down."

"Bastard!" Liz cried, arching her back.

"You're right," he said. "Let me fix that."

Somehow, Zeke took off his pants with one hand while still holding Liz's wrists. She tried breaking away so she could pull him to her, but he was too strong. Finally, Zeke knelt naked beside Liz. "I'll let you go if you'll let me drive this once," he said. "I want to touch every part of you, and I can't have you distracting me."

"What if I want to touch you?" Liz asked.

"Next time. Every time after that if you like," he said. "But let this first time be mine. I've been thinking about it for so long."

"Deal," Liz said. When Zeke let her go, she obediently put her hands behind her head. "I'm not always this easy to deal with, you know," she said.

"That's what makes this special."

He got down to business and lived up to his promise of touching every part of her. He nibbled her ears, he kissed her fingertips, he massaged her toes. When he finally entered her and Liz threw her arms around him, he didn't mind. He felt like she was really his after all this time. He had always been hers, whether she had known it or not, but now every inch of her was really his.

Liz wasn't sorry at all that she followed Zeke's instructions. "Seriously, Zeke. No one makes me come like this!"

"That's because no one worships you like I do, Liz," Zeke replied.

Liz lay in the afterglow, head upon Zeke's chest, savoring these words. His heart thumped reassuringly under her ear, which made her smile. "We need to do that again."

"Well, yeah," he said. "I plan on doing that all the time."

"I mean, since the strike resumes tomorrow—"

"Damn war," Zeke muttered. "I forgot."

"It's good to forget," Liz said quietly. "What we do before dawn doesn't count, right?"

"Doesn't count," Zeke said with confidence. "Are you ready for round two?"

"Sure. It's my turn, now," she said, pinning his arms to the mattress. "Get ready for me, boy."

♥

Liz lay awake staring at the ceiling as Zeke snored softly beside her. Of course, they had mapped all of the possibilities beforehand, but Liz had wanted to be president, and she found disappointment a bitter pill at best. Plus, Beckinger was such a self-righteous asshole. Liz remembered that he was the jerk whose condescension had led to her blind rage and the sex strike.

She rolled to her side so she could stare at the wall instead of the ceiling. She wasn't going to be president. An angry tear burned down the side of her head and disappeared into the pillow. She hadn't admitted to herself how much she had wanted to be president, and she hadn't had time to process her disappointment. She felt cheated.

She turned her head so she could see Zeke's pale shoulders next to her. She traced a shoulder blade with her fingertip and he sighed in his sleep, which made her smile.

She sighed, too. She wasn't going to be the most powerful person in the government, but she was still the most powerful woman in America. She had millions of people doing her bidding, and she didn't want to lose that until the war was ended. She worried about how to fan the flames during the lame-duck session and the transition of power.

Her mind raced in circles, and she eventually realized that she was in no state to solve the world's problems, nor to sleep, so she flicked on the television and muted it.

She flipped through the channels until an image on a twenty-four-hour news station caught her attention. Out of the low glow flickered images of women in traditional Islamic dress waving signs and chanting. Most of the signs were completely incomprehensible to her, but one caught her attention: it was a picture of her. Liz turned on the sound.

"...protests springing up in most corners of Mesopotamianstan with women especially complaining about Liz Stratton's loss of the American election," the newscaster said. In the background, an image of Beckinger was being burned in effigy.

"Holy shit, Zeke. You've got to see this," Liz said, reaching behind her and shaking him.

"What the hell?" Zeke groaned as Liz turned up the volume more.

Soon they were both on the edge of the bed, watching in disbelief as reports came in of women in the Middle East protesting the war. It was assumed that there was a sex strike going on, too, but some cultural barriers are harder to break than others and reports remained unconfirmed.

"Do you know what this means?" asked Zeke.

"It means we have a chance to end the conflict," Liz said. "But we have to go abroad to clinch it."

♥

While Cal slept in post-coital bliss, Nicolas sat in bed watching her sleep. He resisted the urge to pinch himself to make sure he wasn't dreaming. Eventually, he decided that sleep would be a good idea, so to lull his brain, he turned on the television to the twenty-four-hour news channel.

A minute later, he shook Cal awake.

♥

Cal took one look at Liz and Zeke as they walked in to breakfast and beamed. "Jesus, you both look like hell."

"Hell is the best place on earth," Zeke said, Cheshire grin and all.

"I'd buy a condo there," Liz agreed. "You don't look so hot yourselves."

Cal exchanged a warm smile with Nicolas. "Maybe we'll timeshare that condo together."

Zeke sat down. "Cal, did you see the news this morning?"

"I was up most of the night watching, actually," she

said. "Who knew we had such reach?"

Nicolas yawned broadly. "What are you all going to do about it? How are Mesopotamian women going to help us here? We still lost the election."

"You're forgetting that objective number one was not to win the presidency, but to end the war," Cal said.

"And if we have supporters on the quote-unquote enemy side, then we have even more chance of stopping the violence," Liz finished.

"Huh," Nicolas said. "Jeesh. I was hoping that you would have been so charmed by last night that you'd have forgotten about the whole sex strike thing." He grinned as Cal slapped him playfully.

"Had to think about it, honey." She laughed. "But as of now, the no nooky rule is back in force."

Chapter 14

President-Elect Oscar Beckinger hadn't even been sworn in yet, but he was still being pressured about the damned war.

He sat in a dress shirt and boxer shorts in his hotel suite in DC, gnawing on the end of a pencil as Megan got the boys ready for school. They marched in for his inspection before they left.

He stood and walked around them with mock criticism on his face as he inspected their new uniforms. "So, first day, boys?"

"Yeah," they moaned a little.

He clapped them both on the back. "You'll be fine," he said. "I know you miss your friends, but it'll be easier to just start now and not wait until we move into that big house, right?"

He shook each of their hands. "Curt," he said to his

thirteen-year-old son. "Make sure your brother is taken care of."

"Yes, sir."

"Ben?" he said to his fifteen-year-old son. "Make sure your brother is behaving, okay?"

"Okay!"

They ran to the door and flung it open on their way to the elevator. Beckinger grabbed Megan's arm as she passed and gave her a kiss on the cheek. She smiled at him and disappeared after the children.

Beckinger sat back down at his temporary desk and resumed gnawing on his pencil. The situation in Mesopotamianstan was impossible to fix. Both sides wanted the complete annihilation of the other. People in the West, who had admittedly caused the problem by creating Mesopotamianstan by squashing several sovereign states together willy-nilly, had been looking for a way to end the conflict and save face for fifty or sixty years. Now, it was his problem.

He glanced at his watch and sighed. It was time to put on pants so that his choice for Secretary of State wouldn't be offended. Foster was a little particular about that sort of thing. Sure enough, he was just slipping on his jacket when there was a knock at the door.

The first words out of Soon-to-be Secretary Foster's mouth were, "You couldn't be bothered to button your jacket for me, huh?" as he stepped gruffly into the suite.

Beckinger laughed. "We may have to work on your bedside manner, Jack, if you're going to be my liaison to world leaders, you know."

"Fuck 'em." Foster's grumble had a bit of mirth behind it as he trundled over to the breakfast cart and poured himself some coffee. "They're all a bunch of damned foreigners, anyway," he said and sipped the coffee. "Mmph. Good."

"Yeah, it's not bad here," Beckinger said as he poured himself another. He and Foster sat at the desk together.

Foster picked up a gnawed-up pencil. "Been thinking about the Middle East, have you?" he guessed, tossing the chewed wood into the trash.

Beckinger sighed and rubbed his eyes. "What do we do, Jack? It's an impossible situation."

"Fifty years of trying, and no results."

"Every president has tried to fix it, thinking it will be a coup, a feather in his cap, and they have all failed with the same black smudge on their records."

Foster took a long noisy sip of his coffee. "Only one thing to do."

"What's that?"

"Talk the talk and stall until you're out of office. Just like everyone else."

Beckinger shook his head. "We need to try something different, man. I mean, we did kinda run on the idea of ending the war."

"Eventually," Foster said. "I see no reason why we should try something that will fail. We'll look even more ridiculous than those who've tried before."

Beckinger sat back. "This would be easier if we hadn't had to up the rhetoric because of that Stratton bitch."

Foster nodded. "She did make this more difficult."

"You know she won't quit now, either. She's already making noises about going over there. Plus, the strike is still on until the war is over."

Foster nodded again and looked carefully at Beckinger. "Mrs. Foster has been…feeling poorly in the evenings for months now."

Beckinger shook his head. "All the women in my life, man, are 'feeling poorly.' I'm getting a little desperate."

Foster had a habit of blinking slowly when he was formulating an idea, so when Beckinger saw the old man's eyelids creeping down and then up, he said, "What is it? What?"

"Stratton wanted to be president so she could end the war, correct?"

"Yes, yes. Go on."

Foster's eyelids slid down and up again and he looked at Beckinger askance. "Let's let her do it."

"What? Be president?"

"No, stupid. End the war."

"I'm confused."

"Send the little minx and her troupe of tarts to Mesopotamianstan and let them end the war."

"They won't be able to do that if we can't, Jack," Beckinger protested.

"Doesn't matter, Ox," Foster said, leaning back and smirking. "If they fail, we don't lose a thing, and we don't have that black mark of history on us. Plus, on the remote chance that they do bring peace to the region, you and I smell like a fucking rose garden for sending such a talented envoy."

Beckinger grinned. "I knew there was a reason I pulled you away from California to be in my cabinet."

♥

"I don't understand," Liz said again. She was tempted to turn the letter from the president-elect's office upside down in case it made more sense that way. "Am I reading this right?" she asked, thrusting the letter back into Zeke's hands.

"Yes, you are," he said, trying to give it back to her. When she wouldn't take it, he read aloud from it again.

"'Dear Ms. Stratton,

"'In light of the recent election and demonstration of the strength of your convictions on ending the war in Mesopotaminastan, our administration in conjunction with the sitting administration would like to send you as our envoy to the Middle East with the goal of ending the conflict there. If you accept this position please contact us at...'"

"I can't believe that's only two sentences," Cal muttered.

"I can't believe any of it," Liz said, sitting down.

"I don't trust these snakes. What are they up to?" Elektra said. "I smell a rat."

"Me, too," Liz said. "But what do we do?"

"We pack layers," Cal said. "And we call the Poli Sci Department at our alma mater."

♥

The American involvement in the ancient war in Mesopotamianstan was begun on a fear-based agenda. It was sold as a pre-emptive move to secure the region because factions were going to invade Israel and steal her nuclear bombs, which would then be trained on Europe and the US. The little countries of the Fertile Crescent were then invaded and combined into a Western-controlled country that separated Israel and Iran, which comforted the former and enraged the latter.

Naturally, the little countries did not recognize Western control, and numerous uprisings plagued the pseudo-governing bodies. Iran pumped cash and weapons into the insurgency and nobody in the world blamed them.

This had been going on for years, and it looked as if there would never be a solution. If the little countries were given their autonomy back, they might retaliate against Israel. If Mesopotamianstan were given complete autonomy, it would probably dissolve into either civil war or be overtaken internally by Iranian supporters, who might then decide to invade Israel. If the West continued its puppet government, it would run out of money and troops before the region ever settled down.

These were the problems Liz was trying to fix.

♥

"It's an absurd, impossible problem," Liz said,

throwing down her pencil. It was very late, and the fluorescent lights of the hotel conference room made everyone look very, very drained, which they were. "I don't think there is a rational answer here."

She was particularly irritable because the trip to France had been so surreal. First, they were told a time and hanger to arrive at, but they weren't told where they were going until the plane was in the air for an hour. When she asked why they were being taken to France instead of a locale in Mesopotamianstan, she was told that she didn't need to know. In addition, she was given notes on the negotiation strategy that were so contradictory and unyielding, she didn't know how she would be able to bargain with them at all.

"You're still thinking rationally, Liz," Elektra said. "Stop that. Are there any irrational answers?"

"What, like a wife-swap?" Zeke laughed. The six Red Bulls he'd downed gave him the giggles.

In spite of herself, Liz snickered at the thought of First-Lady Beckinger with the Shah of Iran and vice-versa. "I don't think that would go over well."

"How about a yearly 'get-high-and-naked-with-your-enemy' day?" Cal suggested. "It worked at the frat houses at UMASS on Homecoming."

Liz smiled. "I don't think we can base foreign policy on one frat party we went to in college, Cal—though that was, indeed, a night to remember."

"I still like the wife-swap idea." Zeke giggled. "Which probably means I should go to bed." He stood and stretched, then leaned over and gave Liz a smooch.

"G'night, sweetie," he said and left the room.

Liz watched him go. "He does have a point, doesn't he?"

"How do you mean?" Elektra asked.

"Well, the sex strike is what got us here, right? Maybe something like it can help us."

"So, the question is, 'What would the leaders involved be willing to give up for sex?' isn't it?" Cal asked.

"Yes. Let's work that angle," Liz said.

The women bent their heads over their budding plan.

♥

"Madame?" the polite French voice called from the doorway.

Liz raised her head from the table where she and Cal had fallen asleep sometime during the night after Elektra had excused herself and gone to her room.

She sat up and rubbed her eyes. "Yes?"

The manager of the hotel looked apologetic. "The delegation from Mesopotamianstan has offered the services of their envoy for designing a plan."

Great, Liz thought, kicking Cal awake. *Just what we need. Some chauvinistic Persian man to try to push us around until he gets what he wants.* She smiled sweetly. "Send him in."

"Oui," said the manager. He waved at someone behind him, and a cart with steaming dishes of eggs and sausage rolled in.

"What's this?"

"They also sent *petit déjuner*—er—breakfast." The waiters heaped two plates with food, and Liz realized how hungry she was. As she lifted her fork, she noticed that the manager hadn't left.

"Is there anything else?" she asked.

"Madame will notice that we have very elegant mirrors hanging at both ends of this conference room."

Liz frowned in confusion. "Yes, they are very nice."

"Perhaps madame would like to examine them, up close?"

Still frowning, Liz stood, walked to one of the mirrors, and was immediately grateful. Her hair had come loose and was poking about in all directions. Her lipstick was gone and her mascara had run down the corners of her eyes making her look like Cleopatra. Her glasses were so smudged she could barely see out of them.

"Holy cow," she said. "These mirrors are fantastic! Monsieur, give yourself a $50 tip on our account."

"Very good, madame," he said and backed out of the room.

"Cal, wake up and fix yourself up!" Liz called from the mirror as she tidied herself. "We're getting company in a couple minutes!"

"Who?" Cal moaned. "Can't it wait until after I shower?"

"No, the envoy from Mesopotamianstan is coming, presumably now. The manager is probably stalling him for a few minutes. Run a comb through your hair and splash some water on your face."

They were almost presentable and nearly finished with a second helping of breakfast when there was a discrete knock at the door. The manager stepped in. He nodded at the improvement. "The envoy from Mesopotaminastan: Anusheh Ebrahimi."

Cal and Liz stood and smoothed their lapels expecting a forceful man with heavy, dark eyebrows to bluster in.

Instead, a petite woman in a headscarf and power suit walked up to Liz, hand extended. "You must be Elizabeth Stratton," she said with a distinctive British lilt to her voice. "I'm Anusheh Ebrahimi. Please call me Anu."

"Call me Liz." She stood stunned for a moment. "You're the peace envoy?"

"Oh, yes," Anu said firmly. "I insisted when I heard that you were the one the new American President sent here. I want to work with you so badly."

Liz stood another moment, shaking Anu's hand, until Cal cleared her throat. "Oh, shoot. Anu, this is my most trusted advisor, Calliope Talmadge."

"Cal," she said as she shook Anu's hand. "Did you say you insisted? Who are you that you can insist on such things? If you don't mind my asking."

"I used to be—I mean, my father used to be a sheik. We were quite a powerful family until the war. I suppose we still are powerful. I've made my way up the foreign relations department of Mesopotamianstan to a respectable level. Also, I was able to convince my father and other officials that I should be the envoy. Not only do

I speak perfect English, but I am a woman and negotiate like one."

"How do you mean 'negotiate like one'?" Liz asked, sitting at the table.

"Oh, well, suppose I had been a man. Would you be as receptive to a Persian man? Or, rather, would he have been as willing to negotiate with you?"

"I admit, I was worried about that," Cal said. "I hate to stereotype, but the Middle Eastern men I've known haven't always listened to me as carefully as they could have."

Anu smiled. "I have certain assumptions about Americans, too," she admitted. "I went to school in England, so I know that not all of my countrymen's beliefs about Westerners are true."

"You have us there," Liz said. "I'm afraid Cal and I went to Europe for a summer after graduation, and that's the extent of our foreign travels."

"That is peculiar," Anu said. "Why were you sent to negotiate this treaty, then? I don't mean to offend, but why didn't the United States send the most experienced foreign specialists?"

Liz blinked. "I had not thought of it that way, Anu," she said slowly. She turned to Cal. "Do you think—"

Cal threw herself back into her chair. "Shit. The bastards mean for us to fail!"

"Jesus," Liz moaned. "I'm so fucking arrogant. I thought they had faith in us and our skills, but they want us to fuck up."

"I'm sorry, I don't understand," Anu said. "Why are you so distressed?"

"Oh, Anu. I'm so sorry," Liz said. "We were sent here by—I ran for president in this election."

"I know. I watched from here."

"Then you know I lost."

"Yes."

"The person I lost to sent me here to end the war."

"Yes, yes. I know this."

"Anu, he sent me here because either he doesn't want the war to end, or he knows that it's impossible to find peace—"

"Or both," said Cal.

"Or both. He's sent us here, set us up to fail—"

"So he looks good either way. If we get peace, he looks like he chose the right negotiation team. If we fail, then he blames us," Cal explained.

"Oh." Anu sat back in her chair, too. "Perhaps that is why my father allowed me to come as envoy, instead of better negotiators. I thought I was just lucky."

The three women sat under the large gilt mirrors, dejected, each watching her personal fantasy of ending the war dissolve. Liz wondered if she moved to Wyoming if anyone would recognize her. Cal made a list in her head of all the people who would have to pay for humiliating her like this.

But after a moment, Anu stood up and pounded the table with the flat of her hand, scaring the wee out of both Liz and Cal. "Damn it!" she spat in her clipped British accent. "I don't care if they sent me here because they thought I would not succeed. I want to show them that they are wrong! That would be the best revenge—to bring peace to my land!"

"She's right," Cal said. "Wouldn't Beckinger just eat his heart out if we came home with a peace treaty to flap in his face? Who'd get elected for a second term then?"

"All right," Liz said, standing. "We'll do it. We'll show those sons of bitches who can end the fighting—the bitches can!"

♥

Anu, Liz, Cal, and Elekta worked with the fury of women scorned. They realized that part of their problem was that their plan had to be accepted by the men who ran the countries. These men had very big egos and, like all men with big egos, were very keen on making sure everyone knew how strong they were.

"I hate protecting all these frigging male egos," Cal growled. She threw down her pen in disgust. "I mean, we can't give up anything without our guys raising a stink."

"And my father refuses to move on any of these items, too," Anu said. "Is this really hopeless?"

Both women turned to Liz who was bent over a stack of paper holding her head up with fistfuls of hair.

Finally, she sighed and leaned back. "It's pretty bad, ladies," she said. "Treaties are a compromise. That's why they are 'negotiated.' We haven't been given the tools to negotiate."

"So, we are screwed." Cal stood and started pacing. "Those fuckers in Washington are going to pay. Just wait till I get back to the States and raise the troops."

"I thought that America was ready to negotiate because of the…uh…strike," Anu said.

"You are right, Anu," Elektra said. "They should be much more willing than they are. Maybe they need another reminder?"

Cal grinned. "That would just take a couple phone calls."

"Could I be of help?" Anu asked.

"Of course, Anu," said Liz. "How would you like to help?"

"Well," she began. "You might not have noticed, but there is a strike going on here, as well."

"I had heard rumors, but I thought they were just wishful thinking," Elektra said.

"Oh, no. It's very quiet, but several women of high-powered men are not…as available as they were."

"Oh, that's great news, Anu!" Liz said. "We can hit them on two fronts at once, so to speak."

When Zeke joined them for lunch, the women were a-twitter.

"I didn't expect to see you all so happy," Zeke said as he sat next to Liz. "Have you made good progress on the peace agreement?"

"Nope." Liz stabbed her salad with a grin. "Both sides have hamstrung us by not allowing us to concede anything."

"Okay, so why the grins?" The smile slid off his face. "Oh, no. You girls are up to something, aren't you?"

"Creative negotiation, darling," Elektra said.

"That sounds bad," Zeke said. He braced himself against the edge of the table and closed his eyes. "Okay, I'm ready. Let me hear it."

"First, we need to call some wives of some influential people," Liz said. "Then we're going to need to get some girls. Pretty ones with a strong conviction to end the war and...um...loose definitions of decency."

"Oh, boy," Zeke said.

"Then we need to get the president and president elect over here."

"And I'll get my father and the officials of my country," Anu said.

"And we'll all meet back here," Cal said. "For the party of a lifetime."

The wives they called were very supportive. They took the mistresses on week-long spa vacations and arranged to visit to old girlfriends, and so the leaders of the countries in conflict were once again faced with cold, lonely sheets.

Finding the girls proved to be easier than expected, too. One or two modeling agencies were contacted and women flew to France from all over the world to participate. The hotel was suddenly full of long legs, flowing hair, and high cheekbones.

Getting the sitting president and president-elect and the sheiks to show proved a little more difficult, but the little consortium wasn't above a ruse.

On the appointed day, the most powerful men of the "free" and the Islamic worlds smugly entered the same glittering ballroom in the French hotel. Their first indication that something was awry was the fact that their opponents were smug as well. Lame-duck President Bernstrom leaned over to President-elect Beckinger and whispered, "I don't like the looks on their faces."

"I know, but look at that one," Beckinger said, pointing across the table with his thumb. "He looks as confused as us."

"Something's up," Bernstrom said louder. "I think those girls have something planned."

"Oh, you are right there, Mr. President," Elektra said as she entered the room in a slinky little number that her spry body looked surprisingly good in. "We have quite a show planned for you gentlemen."

On cue, a flock of models glided into the ballroom wearing couture eveningwear—on loan from sympathetic designers—opera length gloves, and impossibly high heels. There were three gorgeous women to every uncomfortable man in the room. Beckinger kicked President Bernstrom so he would close his mouth.

"Haven't we seen this show before, Ms. Stratton?" Beckinger said as snidely as he could. "Wasn't this your 'Spectacle' just before the election?"

"What a good memory you have, Mr. President-Elect," Liz strode into the room with loose hair and in long gloves and a striking red gown.

It was cut down to her navel and draped cloyingly at the base of her spine and suspended as if by magic everywhere else. Even Beckinger had to admit that it had the intended effect on him.

"We didn't see any reason to fix something that wasn't broken."

"But we did decide that we could push it further," Anu said, stepping into the room. She wore a beautifully draped gown as well, and though it was somewhat less daring than Liz's, it had the same effect.

"Anu!" Her father stood and pounded the table with his palms, his robes flying. "What on earth are you wearing? Where is your headscarf? Have you lost your mind?"

"I am doing what I think it will take to get a peace deal," she said.

"What does that mean?" her father demanded. "You told us that the Americans were ready to concede everything to us, that we were now victorious!"

"Wait a minute! That's what Stratton told us!" Beckinger stood and glared at Liz.

"You mean that little bitch lied to us?" the president stood, too. "Those towel-heads don't want to roll over and sign their oil reserves over to us?"

"Towel-heads?" Sheik Ebrahimi roared and lunged across the table at Bernstrom, a knife appearing in his hand from nowhere. Suddenly, the room was full of men in black suits and sunglasses. The deafening clicking of guns being cocked brought a furious tension to the room.

"Shut up, you morons!" Everyone was so stunned that they all turned to look at Liz who had leapt up on the table and stood in her three-inch heels like a goddess parting the sea. "Now sit down."

To her surprise, everyone sat obediently.

Liz pointed at Bernstom with a red-gloved finger. "You, you will shut your racist face, you son-of-a-bitch." She swung her arm to Sheik Ebrahimi. "You will relinquish your weapon, as you were supposed to before you came in here."

The sheik placed his knife upon the table and security took it away.

After a pause, Beckinger asked, "How is 'your way' different?"

"Simple," Liz answered. "We make it worth your while." And she pulled off a glove, first tugging on the fingers with her teeth, then easing the fabric over her arm until it slid off her hand. She slipped the satiny fabric through her fingers before finally tossing it to Beckinger, where it landed on his lap.

"A strip-tease?" He tried to snort derisively. "It's not like I haven't seen one of those before."

Then she waved her arms in an arc that encompassed the whole room. "We are here to make peace with each other. We have tried it your way for years and failed. We are now going to try it our way because we have nothing to lose and everything to gain."

"No kidding," Elektra said.

"And you're not…well, you're not a stripper." Beckinger's snide-ness had returned.

"Perhaps not," Liz said. "But I'll bet there are a few girls here that pass that test." She waved a hand, and at once the air was full of left-handed opera gloves. They landed all over the conference table and on each of the men. The Americans all turned to get a better look at the models who were now all sporting one bare arm.

The Arabs ranged from deeply offended to wildly excited by the situation. "This is outrageous," fumed Sheik Ebrahimi. "Anu, I forbid you to participate in this!"

"You sent me to negotiate for peace, Father," Anu said coldly as she tossed him her glove. "I believe this will work better than any other method."

"The first thing on the table is the reduction of American forces in Mesopotamianstan," Liz announced.

"The region is too unstable," Beckinger began as another opera glove hit him in the face. He swiped it away angrily. "The region would fall apart if..." He trailed off as he saw a girl behind the sheiks toying with the shoulder straps of her dress and batting her huge blue eyes at him. "Fall, fall apart—" He struggled. One of the straps fell off her shoulder and an enticing curve of her breast was exposed. She toyed with the fabric and licked her lips.

"How about if we reduce the forces by half each year for the next three year and pull out entirely in the next four?" Liz asked.

"Yeah, sure," Beckinger muttered.

At Liz's signal, the girl he was watching dropped her hand, rewarding him with a full, pert nipple. He sat back, rapt.

"Next on the table is the eradication of the splinter terrorist cells in Mesopotamianstan by the ruling parties. Gentlemen?" Liz turned to the sheiks.

"It's impossible," Sheik Ebrahimi began. "We cannot possibly eradicate them. There are too many, and, and..." He trailed off as he noticed the girls behind the

Americans were also losing control of their straps. "And besides, they are our countrymen and—Oh heavens!" He caught sight of Anu, his daughter, fiddling with her straps as well. "Anu! What do you think you're doing?"

"I am negotiating for peace, Father," she said.

"You will shame our entire family, you stupid girl!" he shrieked.

"If I have to," she said, leveling a cold stare at him.

As the sheik stood and glared at her angrily, Anu dropped a shoulder strap and held the front of her dress up by a finger and thumb. The room was very quiet for a long, long moment. Finally, Sheik Ebrahimi crossed his arms. "We will eradicate the terrorist cells," he said and looked away from Anu. She tied up her dress and sat.

"That went well," Liz said brightly. "Let's see what else we can get done today!"

♥

By the time an hour had passed, the treaty was agreed to and signed. The room was also filled with beautiful naked girls who chatted happily with each other and the equally happy men in the room. The only women who still had on even a scrap of clothing were Liz, Cal, and Elektra because they had been too busy with the treaty to strip, and Anu because her father had agreed to everything in the treaty.

As they celebrated, Liz took Anu aside and asked, "Is everything going to be okay between you and your father? He seems pretty upset."

"Perhaps in time," Anu said quietly. "I have never been a very traditional daughter, and I know he is very angry. I have just blackmailed him into this treaty."

"Oh, Anu. I'm sorry."

"It will be all right, Liz," Anu said. "My father will either forgive me or he won't. We have all made sacrifices for this peace. This is my sacrifice."

"I am so grateful," Liz said. "Let me know if there is ever anything I can do for you."

"No, I am grateful to you, Liz Stratton," Anu said. "Without you, none of this would have happened. You are an amazing woman, and you are a hero. I am glad to count you as a friend."

"You can certainly do that," Liz said, hugging her.

♥

In the era of twenty-four-hour news channels, information like the end of the war, and subsequently the ending of the sex strike, traveled like lightning across the sea to America. Happy little beams bounced joyfully off the satellites and were reported by talking heads so giddy they could barely contain themselves.

"Really?" asked Westly Chu, morning news anchor at one of the always-on channels. He looked off-camera for confirmation. "Really? I can go home and screw my wife? Crap, did I just say that on live television? Hell, I don't care. America! I'm going to get laid tonight!"

On other channels, the cameras were simply left on to record the general melee of people whooping in joy, and abandoning their desks to race home. Office buildings emptied, spilling people onto the street as if they had steady leaks. The traffic jams were horrifyingly slow and happened throughout the day because people got the news at different times, but the instantaneous urge to go home was universal.

Even some of the sad, lonely souls who hadn't had anyone to sleep with during the strike found themselves getting "lucky" that evening since the air was heady with the smell of sex, and the bars were full of people who wanted to "participate" in the cross-country celebration.

Commerce essentially ground to a halt. The stock exchange averages leveled off after the news broke because everyone went home, but no one turned it "off." Stores closed, not that anyone was around to buy anything. Government offices were all officially open, but you were double-damned to find anyone to help you if you went inside.

And while there was a month-long lull in the maternity wards around the country, nine months after election day and the declaration of peace, the hospitals couldn't keep up with the boom of babies. The boom continued for a while because once the war was over, the troops started coming home, and everyone knows what happens when troops come home from extended tours of duty.

♥

The list of concessions was not long, but it was

insurmountable enough that neither side would ever be able to complete any of them. The US swore it would never meddle in the affairs of another country's policies—a twenty-first-century prime directive. The governing bodies of Mesopotamianstan were to give their women complete rights equal to their men on the pain of humanitarian sanctions. The US was to abandon Israel to its fate and Mesopotamianstan was to abandon all intentions of eradicating that country.

The idea was that with so many impossible concessions on both sides, that each could withdraw with contempt and spout anger at the other side without actually conceding anything, nor expecting any concessions from the other side. It would be a tenuous peace, but it would work as long as the two sides continued shouting, but doing nothing else. It saved face, enabled an "end" to the war, and it satisfied the hawkish with a continued verbal conflict.

Unofficially, it was called the Passive-Aggressive Peace Plan, or "PAPP Smear." Nobody wanted it, but it had to be done, and it would have to be revisited yearly to keep it healthy. It did not, however, involve cold instruments or cotton swabs.

President-Elect Beckinger and the current President Bernstrom were both skeptical of the plan. President Bernstrom even went so far as to call it preposterous and impossible to enforce, although he realized it wouldn't matter to him in a after Inauguration Day. He signed it as a welcome present for Beckinger and sniggered about it in his sleep for months afterward. His wife had opened the store again, so what did he care? His next worry was where to put his Presidential Library.

"Isn't this a little precarious?" a reporter asked Liz at the "Welcome Home" press conference. "I mean, this doesn't sound like a lasting peace."

"You'd be surprised," Liz said. "I know families whose lives are ruled by ideas like this, who go for decades not talking about certain events. Granted, even a stiff breeze can wreck arrangements like these, but many have legs that last for years."

"So, which side won?" asked another reporter.

"Oh, please." Liz laughed. "This is like a marriage. There were so many concessions that people can claim victory or defeat as they like, as it fits their political positions. That's what makes it so perfect."

"So, the sex strike is over?"

"The war is over, kiddo. So is the sex-strike," Liz replied with a huge smile. "And no one is happier about it than I am."

The party after the signing of the non-treaty was world-wide, as the baby-boom later attested. Most parties were impromptu, but a few optimistic souls had laid in supplies, just in case.

Maureen was one of those, so when Liz and Cal, Elektra, and Zeke arrived at the hotel ballroom in DC after the press conference, they were greeted by three hundred of their nearest and dearest friends with free-flowing champagne and a balloon drop. Somehow, Maureen had even snagged the remaining members of the Grateful Dead to play the event.

"Where did she get a 'PAPP Smear' banner so quickly?" Cal wondered.

"Maybe she knows someone from an OBGYN convention?" Liz suggested.

They roamed the room shaking hands, laughing, joking, and sipping bubbly until midnight when the blue and white balloons were dropped after a countdown to the first whole day of World Peace. People kissed whoever was nearest at that moment. Zeke made sure he was nearest Liz.

Cal found herself staring into the shining brown eyes of her fantasy professor. "How did you know I would be here?" she asked.

"Your friend Maureen called and threatened to hurt me if I didn't show up," he smiled.

Cal could swear that the man's dimples twinkled.

"I'm glad she tracked you down. She's about a subtle as a rhinoceros, isn't she?"

"I was thinking grizzly bear," he said. "I'm glad I showed up."

"Really?" Cal could kick herself for sounding like such a teenager.

"I owe you a drink," he said, reaching for champagne as a waiter passed.

"I think we're past that," Cal said, flinging her arms around him. "I think it's time for a round two, don't you?"

Nicolas laughed. "And round three and four!"

Late that night when people began filing out of the ballroom in happy hazed stupors, Zeke took Liz into his arms and smiled at her. "So, did you get what you wanted out of this?" he asked.

She smiled. "Oh, yes, and more." She gave him an adoring peck. "I wanted to live in the White House, but that's because I wanted to change the world."

"Oh, really?"

"Yes."

"So you're not disappointed about the election?"

"Oh, I'm disappointed," Liz admitted. "But we changed the world, didn't we?"

"Yes, we did."

"Well, I've proven that you don't need to live in DC to do that," Liz said. "So, what's stopping us from doing it again, from the comfort of LA where the beach is just down the road and the air isn't thick with lobbyists?"

"What, indeed?" Zeke laughed and kissed her. "I adore you, you know."

"I know," she said. "But you haven't asked me to dinner in absolute ages, Zeke. What's up with that?"

"Oh, I'm saving it for a special occasion," he said.

"World peace isn't special enough?" Liz asked.

"You're right, it is," he said, and slipped a little box into her hand. "Happy World Peace."

Liz blinked at the sparkly diamond ring in the box and grappled for something to say. "Are you sure, Zeke?" she asked. "I mean, we've only had sex once, you know."

"That was enough to convince me," he said. "Besides, Liz, I've been fantasizing about living with you since I met you ten years ago. Why would I want to put it off any longer than necessary?"

"But, isn't it a little trite to have an engagement at a moment like this?" She wasn't sure if she'd said this aloud until Zeke answered.

"I can take it back until a more mundane moment, if you like."

"No, no. I'll just suffer through a happy-movie-ending, thank you," she said, kissing him.

"I can take that as a 'yes' then?"

"Yes, yes, you can," Liz replied. "Shut up and kiss me, you."

THE END

About the Author

Maren Bradley Anderson is a writer, teacher, podcaster, blogger, and alpaca rancher who lives in the Willamette Valley of Oregon. She teaches literature and writing at Western Oregon University, and blogs about alpacas and writing. Her alpacas win ribbons, and she thinks they are darned cute.

Connect with the author online!

Website: http://www.marens.com
Twitter: @marenster
Facebook:
http://www.facebook.com/MarenBradley Anderson